DATA JACK

A DETECTIVE JACK STRATTON NOVEL

CHRISTOPHER GREYSON

GREYSON MEDIA

Novels featuring Jack Stratton in order:

AND THEN SHE WAS GONE
GIRL JACKED
JACK KNIFED
JACKS ARE WILD
JACK AND THE GIANT KILLER
DATA JACK
JACK OF HEARTS
JACK FROST

Also by Christopher Greyson:

PURE OF HEART

THE GIRL WHO LIVED

DATA JACK
Copyright © Christopher Greyson April 15, 2015

Find out more about the author and upcoming books online at www.ChristopherGreyson.com.

ISBN: 1-68399-060-9
ISBN-13: 978-1-68399-060-4

CONTENTS

1

HUNTING WILD BOAR

Jack waited behind the seedy bar, hidden in the shadows at the end of the alley. Like a hawk, he watched the motorcycles parked there. Two were sport bikes, but his attention was focused on the leather, saddle-bagged Harley.

Jack's body stiffened. He reached for his gun, but felt nothing but air. He grimaced. After his latest run-in with the sheriff's office, Sheriff Collins had pulled his license to carry a firearm. He was also out of Taser cartridges and mace. The medical bills had emptied his savings, and his day-to-day expenses had wiped out the reward he'd received for catching the guy the news had dubbed the "Giant Killer."

Now I'm hunting wild boar barehanded. Great.

The fall night air had a chill to it. It had rained earlier. That and the smell of the autumn leaves helped alleviate the stench that rose from the trashcans along the wall.

Jack looked at his phone: 2:52 a.m. The bar had closed at two, but his prey remained inside. Jack would continue to wait; he needed to get the man alone.

The back door burst open and "Mad Dog" Jenkins stomped out. Jack instantly recognized him from the wanted poster. Jack snickered. He doubted the other bikers knew Mad Dog's real name was Marvin.

Marvin stood just shy of six feet, and dressed the part of a wanted fugitive who'd just left a bar filled with reprobates. Clad head to toe in leather, he was the kind of man most people wished would never cross their path. But not Jack.

Jack grinned as he pushed away from the wall. The hunt for Marvin had lasted three weeks. Right now, he struggled to restrain himself from running up and tackling the man.

Jack let Marvin get on his bike before he stepped out of the shadows.

"Hold on a second, Marvin," Jack called out as he approached.

"Who the hell are you?" Marvin glanced up as he started his bike.

"You skipped bail. Titus wants his money."

Marvin scoffed. "Tell Titus to screw himself." He revved the engine louder.

Jack stopped ten feet in front of the bike. "I wouldn't try to leave."

"Try to stop me." Marvin dropped the bike into gear and pinned the throttle.

The motorcycle surged forward, and an earsplitting metallic crack filled the alley. The motorcycle shot up on its front wheel and Marvin flew up and over the handlebars. The bike crashed onto its side; Marvin face-planted on the pavement.

Jack sprinted forward and pinned Marvin to the tar. "Boy, that sucks, Marvin." Jack patted him down. "Looks like someone put a heavy-duty lock on your front wheel."

He took a knife from Marvin's belt and another from his back pocket. "Guess you should've listened to me."

Jack clicked a handcuff around Marvin's wrist.

The back door of the bar burst open. The metal door rang like a bell as it clanged off the railing. Four guys poured into the alley. All of them wore jeans, black shirts, and black leather vests. One big guy with a pot belly clenched a pool cue in his hands. When they saw Marvin lying flat out in handcuffs, they glared at Jack.

Damn.

Jack snapped the other cuff on Marvin's other wrist, then stood and read the road names on the patches on the bikers' vests. The pot belly was Chunk; the others were Vegas, Hammer, and Ice. Jack had never understood why bikers who broke the law wore their names on their vests; it made identification so much easier.

"He jumped bail, Chunk," Jack said. "I'm taking him in."

Chunk hesitated when he heard his name. His nose wrinkled as he peered at Jack.

"No, you ain't," Vegas snarled.

Jack yanked Marvin to his feet while he stared them down. "Believe me, he's not worth it."

"Hammer. Ice. Kick his ass!" Marvin barked.

Chunk charged forward with the pool cue raised over his head.

Jack shoved Marvin into the way of the oncoming onslaught. Marvin swore as the cue slammed into his arm. Jack grabbed the cue with his right hand while his left fist slammed into the side of Chunk's face.

But hockey players, boxers, and Chunk had one thing in common—they were all used to getting punched in the face. Even though the blow solidly connected, Chunk only stumbled to the side a bit, and he still held on to the cue.

Meanwhile, the two other guys, Hammer and Ice, did something Jack didn't expect. They dove over the bike and tackled him. Hammer caught Jack around the chest while Ice's arms wrapped around Jack's thighs. The three of them crashed to the ground next to the still-running motorcycle.

Jack lay flat on his back. He ripped his right hand free. Two rapid punches to Hammer's head, and Hammer slumped to the ground.

Vegas ran forward and kicked.

Jack rolled onto his side and blocked Vegas's boot, even as Ice kept his hold on Jack's legs.

Marvin, handcuffed and standing over Jack, kicked Jack in the back. But as Marvin drew his leg back to kick Jack a second time, Jack grabbed behind Marvin's knee, yanked him forward, and punched him in the groin.

Marvin dropped to his knees.

Vegas then leapt on top of Jack and tried to pin his arms while Ice continued to wrap up Jack's legs. Vegas punched Jack in the face. The blow caught him on the ridge of his left eye, and he felt the skin tear.

Ice let go of Jack's right leg in order to pull a knife, and Jack seized the opportunity. He planted his heel against Ice's shoulder and his foot against the side of Ice's head. Jack pushed Ice's face against the hot muffler of the bike.

Ice screamed. He dropped the knife and rolled off Jack.

Vegas tried to grab Jack's feet, but Jack drew both legs up toward his chest and slammed his heels into Vegas's knees.

Chunk swung the cue at Jack's head, but it smashed into the handlebars next to Jack's face.

As Marvin staggered to his feet, Ice recovered enough to grab Jack's legs again, and Vegas stumbled forward and fell on Jack. Then Hammer covered Jack's upper body like a wrestler going for the pin.

Three bikers held Jack down.

Chunk lifted the pool cue over his head. Blood ran down his chin from his cut lip. He sneered as he aimed for Jack's face.

Jack grabbed the throttle of the motorcycle and twisted hard. Chunk screamed as the tire whirled against his shin.

Jack kept the throttle down. The rear tire made contact with the ground. The bike started to spin, and Jack held on to the handlebars. Like a water-skier lifted out of the sea, the motorcycle pulled Jack free from the pile of people on top of him. Jack grabbed both handles, and the motorcycle pulled him to his feet.

The lock on the front wheel held, but smoke poured from the rear wheel. Jack kept the throttle down, and the motorcycle spun in a circle. The bikers screamed and swore as Jack used the motorcycle as a battering ram. After three circles, he heaved the bike toward the men. They stumbled and fell back into some garbage cans.

Jack grabbed Marvin and dragged him down the alley. He lifted up on Marvin's hands and forced him forward.

"You're gonna pay for this—" Marvin's threat stopped short when Jack yanked up on his arms.

"Keep moving," Jack ordered. He needed to get Marvin to his car before the other bikers caught up.

Marvin swore as he stumbled onto the sidewalk. Jack's Charger was parked five cars down.

The front door of the bar swung open, and five guys hustled out. They now stood between Jack and the Charger. A second later, Chunk ran out of the alley, followed by Ice and Hammer. Ice had a look of murder in his eyes as he cradled his burnt face.

"Over here!" Chunk yelled to the men from the bar. He turned to glare triumphantly at Jack. "You're screwed."

I'll never make the Charger. I can outrun them, but there's no way I'm letting Marvin go—I need the money.

One of the guys stepped forward and held up a baseball bat. Jack pulled out his retractable billy club and snapped it open.

"You think that little dinky thing is gonna hold them all off?" Marvin laughed.

"Shut up."

Jack pushed Marvin back beside the large glass windows surrounding an ATM; the entrance to a bank was a few steps away. The men fanned out and circled them.

"Looks like it's not your night." Chunk laughed.

Jack swung his billy club with one swift motion. It struck the ATM glass behind him. The whole sheet of glass cracked, and shards of glass hit the sidewalk.

Lights flashed and alarms blared inside the bank.

The group of men stared at Jack in disbelief.

"Stop, thief!" Jack shouted, a smirk spreading across his face. "These men are trying to rob the bank. That's a felony!" he yelled.

"*You* did it." Chunk pointed at him with the pool cue.

"Yeah." Ice nodded.

Jack smiled when he heard police sirens start up a few streets away.

"You're right," he said. "Why don't we all stay here and explain it to the police?" Jack tightened his grip on Marvin's arm. "I'm sure they'll believe you."

The bikers looked at one another. Then Vegas turned and ran. And once one bolted, they all followed. Jack smiled as he watched the tough bikers dashing off down the alley.

"You bunch of—" Marvin yelled, but Jack pulled up on his arms, which pitched him forward and cut him off.

"Shut up, Mad Dog. Or I'll tell them your real name."

As Jack stood in the middle of the sidewalk with glass all around him and the sirens getting closer, he surveyed the mess he'd just made.

Great. I wonder how much that window is going to set me back.

2

PIERCE WESTON

"Mr. Weston. Mr. Weston!" A young woman in a light-gray business suit and high heels that revealed a peekaboo butterfly tattoo on her ankle rushed over to the limo as it pulled onto the tarmac. "I'm sorry, sir, but…" Her voice trailed off when a matronly woman stepped out and scowled. "I'm sorry, Mrs. Maier, but I was asked to get Mr. Weston's signature on these forms before he left."

Lydia Maier's ever-present thin smile did nothing to disguise the displeasure in her eyes. "Miss Moran, that paperwork should've been interofficed to my desk. There was no need to bring these out and disturb—"

"It's fine, Lydia," said a man's deep voice from within the limousine. His tone was refined but firm.

Lydia stopped short and stepped aside. A tall, handsome man with wavy brown hair and deep green eyes stepped out of the car. The young woman gulped as she looked up into his attractive face.

"It's not a bother." The polished young man took the clipboard from the girl. He scanned the paperwork on the Weston Industries stationery before signing. "Here you are, Miss…?"

"Tiffany." Her voice rose along with the color in her cheeks. "Thank you, Mr. Weston."

"Thank you for your diligence. And please, call me Pierce."

Tiffany nodded and clutched the folder against her chest.

Pierce nodded to Lydia before walking over to the waiting private jet.

Lydia motioned to the limo driver to take the luggage on board, then caught up with her boss. Her heels clicked on the tar as her short legs moved rapidly to keep up with Pierce's long strides.

She scanned an itinerary page on her tablet. "You just have the weekend meeting coming up at your house—apart from that, I've cleared your appointments for the next two weeks." She looked around and lowered her voice. "Are you sure you don't want me to reschedule that meeting so you don't have to do it right in the middle of your vacation? I can put it off until you're back."

"No, the whole idea was to get everyone out to my house for some offsite time. It'll only be two days, and I really need to hear some feedback from a trustworthy source before we present it to the board," Pierce said. "Besides, it won't be *all* work."

Lydia clicked her tablet and smiled. "Well, you'll have two full weeks after that to relax and do whatever you want."

"Relax? I want to code. It's all I've been thinking about for weeks and the only thing I haven't been able to do. That's why I'm getting a head start and leaving today."

"Well, that'll give you a couple of days to get settled. The rest of us will be flying in Friday evening. After that, should I follow the standard operating procedures for who's allowed to interrupt you?"

"No. I have an idea I need to program, or I'll go out of my head. Unless it rises to an issue that the board can't deal with, I'm unavailable."

"Understood."

"That is to say—for anyone except you." Pierce gave her a little wink. "I'm sure you'd go completely mad if you didn't check up on me at least a few times."

Lydia skimmed over the long list on the tablet, and her smile thinned. "It's my responsibility to see you have everything you need at your disposal. I wish you'd let me make sure the house was settled. I don't know if the contractors had time to finish. No one planned on you arriving early."

"All I need at the house is electricity and peace and quiet. Besides, I thought we agreed this would be the perfect time for your vacation."

"It's the perfect time for me to catch up on a million things back at the office." She huffed but smiled.

"After the meeting, take the time to get some rest. When I get back, things are really going to get busy."

Pierce hurried up the steps of the private jet. His hand instinctively tightened around his laptop case. Two stewardesses waited for him at the door.

"Mr. Weston." The blonde nodded politely.

"Mr. Weston." The brunette looked as if she was trying to hold back a bubbly smile.

Pierce scanned their hands. The blonde wore a wedding ring; the brunette didn't. "Ladies. Your names?"

"Maggie," the blonde answered.

"Stacy."

Pierce nodded. "I'm afraid this will be a very boring flight for you. The only thing I'll require is an occasional water."

"We'll be happy to get you *whatever* you want." Stacy flashed a perfect smile that matched her surgically enhanced form.

"Please let us know if you change your mind." Maggie took a small step forward, and Pierce caught the slightest disapproving glance shot back at Stacy.

"I'll ring," he said. "Thank you."

A man in a dark-gray suit waited behind them in the galley. Standing ramrod straight, the man gave Pierce a confident, tight-lipped nod.

Pierce nodded. "Manuel."

"Sir." Manuel's tone was clipped. His eyes only met Pierce's for a brief moment before they returned to sweeping the tarmac.

Pierce sighed. "How many men did Bagwell send to the house?"

"Just five, sir."

Pierce shook his head. His overenthusiastic head of security, Leon Bagwell, was a former career Marine who approached his new profession with an even greater intensity than he had his outstanding military service. That zeal, while appreciated in all other areas, was trying when it came to Pierce's personal life.

"Bagwell did understand that it's a vacation?"

Manuel, also a former soldier, met Pierce's gaze. "I understand, sir."

"I know you do. You're just doing your job. Thank you, Manuel. I'll speak with Bagwell."

"Yes, sir."

As Pierce walked through the plane, he took in a deep breath and smiled. But it wasn't the opulent wide leather seats and mahogany tables with cherry inlays that made him smile—it was the fact that he was alone. No endless meetings, no dealing with hungry investors, and no security issues to address. He loved the feeling of being in a bubble on a plane.

He put the laptop case down, took his seat, and leaned back. The jet engines hummed, and he shut his eyes. The solitude welcomed him, and the quiet inside the cabin seemed to hush even more with the engine noise wrapped around it.

After a few moments' respite, the plane took off. When they reached cruising altitude, Pierce's eyes flicked open like a soldier snapping to attention. He stared at the beat-up black laptop case that stood in sharp contrast to the high-polished wood of the tabletop. He'd ordered the specialized case four years ago, and it had turned out to be one of the few things in his life that had exceeded his expectations. He'd wanted security for the laptop that would travel inside it, and that's exactly what he'd gotten. Waterproof, fireproof, and impact-resistant, it was the trusted guardian of Pierce's most prized possession: his personal laptop computer, and more importantly, the code he had written that was contained within it.

With the touch of his fingers, the tumblers spun and the lid of the case silently rose. The laptop was a beast by computer geeks' standards, but its outward appearance made it look dated. It was thick, heavy, and boxy—but the custom-built machine cost as much as his Porsche 911.

He remembered the sleepless nights in college when he toiled on his old secondhand computer until he collapsed. He glanced around the private jet and smiled; his hard work had paid off.

Pierce drummed his fingers on the armrest. He felt anxious. He had been trying to quit smoking for months. He pulled out his interim crutch, an e-cigarette, inhaled deeply, and frowned. It had been three months since he'd quit, but the cravings were still there. He exhaled slowly, and as he gazed down at the faux cigarette, his expression soured. It did little to satisfy his craving. He yearned for the real thing.

But the cigarette wasn't his biggest vice. The need for what he couldn't have was. He plugged the e-cigarette case into the USB port of the laptop before settling back in the chair.

Stacy approached with his drink. "Here's your water, sir." She set the glass down and scanned his face with rapt attention.

"Thank you, Stacy."

"Would you like anything else?" She leaned over so her eyes were now level with his.

Pierce looked into her big blue eyes and paused. "Well…"

"I just have to tell you, I love VE-Life. I use it for everything."

He nodded modestly. "Thank you."

"Are you making a new app?"

"We're always working on moving forward."

"It's just great. I link up to all my friends just like that." She snapped.

Pierce nodded. The fact that he was having a one-on-one conversation with a woman—and he wasn't in the office or a carefully organized dinner party—was not lost on him. He sat up straighter.

"If you need anything, just press this button for help." Her finger traced along the contour of the switch on his chair.

"I should write F1 on it." He grinned.

She made a face. "I don't understand."

"You said if I needed help, I should press the button, so… I said I should write F1 on it."

Her eyebrows rose higher, and a smile that screamed *I have no idea what you're talking about but I'll pretend that I do* appeared on her face. "Oh, yes."

"It's a computer geek joke. F1 is the help button."

"Oh." She chuckled, but he knew she still didn't have a clue.

"Do you know anything about computers?"

"Just that I hate them. I can never get mine to work right." She shook her head.

He nodded, but internally he cringed as the oh-so-brief possibility flew right out the cabin window. His phone buzzed in his pocket. Grateful for the distraction, he held up his phone. "Sorry, I have to take this."

Stacy smiled and backed away.

"Hello?"

"Miss me, buddy?"

"What part of 'leave me the hell alone' don't you understand, Roger?" Pierce asked.

"You haven't gotten to your destination, so technically your vacation hasn't started yet."

"You're keeping close tabs on me."

"What're friends for?" Roger laughed. "Did you meet my new secretary?"

"Tiffany? Yes."

"What do you think? Smoking hot and completely dedicated to her new boss."

"I'm trying to understand what you're going through with your home life, but I don't want to see a sexual harassment complaint come across my desk."

"Hey, I didn't pick her. It was HR, but I'm not complaining. It was totally aboveboard."

"And you had no input?"

"I may have peeked at the candidates when they came in for their interviews. I'm just saying she's easy on the eyes."

Pierce loved his old friend. He was a good guy, but his love life was a human train wreck. "Well, I signed her papers. What now?"

"I'm just calling because I know how you get when you start programming. You'll stick your head into that computer, and I won't hear from you for a month."

"Two weeks and I'm almost done," Pierce said.

"I thought the new version was already a done deal. You've gone over it. We've had two test groups clear it. Seriously, if you decide to change anything, it's going to set everything back."

"It has to be right, Roger. It's my name on it. Besides, I'm working on something else. When it goes out, it'll be huge."

"We're already huge. It's kinda hard to top number one."

"Then this will keep us there." Pierce's thumb ran along the metallic edge of the keyboard.

"What is it?"

"I'm going to reveal it at the meeting."

"Now I'm curious. Give me a clue."

"Not yet. I'm still working on it."

"Creative geniuses—you're a pain in the ass, Pierce. Put your bow on it, and let's get it out the door. Is that what this meeting is all about? All I know is the Iron Lady told me I had to come. I just don't want this to be a 'you threw your poor old college roommate a bone' thing. You already made me assistant vice president of marketing twice removed."

"Roger, we've been over this…"

"I'm kidding. I appreciate the job, but if I don't toot my own horn, who will? I'm gunning for Allister's job when he retires. Everyone knows that."

"And they know you're my friend."

"What's a little nepotism between friends? Besides, I'm rocking it, right? That new ad campaign has skyrocketed with eighteen- to twenty-four year olds."

"That's why I need you at the meeting. And I want input from people at the company I trust. We'll discuss the job when Allister really does retire."

"Sure. We'll talk about it over a couple of dozen beers."

"Roger, I'm serious. Apart from this meeting, I'm not to be disturbed. Two weeks. I want to go over all the code, and I can't when I'm interrupted every second. There are already more people with me than I want."

Roger laughed. "How many did Leon send?"

"Five."

"Seriously? Only five? Didn't someone make another threat?"

"It wasn't a threat."

"Oh, really," Roger quipped. "So why did we have all those federal investigators swarming the building?"

"That was for a different situation. It's not a big deal. It's probably just some psycho with an ax to grind."

"Maybe I should check on the whereabouts of my ex-wife?"

"Roger, I have enough on my plate."

"That's what I'm saying. You need to blow off steam. One night we'll go out and—"

"No."

"When was the last time you ran a little wild?"

"Your house party two months ago."

"That's a long time ago."

"Thank you, but no. Besides, it's a sleepy town. You'd be bored out of your mind."

"So why'd one of the wealthiest guys in the country buy a house in some backwater community when he could live it up in LA or New York?"

"I like the quiet."

"Seriously? That's all you've got?"

"It has special memories for me, that's why I picked it. Besides, nothing happens there; it's trouble-free and peaceful."

"What's the name of the town again?"

"Darrington."

3

OUR NETWORK GIRL

Replacement's foot stopped tapping when she saw the late-model brown BMW round the corner. A man in his late fifties was driving. A heavyset man with a bushy beard sat in the passenger seat, and another man sat in the back.

She waved as they pulled up to the curb. "Hi, Gerald," she said to the driver. She hopped into the back seat and shut the door.

"Morning, Alice." Gerald gave a little wave and pulled right back out. "This here is Bruce. He's our wiring expert."

The car rocked as the heavy man turned around to look at her. His eyes all but disappeared when he smiled. "I cable and network, too." Bruce looked to be in his mid-thirties and a frequent flier at the all-you-can-eat buffet.

"And that's Phillip." Gerald gestured to the man next to her in the back seat. "He's our AP guy."

"Nice to meet you, Phillip."

Phillip gave a tiny wave and slid as far away from Replacement as the seat would allow. Replacement knew his type: shy computer geek. His short, straight brown hair did little to cover the flush of red on his ears. He pushed his round glasses higher up his nose and stared out the window.

"And Alice here," Gerald said to Bruce and Phillip, "is in charge of config. She's our network girl." Gerald angled his thumb her way.

Replacement clicked on her seat belt and put her bag at her feet. The BMW was clean, but the odor of stale smoke was everywhere. She tried not to wrinkle her nose.

"Do you still expect the job to run the full week?" Replacement asked.

Please say yes. Please say yes. Please say yes. We need the money.

"It actually could run a little longer. I hope not, but the Bellmore estate's huge, and it's smack in the middle of the Blue Hills. Getting wireless coverage up to spec in every room is going to be the tough part. The main line went live yesterday. I've got a plan written out. We can go over the specifics when we get out there." Gerald ran his hand over his short graying beard.

"Will the client be there?" Bruce asked.

"Not today. He's supposed to be there later in the week."

Bruce huffed. "Good. I hate when they stick around while you work. They end up hovering around like a buzzard, waiting for you to screw up. It makes me nervous."

"Who's the client?" Replacement asked.

"Pierce Weston," Gerald replied.

"Pierce Weston? The CEO of Weston Industries?" Replacement's voice went up an octave. "*He's* the one who bought the Bellmore estate?"

Bruce looked over at Gerald, shocked. "Weston Industries is one of the hottest software firms. They make VE-Life. That's our client?"

"One and the same." Gerald sat up a little straighter.

"Seriously?" Replacement beamed. "How'd you get this job? He's like a legend. He wrote his first computer program when he was seven!"

"On a PC I built for his dad." Gerald angled his head. "Back when I had my computer fix-it shop."

"Get out!" Replacement's hand flew to her hair, and she checked her reflection in the window.

Bruce said, "I thought he lived in California?"

"He does. I saw his mansion on the news once."

"So why'd he buy a house in Darrington?" Bruce scoffed.

"It's a great area." Gerald shot him a sideways glare.

"Yeah, it's okay," Bruce said, "but the guy's used to Malibu and the Riviera. Not Lake Onopiquite."

"It's beautiful out here." Replacement waved her hands at the changing foliage. "Great score getting this gig, Gerald."

"I can't believe you've known Pierce Weston since he was a kid, and you never said anything," Bruce said.

Gerald rubbed the top of his receding hairline. "It never came up. It's no big deal. His parents owned a nice summer house near this cottage Tammy and I had. Down near South Pond. He and Tyler used to hang out."

Phillip leaned forward but kept his hands flat on his legs. "Who's Tyler?"

"My son." Gerald tapped the steering wheel. "Every summer, Pierce's family would come up. He practically lived at our house. Still, I couldn't believe it when Pierce called about this job. I haven't talked to him since he was in college."

He rolled down his window. "Does anyone mind if I smoke?"

Both Bruce and Phillip rolled down their own windows and reached into their pockets.

"Is there any way you could hold off?" Replacement asked. "I'm sorry, but smoke kills me."

"Sure." Gerald's window rose.

Phillip put his window up too, but Bruce groaned. "Could you try to breathe out the window?"

Gerald pressed the button for Bruce's window and frowned. "We're not far."

"Sorry," Replacement said. "And I really appreciate the job, Gerald. It couldn't have come at a better time."

"Well, you're needed, Alice, so I appreciate you. How's Jack doing?"

"He's doing great. All healed."

"Healed?" Phillip asked.

"Her boyfriend's Jack Stratton." Gerald pulled down the rearview mirror and gave Phillip a look that said the name should tell the whole story.

Phillip looked back blankly.

"You know, Jack Stratton?" Gerald repeated.

Phillip shrugged. "I'm sorry, I—"

"It's okay." Replacement waved her hand. "My boyfriend's been in the news a little bit."

"A little bit?" Bruce scoffed. "That guy's your boyfriend? The guy who caught the Giant Killer?" He struggled to turn his large bulk around to look at Replacement. "I heard he got shot and kept going. I've got this friend who knows this cop who used to work with him. Guy said Stratton's one hundred percent bad-ass. I heard he's a bounty hunter now. Is that true?"

Replacement nodded and tried not to appear too proud, but the color rose to her cheeks.

"I hope he's taking it easy now at least," Gerald said.

"He promised me he would. No excitement. None at all."

4

ZOMBIE HUNTER

Jack finished the paperwork for Marvin and hurried out of the jail, grateful Replacement hadn't called to check on him. His ribs hurt, and his head throbbed. He slid behind the wheel of the Charger and pulled down the rearview mirror. The nurse at the jail had given him two butterfly strips for his eye and three aspirin. The cut was close to his eyebrow, so if it did scar it shouldn't be that noticeable.

His phone barked, and he looked at it before answering. An unknown number.

"This is Jack."

"He's on his way," a woman whispered into the phone.

He recognized Kimberly's voice. "When?"

"Now. How do I tell you when he comes? There's no phone in my room."

"You're on the third floor facing Vine Street, right?" he asked.

"Yeah."

"Closest to the barber shop?"

"Yeah."

"Put your shade up when he knocks," Jack instructed.

"I've got no window shade."

"Do you normally keep the window open or closed?"

"Open. I get hot."

"Close it when he comes."

"Okay. Bye."

Click.

Jack looked at the clock and groaned. Between getting Marvin processed and the hospital, it was already after nine. The last thing Jack wanted to do was go after another bounty, today especially, but now he didn't have a choice. He turned the Charger around and headed for Vine Street.

When he got there, he pulled over across the street from the dilapidated three-story tenement. It sat at the end of the block and had exits on three sides, but he could only watch one and still see Kimberly's window.

He looked down at the two pictures on the passenger seat. It was hard to believe both photos were of the same man. One showed a businessman in his early thirties. Muscular and handsome, he sat confidently as he posed for the camera. The other photo was taken only two years later, but already the man in the picture was a ghoulish shadow of his former self. Peter Marshall had become a meth addict. In the two years since taking his first hit, he'd lost his job, his house, and his wife and kids.

Jack stared at the hollowed-out eyes in the picture and adjusted his bulletproof vest.

Peter's first mistake wasn't the drugs; it was sex. That's what started his downfall. Kimberly was a high-class escort. Peter had met her monthly for a little tryst, and then it quickly turned into a weekly thing. He thought he could keep the genie in the bottle. But when he introduced her to a deep-well bank account, she introduced him to meth. They held hands and threw themselves over the cliff.

Peter had fallen farther, but Kimberly landed just as hard. When Jack had met with her two nights ago, he'd found it difficult to look at her. Scabs covered her face. He knew it wasn't that long ago that she had charged a thousand dollars a night for her company. Now only the most desperate man would even go near her.

It took only twenty bucks for her to agree to help Jack. She didn't say so, but he could tell she was scared of Peter. She wanted him away from her.

For an hour, Jack watched the building. People went on with their lives while he scanned their faces.

Then Kimberly's window closed.

Jack slid out of the Charger and hurried to the hole in the wall where a back door should have been. Instead, the broken back door was off its hinges and leaning against the outside wall nearby. Inside, trash littered a darkened staircase.

Jack hugged the wall as he moved silently upward. The stench of urine hung in the air. The door on the first room he came to was wide open. Two mattresses in the corner had three people lying on each of them, asleep.

The next room he passed was a large common room. Two dilapidated couches ran along the walls. The place was packed with addicts, sleeping anywhere they could. No one lifted their head as he hurried by. Jack slowed as he climbed the last staircase. The carpet on the stairs had been ripped out and the staples caught at the soles of his shoes. He stepped around the shell of a man who sat halfway up—his eyes glazed and unfocused.

He found Kimberly's room on the third floor. Her door was closed, but he heard raised voices.

"I don't have any more," Kimberly said.

Jack moved to put his back against the wall.

"I need a hit. You've only got ten bucks? I saw the guy who left. You've got to have more."

"He paid me with a hit. I swear. It's all I've got. Take it and just—"

Her words were cut off by the sickening sound of flesh slamming against flesh. Kimberly cried out.

Jack stepped back and smashed his foot into the door. The wood splintered and the door flew open.

Peter spun around.

One look at Peter's wild eyes told Jack that Peter had not only boarded the crazy train, but he was going full steam ahead.

Peter held Kimberly by the shirt with one hand. He flung her roughly aside, and Jack had to leap forward to catch her before she slammed headfirst into the wall.

Peter seized the opportunity to dash out of the room and down the stairs. "Cops! Cops!" he screamed as he ran by the common room on the second floor.

Damn it.

Jack ran down the stairs. People had already flooded the hallway. He pushed them aside as he tried to catch up with Peter. Most just ran, but one tall guy with brown teeth blocked Jack's way and raised his fist. Jack shoved him backward and kept going.

People were now tripping over one another as they rushed to escape. One look at the crowd blocking the stairs convinced Jack he couldn't catch up with Peter that way.

He darted through the common room, pulled open a window, climbed out onto a rusted fire escape—and stopped.

He was looking down two stories, and the bottom of the fire escape was gone.

I can't catch a break.

He grabbed the metal railing and swung over the side. His legs dangled down… and he let go.

The packed dirt felt like cement when he hit. Pain shot up his legs as he landed and fell into a roll. He tried to shake his head clear, and he saw the side door slam open and Peter scramble out.

Jack felt his thigh muscle seize as he stood up. He forced his leg forward and limped for two strides before he was able to break into a sprint.

Peter yelled as he raced down the sidewalk. People scrambled to get out of the way of the disheveled man with crazy eyes.

"Freeze!" Jack ordered, but Peter broke left and dashed into traffic.

Horns blared as a truck swerved around Peter. Jack jumped sideways to avoid getting hit; the truck's side mirror barely missed his face.

As Peter glanced back, he tripped over the curb. He stumbled forward and fell onto the sidewalk, hard. Stunned pedestrians stared down at the man who was now curled up into the fetal position, moaning and writhing. He burst out crying.

Jack stopped beside Peter and tried to catch his breath. His chest heaved, and he put his hands on his legs as he breathed in huge gulps of air.

A man stepped toward Peter. Jack held up his hand, warning him away. "He's wanted."

The man jumped back as though he'd almost patted a rattlesnake.

Jack stared down at the pitiful man lying on the sidewalk. Peter was whimpering loudly. Jack cringed. Peter buried his face in his hands and wailed.

Jack squatted down next to Peter and softened his voice. "It'll be okay. They'll be able to give you something to take the edge off. Let's—"

Peter pounced.

His hands smashed into Jack's chest and pitched Jack backward. They fell onto the sidewalk, Jack on his back, Peter on top of him.

Jack had to grab Peter's wrists to keep Peter's broken fingernails from clawing out Jack's eyes. Peter's mouth opened, and his head shot forward. Broken brown teeth clacked together as he tried to bite Jack's face. Jack could feel Peter's rancid breath on his face.

Peter's snarling mouth got closer.

Jack punched Peter on the side of the head. The blow was fast and hard. Peter's head snapped to the side, but it swung right back and his mouth sought out Jack's face again.

Two more rapid punches had no additional effect.

Damn. It's like fighting a zombie. I'll kill him if I hit him any harder.

Jack held his hand flat and aimed for Peter's throat.

The blow hit home. Peter's eyes bulged, and he fell off Jack.

Jack's karate instructor's words echoed in his head: *If you can't breathe, you can't fight.* Jack quickly yanked Peter's hands behind his back and cuffed him.

Jack then carefully patted Peter down. He knew one used syringe could be as fatal as a bullet. Finding nothing, he dragged Peter to his feet.

Peter doubled over, wailing, and begged, "I have to see someone. Please."

"Shut up, Peter," Jack growled as he pushed him forward. "I felt sorry for you a second ago, and you tried to bite my face off."

"Please," he cried. "I can't go in. I can't go in. I can't—"

"Shut up. You just want to get a hit."

"Take me to the clinic. They'll give me something."

"They'll give you something at the jail."

"Okay. Okay." Peter walked with his head down as Jack pushed him across the street and toward the Charger.

Jack tried not to limp as he prodded Peter to keep moving. He added up all of the hours he'd put into chasing this junkie, and his scowl deepened. People hurried out of the way of the handcuffed junkie and the bounty hunter with the blazing eyes.

Great. I'm a zombie hunter. Can things get any worse?

5

ANATOLI

UKRAINE

Anatoli Belarus walked with his head high despite the rain. Fifty plus years had taken some of the edge off his staunch strut, but he still walked in such a manner that men would get out of his way—even if they didn't know who he was. The man was the size and shape of a grizzly bear. With his barrel chest and head that hung slightly forward, he cast an imposing shadow on the cobblestones of the old quarter as he ambled down the street.

Because of the rain and the early hour, only a few people stirred. The ones who did gave Anatoli a wide berth. None met his eyes. They didn't need to look at his face to know the man. His silhouette was enough.

He headed for the old coffee shop in the middle of the block. The glow from the yellow lights shimmered on the wet cobblestones. Pastries, cookies, and cakes sat on shelves in the display window.

Anatoli paused before stepping over the threshold. He always did. He regarded his family's crest carved ever so faintly in the lower right-hand corner of the marble threshold. It was the Belarus mark. For generations, all the men in his family had been stoneworkers. Artisans with rock. Every male had gone into the trade—until Anatoli broke with tradition.

He pushed open the old wooden door, and the little bell chimed. Behind the counter, an old woman raised her gray head, and her smile vanished. Her eyes darted to the floor. Anatoli could hear her mutter a curse from where he stood.

She leaned around the corner and spoke toward the back room. "Він тут." Her tone was as cold as the water that fell from his jacket as he hung it up.

Anatoli made his way to the little table in the back. The smell of fresh bread hung in the air. He pushed the table back as he slid into the booth. He glanced up at the clock. The little coffee shop wouldn't open for another forty minutes.

A man in his seventies, bent from years of hard work, shuffled forward and locked the front door. He smiled and nodded to Anatoli as he shuffled back over to the counter. Minutes later, he came back with a plate of warm bread and cold ham. In his other hand was a cup of thick, strong coffee.

"Good morning." The man spoke in a heavy accent. He smiled, but his eyes stayed narrowed. "It's supposed to rain the whole week."

Anatoli looked the old man over. "You should take a holiday, Petr. Go down to the coast. It would be good for your back." He gripped the delicate handle of the coffee cup.

The old man shrugged.

Once the words were out of Anatoli's mouth, he realized how wasted they were. The old man would never take time off. Men like him worked until they were dead.

Petr had been Anatoli's father's partner in his stonework business until Petr injured his back. Anatoli's father and others in the village had built this bakery for Petr. The people of the village had respected Anatoli's father.

They feared Anatoli.

Anatoli humphed as he glanced back at the clock. His bushy brows knit together, and he scowled. Petr, seeing Anatoli's changed demeanor, retreated to the kitchen.

Anatoli closed his eyes and focused. He never wrote anything down—only stored things in his head. That's why he came to the coffee shop. To think. To go over his plans.

Right now, he had many gray areas that lacked detail and form. He didn't like that.

Anatoli had paid his nephew Luka's way through university. Since he'd graduated, Luka's plans had grown larger, and so had the profits. They'd started small, pillaging the old countries unaccustomed to new technology. Luka made up a fake website and used it to get people's credit card numbers. Anatoli used his connections to sell the numbers.

Anatoli never touched a computer, but he understood more about them than most. And Luka's computer skills, combined with Anatoli's knowledge of manipulating people, turned quick profits. Modified banking emails filled with tales of fake riches only if the recipient acted quickly unlocked a few bank accounts, which were quickly emptied. Bogus porn, concert, and event websites followed. Here in the old Eastern Bloc nations, with little to no governmental oversight, it was easy. Anatoli had Luka hire a programmer, and they took existing viruses and modified them into ransomware. Now people had to pay if they wanted access to their own data.

Anatoli took a big bite of bread. He humphed again. What he was doing now in virtual reality was no different than what he did in the real world. It was kidnapping and ransom, except it was done with bits and bytes instead of flesh and blood.

But Luka's latest scheme was too grand. Anatoli worried it would never work the way Luka planned it. Luka had spent months trying to gain access to a tech company's computer system, but the cyber security had stopped him cold. But he hadn't given up; the prize was too tempting. He had told Anatoli just how much information people stored within the corporation's latest app: VE-Life.

This time, the target went beyond credit card numbers and bank accounts. Those were small change. A credit card sold for ten American dollars—but a clean medical record with a good Social Security number? That would clear twenty times as much. That kind of information was digital gold. And Weston Industries had tens of millions of users who used VE-Life to store this information.

For a month now, Anatoli had done nothing but think about how to get his target. Luka had just about gone out of his mind with impatience. They spoke every day, and every day Anatoli asked a new question, or wanted more information. But young, impetuous Luka wanted action.

Finally, Anatoli had had enough of his nephew's whining. He slammed his nephew's head against the table where he now sat. "Michelangelo studied a block of marble every day for four months before he lifted a chisel to the statue of David. Each day he came and looked at the stone. He watched it. Analyzed it. Until he was ready. When *I* am ready, then we will move."

Anatoli realized they needed to get the data when it was *outside* the company. His idea was the same as robbing a bank. "Do you go for the main vault with security cameras, alarm systems, and armed guards, or do you hit the lightly guarded armored car where you can change the environment to suit your plans?"

They lacked inside information, but Anatoli had solved that issue too. He smiled faintly as he swirled a piece of bread in his coffee. It had been far too easy to find possible targets to blackmail inside Weston's headquarters. All executive staff had their own webpage that detailed their personal lives, and they were all very active on social media. Not only did he have access to their carefully prepared business lives, but he could also peek behind the curtain. Simple Web searches revealed their pasts— and Anatoli targeted the ones he felt were hiding something. From that culled list, he had hired a private investigator to dig deeper. He had so many candidates it was easy to discover which ones he could manipulate.

The strong coffee warmed his mouth as he took a long sip. He never left the village, yet he had put a plan in motion on the other side of the world. Technology had made the world a smaller place. He wondered how many knew how dangerous it was now that a man like him could be anywhere.

Of course, Anatoli knew well that a stolen item was only as valuable as the price you could move it for. Steal a Rembrandt, and it would be so hot you'd only get pennies on the dollar. Because of that, Anatoli always put feelers out to gauge the possible return on his investment. And he had done the same with this particular investment. Unfortunately, he made a mistake: he brought Luka with him.

His nephew's biggest fault was pride. When the buyer scoffed at the idea of anyone getting their hands on tens of millions of accounts, Luka had blurted out the intended target—Weston Industries. That information had traveled on the black winds. Now his contacts in Russia were intent on having it as soon as possible. There had been no pressure—yet—but the Russian mob was not known for patience; they expected results.

And if Luka failed, it would be Anatoli's neck on the line.

Anatoli set the coffee cup down so hard that it chipped the little saucer. He frowned. He knew there must be many others who were aiming to steal the data first. Now he had to act quickly.

That was why he had sent his nephew to the States with the team Anatoli himself had handpicked.

6

I'M A FAN

As the Bellmore estate came into view, Replacement sat up straight. Bruce whistled. "That thing's the size of a Star Destroyer."

"We may be here longer than a week," Phillip added.

The mansion was a magnificent two-and-a-half-story residence built in English Tudor style. It sat on a hill overlooking the Onopiquite Reservoir. Built in the early forties, the brick and stonework home rose majestically from the surrounding mountainside. At each corner and evenly spaced along the front were square towers that made it look like a castle. It had fallen into some disrepair over the years—until Pierce Weston purchased it. Over the last few months, a host of construction workers had upgraded and restored the estate back to its former glory.

"They want it all wireless, right? Top to bottom?" A smile spread across Replacement's face.

"The whole shebangarino." Gerald's gaze slowly traveled down the length of the huge building. "Maybe I priced this job too low…"

They drove through a grand stone entrance with two opened iron gates. On the right side of the driveway stood a small cottage house. The door opened as they approached, and a tall man in a sharp gray suit walked out.

Gerald rolled down his window. "Good morning. I'm Gerald Mathis. We're doing the wireless work."

"Good morning, Mr. Mathis." The man scanned his tablet. "May I please see everyone's identification?"

Everyone handed over their licenses, and the man checked them off his list.

"Thank you, sir. Do you know where you're going?"

"I know where to park. Thank you."

The man handed back the IDs and stepped away from the car. As his tablet pressed against his coat, Replacement noticed his gun holster.

Gerald drove forward. The long driveway wound its way past a manicured lawn and perfectly trimmed bushes. On the left end of the house stood a seven-bay garage. A massive stone stairway led to the main entrance in the middle. Gerald headed over to the right, to a smaller covered entranceway.

"Today's going to be just prelim work," Gerald explained as he parked the car and they all got out. "I want to confirm a list of questions I have before we get started." He opened the trunk and rummaged around.

Replacement looked around. "Are there other people working here now?"

Gerald glanced up. "Nope. They all finished up. Ow!" He bashed his head on the trunk. Swearing, he walked in a circle and rubbed his head.

Replacement grimaced while Phillip and Bruce looked as though they were trying not to laugh.

"Are you okay?" Replacement asked.

"Fine. Fine," Gerald grumbled. "I spoke with the electrical contractor. They've upgraded all the electrical in the house and tested it, so we're good to go."

"Everything's getting its own UPS and surge protector?" Bruce asked.

"Everything." Gerald nodded. "Today I need to confirm the locations for the access points. Do you all have your phones with you?"

They nodded.

"Good. I sent a spreadsheet to your numbers, along with everyone else's contact information. Everything is marked on the spreadsheet. Alice, you'll take the top floor, Phillip, you have the first, and Bruce, you've got the basement. I'll take the guesthouse."

Replacement pointed down the hill at a huge cottage home. "That's the guesthouse?"

Bruce chuckled. "It's good to be a king."

Gerald looked like a computer-nerd herder as he pulled them all into a huddle. "I need you to confirm the physical location of the APs, jack placements, structural materials, and power outlets."

Phillip took out his cell phone. "What do we do if we have a question? Should I just call you?"

"Give me a ring-a-ding-ding. Remember, you don't know everything, and everyone can't know it all." Gerald smiled awkwardly. "I mean that it's better to ask than apologize. If you have any questions or doubts, call me. Let's get started and meet back here at ten, okay?"

Everyone nodded.

"Any other questions?" Gerald asked.

"I'm good," Replacement said.

"Me too." Phillip tapped his phone.

"Ah, what're we going to do about lunch?" Bruce asked.

"There's a refrigerator inside. I'll put everyone's lunch there." Gerald held out his hand, and Phillip and Replacement each handed him a brown bag.

Bruce rubbed the back of his head. "I meant, where can we get lunch?"

"There's no place around here. I thought I told you to bring your own lunch," Gerald said.

"You did. I ate it while I was waiting for you to pick me up." Bruce smiled crookedly.

Gerald ran his hand up the back of his head and rolled his eyes.

"I made two peanut butter and jelly sandwiches," Replacement said. "You can have one."

"Thanks."

"Great. Problem solved." Gerald walked toward the main house.

They all followed Gerald inside. The old, thick oak side door swung inward with surprising ease. Replacement's mouth fell open, and Bruce whistled.

Dark wood, stone, and brass led to a huge kitchen. The lights sparkled off the glass and stainless steel.

"Wow. What a kitchen." Phillip pushed his glasses up the bridge of his nose.

"Which way to the basement?" Bruce turned in a circle.

"Through those doors." Gerald pointed toward the end of the kitchen. "First door on your left leads to a staircase down."

"Do you have a map?" Bruce quipped as he walked away.

"I should make something up," Gerald muttered. He typed himself a note.

"The kitchen is like three of my apartments," Replacement said.

"I'll start here." Phillip set his big bag down. "The walls look ten feet thick. The wireless signal is going to go crazy with all the stone, stainless, and tile. Like a pinball."

Replacement smiled. "I'm heading upstairs. Call me if you need me."

She waved and started down the hallway. The house had two hallways on each floor. The hallway in the back was a straight run, but the front hallway consisted of straight sections and corners. The architect had evenly spaced the front rooms. It gave the mansion its battlement-castle feel and kept the hallway from being one long, dark corridor. At the end of every section Replacement turned left and walked along a hallway that faced the outside.

She tried to keep focused on her job, but her head kept swiveling around as she passed beautiful paintings, ornate vases, and other expensive trappings. She ran her fingers along a dark mahogany table, then rubbed the tips of her fingers together. There wasn't a speck of dust.

"He must need an army of servants to keep all this clean," she mumbled to herself.

The hallway opened into a wide front entranceway with an enormous marble staircase that led to the second floor. Two full suits of armor stood guard against each wall. Family crests, shields, and crossed swords covered the walls. A massive medieval chandelier hung suspended from the arched ceiling. She gawked as she started up the stairs.

At the top of the stairs, hallways led off to the left and right, but it was the view in front of her that took her breath away. The back wall of the huge room was all glass, presenting a commanding view of the countryside. The lake below reflected all the glorious colors of the changing leaves, and the mountains stretched out beyond.

She rubbernecked for a minute, taking in the view, before she forced herself to go to work. She decided to start at one end of the house and work her way to the other side. She counted several rooms before the hallway ended at a pair of large double doors. On either side of the doors stood two suits of armor. One held a huge broadsword. The other grasped a massive two-headed battle axe.

"Master bedroom, I'd say." She pushed on one of the thick doors. It silently swung open.

The bedroom had the biggest bed she'd ever seen. The huge headboard was carved out of thick mahogany. This room, too, had floor-to-ceiling windows that provided a panoramic view of the lake. A door on one wall was closed, and next to it was an open walk-in closet.

Replacement stepped inside the closet, and her eyes grew even bigger as she gazed at the long line of designer suits that hung neatly spaced every few inches. She checked her spreadsheet and found the power outlet located below a large, gray wall safe. She marked off the boxes as she ran down Gerald's list of questions.

"One closet down. This is going to take a month. Yeah!" The thought of more work brought a wave of relief to her. She'd been doing everything she could for side work, but the jobs were few and far between. And poor Jack had been working like a dog. He never complained, but she knew the strain was getting to him.

She looked back at her phone. A symbol for a data jack was placed on the wall behind the headboard of the bed. She squatted down and tried to peer along the wall to confirm that the diagram was accurate, but the dark wood and huge bed made it impossible to see. She ran her hands through her hair. She grabbed the back of the bed and tried to pull it away from the wall, but the massive bed wouldn't budge.

"Stupid giant bed," she muttered.

She pulled the mattress away from the headboard, revealing a strip of wall. She kicked off her sneakers and climbed on top of the bed. With one hand pushing against the headboard, she pulled back the mattress, lowered her head, and scanned a few inches of the wall. Huffing, puffing, muttering, and swearing, she squirmed to the center of the bed, checking as she went. Lying on her stomach with her head buried underneath the headboard, she finally saw the edge of the plastic plate of the data jack.

"Ha! Now I've gotcha."

"Excuse me?" A man's deep voice spoke from behind her.

Replacement's head snapped around. In the bathroom doorway stood a tall, bare-chested man wrapped in a towel. Steam poured out around him and drifted up to the ceiling. He tipped his head to the side as his eyes traveled over Replacement lying on his bed.

"Contrary to the tabloids, I'm not used to finding beautiful girls sprawled in my bed."

"Uh... uh..." Replacement was so muddled she couldn't think of a response.

Pierce Weston looked her over again and drew his head back a little. "Did Roger send you?"

"Who's Roger?"

"Never mind." He shook his head. "Why are you in my bed?"

Replacement felt her face flush as she rushed to get off the bed. "I'm not in your bed—" Her left foot caught on the comforter. She pitched forward and managed to plant her right foot on the ground, but her other leg was now trapped in the twisted fabric.

Pierce rushed forward and grabbed her before she fell flat on her face.

Replacement pressed up against his bare chest as she pulled her foot free. She jumped back, but not before color rose in her cheeks.

Pierce took a step back and put his hands up. "I'm sorry, I thought you were about to fall."

Replacement shook her head, cursing the dumb blanket.

"You still haven't explained to me why you're in my bedroom."

"I didn't expect you to be here."

"I'm Pierce Weston. This is my house."

"I know who you are." Replacement nodded. "I mean, I know your house. That it's yours. And you're home... Here. Now."

Pierce gaped at her. "And you're in my bedroom because...?"

"I'm a fan of your work. I mean I'm working, but I'm a fan. Not a fan, but I follow you. Your work."

"You're a fan?" Pierce took a step backward.

"Not like *fan* fan, but I really like your work. I'm working now. Here."

"You're working here?" Pierce's eyes darted over to the phone on the nightstand. "And what job do you think you have here?" He slowly reached for the phone.

"What? I'm looking for data jacks. JACK!" She closed her eyes and exhaled. "I work for Gerald Mathis."

"Mr. Mathis?" Pierce put the phone down. "You work for him? Is he here today?"

Replacement nodded. "He's working on the computers at the guesthouse. He didn't think you'd be taking a shower—I mean be home."

"I arrived earlier than planned. I'd better go say hello." Pierce turned and headed toward the walk-in closet.

Replacement looked around. She wanted to crawl inside the wall and disappear.

Pierce shut the door but spoke through it. "I don't know if my being here will change his plans."

"Change his plans for the job?" Replacement's voice rose at the thought of losing all that work. "We can work around you. You won't even know we're here." She rushed back to the bed, grabbed her phone, and pulled her sneakers back on. "I'm very sorry I disturbed you. Now that I know you're home, I'll be invisible."

Pierce came back out in a fitted, dark navy-blue T-shirt and jeans. He carried a laptop. He stopped and looked at her. "I just meant I wanted to take Mr. Mathis out for lunch. It's been a long time since I've been in town."

Replacement exhaled. "Sorry. I thought you meant you wanted to postpone the job."

"No, not at all." Pierce smiled.

Replacement let out her breath.

"But I'd really like to see how you could pull off invisibility."

Replacement blushed. "I'd better get back to the bed—I mean back to work on the bed—to check for the jacks. JACK. I should think about Jack."

Pierce coughed, but she was sure he was trying to cover a laugh. "It was nice to meet you…"

"Repla—Alice." Replacement nodded. "Alice. Alice Campbell."

"Nice to meet you." He paused. "Alice."

7

BABIES

As Jack walked out of the police processing office, he tried not to limp. He crossed the street to the Charger, and a determined grin spread across his face.

I've got enough to pay the bills, get some equipment, and take Alice out for a nice night. Not much, but it's enough.

He quickened his pace as he thought about Replacement. Tomorrow night was date night, and he couldn't wait. For the past couple of months, they'd been skimping on date night with bargain movie rentals and homemade subs. But with this little extra infusion of cash, Jack planned to make reservations at Replacement's favorite restaurant, Antonelli's. He'd swing over to Titus's in the morning and get paid.

The relationship with Replacement had kicked into overdrive recently. In the past, he'd been going out of his mind, trying to take it slow with her, but she seemed different now. Ready.

He opened the door of the Charger, and his phone barked.

Don't get it. Go home. Don't even look.

Jack glanced down, and his chest tightened when he saw the caller ID. Well's Meadow Nursing Home.

"It's Jack. Is everything okay?"

"Yes, Jack," Cristalita's familiar voice answered. "Aunt Haddie asked if I could give you a call. Everything's fine. In fact, she's having a very good day, but she insists on speaking with you."

Jack glanced around. "Today? Can you ask if I can come by tomorrow?"

"She was pretty firm. Do you want me to bring her the phone, or…?"

Jack looked at the clock: 4:30 p.m. He'd been awake for close to thirty hard hours and was still an hour away from his apartment.

"No. I'm on my way."

***

Jack sat in the common room at the nursing home across from the frail old black woman with thin salt-and-pepper hair and stroked her hand. Her eyes were bright, but her face was lined with concern.

"I'm so glad you came, Jackie." She squeezed his hand tighter. "What happened to your face?"

"It looks worse than it is. Is everything all right? Did something happen?"

Aunt Haddie's lips pressed together, and she closed her eyes. "Alice stopped by yesterday."

Jack stopped breathing. A thousand different scenarios of what Alice could have said or done to upset Aunt Haddie spun through his mind. "She's great, right? I mean, we're good. Alice and I. We've been really getting along."

"That's the problem." Aunt Haddie patted his hand and frowned. "She came for a visit the other day, and she just... glowed. She's very much smitten with you. Always has been."

Jack rubbed the back of his neck. "Uh... then what's the problem? I know I'm six years older than her—"

"Shh. My Alton was twelve years older than me. He always said he'd just waited for the right girl to come along." She winked.

"Okay, I still don't understand. If we're getting along so well, then what's the problem?" Jack asked.

Aunt Haddie exhaled and held on to his hand with both of hers. Her eyes locked on his. "My Alton waited."

"I understand that. He was twelve years older than you. So he didn't get married because he was waiting for you."

"No. He waited until we got married." Aunt Haddie lifted an eyebrow.

"What else could he be—oh!" Jack tried to pull his hand back, but she kept hold of it.

"Alice practically floated in here the other day. A woman can tell what's on the mind of a young girl. All she spoke about was you. You and your soft hair. You and your big brown eyes and how your smile just melts her heart. How tall you are and how handsome—"

"Yeah, okay." Jack squirmed.

"Well, I saw that gleam in her eye."

Jack swallowed. "Aunt Haddie, I care for her very much, so—"

Aunt Haddie's eyes grew large and then narrowed. "Don't you *so* me, Jack Alton Stratton. You're one of the last people I thought I'd have to have this conversation with."

Jack's chest tightened, and he cast his gaze at the floor.

"You said it yourself: Alice is Chandler's sister, and she's my baby." Aunt Haddie's voice had gotten louder, and people started to look over. "You're going to wait for marriage before you lie with her."

Jack wanted to bolt. "Aunt Haddie, not so loud." He looked around.

"Never you mind anyone rubbernecking. Look at me, Jackie. Making love is special. It bonds you. Do you love her, Jackie?"

"I do."

"And she loves you. But making love isn't something to be taken lightly." She squeezed his hand harder. "How people nowadays bop from one person to the next, thinking nothing of it—'til it's too late. Are you ready to have babies?"

"Babies? I'm not so sure you understand how things work now." Jack ran his hand through his hair as he gauged how to put it. "I'd... take precautions."

She raised her eyebrow. "I know how things work. I was young once." She leaned in. "Those things aren't foolproof."

Jack blushed.

"You need to wait until you're ready to start a family." She patted his hand. "It's the right thing to do."

Jack exhaled.

"Jackie?"

He looked down at her hand and begrudgingly nodded.

She squeezed his hand and cleared her throat. "Look me in the eyes, Jackie. She's my last baby. Promise me. Promise me you'll wait."

Jack's chest tightened. He knew he couldn't break his word to Aunt Haddie, but he couldn't think of a way out of it, without breaking her heart.

"I promise."

Aunt Haddie beamed. She draped her arms around him and gave him an enormous hug. "Do you want me to speak with Alice?"

"No." Jack drew the word out as if he were pulling taffy. "I'll handle that."

"Okay now. When will I see you again?"

"The end of the week."

She kissed his cheek. Jack stood up and hurried for the door.

But just as the nurse reached out to open it, an old man in the corner waved Jack over.

"Hey, Jack, come here," he called out.

Jack looked at the nurse, who shrugged. "His name's Mr. Hayes. He's harmless," she whispered.

Jack walked over to the old man, who was sitting in an overstuffed recliner. Mr. Hayes sat up straighter, but his back was still curved. He peered out at Jack under big, gray, bushy eyebrows.

"Is your girl the little firecracker who comes to see Haddie?"

Jack grinned. He didn't need any clarification to know he was talking about Replacement. "She is."

The man looked Jack up and down, then settled back into the chair. "You want some advice?"

Oh no. What a day.

Jack had a feeling that no matter what his answer was, he was going to get some. "Sure."

"That girl comes in here, and not that I'm eavesdropping, but all she talks about is you. Now I've been married five times, and I've learned something about women."

"And what would that be?"

One bushy eyebrow rose higher as the man thrust his head forward and stared at Jack.

Jack shrugged as he waited for the man to continue.

The old man huffed loudly. "You're like her sun. She revolves around you."

"Okay. And you think that's a bad thing?"

"A bad thing? Hell, no. That's what you want. If any of my exes had cared about me a quarter as much as that girl does about you, I'd still be married with a smile on my face."

The old man spoke very loudly, and Jack was sure everyone in the room was listening.

Jack cleared his throat. "Thanks for the advice."

"Thank me? Don't thank me unless you take it. That's the kind of girl you keep. If you don't, it's on you. You'll end up alone in some home, talking to some young kid who thinks you're crazy."

Jack nodded his head and straightened up. He looked around the room at the sea of old faces, all of whom were now watching him. Their collective years of wisdom could not be counted. They were all nodding too.

"Thank you, sir. I appreciate it."

The old man smiled.

8

HOW LONG?

On any other day, Jack would have been on guard when he opened his apartment door, but today he wasn't. Tired and overwhelmed, he stood with his head hung down and swung open the door.

The giant one-hundred-ten-pound dog slammed into his chest. She knocked him back, and he fell onto his butt.

"Terrific," Jack groaned.

Lady licked his face.

"Lady, off." He tried to push her back.

"Jack?" Replacement called from inside the apartment.

Jack patted the huge dog. "It's me."

Replacement bounded into the hallway, wrapped her arms around his neck, and gave him a big kiss. She had to angle her back to fend off Lady.

"Welcome home, babe." She helped him up. "I made chicken and—" She squinted at his eye. "What happened to your face?"

"Rough day at the office."

Jack winced as her hand lightly touched his cheek.

She frowned. "Does it hurt much?"

He grinned roguishly and kissed her. "I'm fine."

"What happened?"

"I bobbed when I should've weaved."

Replacement rolled her eyes. "Let's get you inside and cleaned up."

Lady trotted after them.

"I taught Lady a new trick," Replacement said. "Watch. You stay right there."

Jack closed the door behind him and waited.

Replacement held up her hand, and Lady pranced over. They both turned to face Jack.

"Sit."

Lady sat.

Jack clapped.

Replacement put her hands on her hips. "That's not the trick, Jack. She's had that one down forever."

"Sorry."

Replacement put her hands behind her back and looked straight ahead. "Meanie face. Meanie face."

Lady leapt to her feet. In an instant, she went from lovable dog to Hell Hound. Her teeth flashed. Her ears lay back on her head, and she chomped at the air.

Jack held up a hand and moved back against the door. "Nice face. Nice face."

Replacement tossed Lady a biscuit, and she took off into the bedroom.

"That's a good trick if you want to make someone wet their pants," Jack said.

Replacement laughed. "I think she's got the top ten down. Sit, paw, lie, dance in a circle, crazy bark, beg, kiss, stay, roll over, and now meanie face."

"Let's hold off on crazy bark, but good work." Jack inhaled deeply. "Something smells awesome." He looked at the little table set with two places. "What's the occasion?"

Replacement bit her bottom lip. "I thought we could have a little romantic evening." She tugged at his arm. "Come on." She led him into the bathroom.

"I'm okay. The nurse at the jail gave me a couple of butterfly strips."

"I don't know why you don't let me go with you. I could watch your back."

Jack shook his head. "No way. It's not safe for you."

"But it is for you?"

"I couldn't have taken you anyway. You were working. How'd it go?"

"Great."

"See. You shouldn't come with me." Jack grinned.

She playfully punched him in the shoulder. Jack couldn't help but wince.

Replacement eyed him suspiciously. "Shirt." She waved her hand in a circle, and Jack took off his shirt. "I could've gone after work with—dang!"

She turned him to the side, and he groaned as her fingers touched his ribs. "Jack, is anything broken?"

Jack looked at the large dark-purple bruise that ran along his side. He shook his head. "I'm fine. It's just a little sore."

Replacement's eyes rounded in concern.

"So, it's a networking job?" Jack blurted out, trying to change the subject. "At the old Bellmore estate?"

"The place is huge. Mr. Mathis thinks it could take longer than he expected."

"Mr. Mathis?" Jack asked.

Replacement inhaled. "Gerald. His last name's Mathis."

Jack pulled her close. "You're calling him Mr. Mathis now?"

"No. It's just… nothing."

"I brought in two today," Jack said. "I thought we could go out for an extra-special date night. Dinner tomorrow at Antonelli's?"

Replacement purred. "I'd love to, but it may have to be a late dinner." She wrinkled her nose. "Gerald picks us up, and he usually stays late."

"Us?"

"He hired a couple of other guys. Phillip and Bruce. Gerald thought it made sense for all of us to meet in town and drive out."

"I'll drive you."

"Thanks for the offer, but Gerald's a little bit of a control freak. I should stick with his plan."

"How about I make reservations for seven o'clock? Will that work?"

"That sounds awesome." She draped her arms around his neck and pulled him down. Her lips pressed against his, and her hand traveled around his waist. Shivers shot up his back as he pulled her tightly against him. He stifled a grimace from the pain in his ribs and forced a smile, but only the corner of his mouth curled up. Replacement looked up at him and bit her lip again.

"I'm fine," Jack said. "Let's eat."

***

After dinner, Replacement came around to his side of the table. "Why don't you hop in the shower?" She ran her fingers up his arm.

Jack opened his mouth but only nodded. Her eyes followed him into the bedroom. He looked back before he closed the door. Her chin was tucked low into her shoulder, and her green eyes peered up at him.

She's beautiful.

Jack felt his hand tick up in a little wave, and she waved back.

In the bathroom, he pulled his clothes off and turned the shower on. A scratching on the door stopped him getting in. When he opened the door, Lady rushed in and shook. She pulled the bath rug into the corner, turned around three times, then lay down on the tile floor with a satisfied huff.

"You big baby." Jack stroked behind her head before he climbed into the shower.

The hot water stung his wounds, and he growled low. Lady growled too.

Jack pulled back the shower curtain. Lady's head was raised as she stared at him.

"I'm okay, girl. Thanks."

Seemingly reassured that everything was okay, the big dog laid her head back down.

After a few minutes, Jack leaned his own head against the wall and sighed. His muscles relaxed, and he let his head droop forward. His eyes closed. The water splashed against his chest, and he breathed in the warm, moist air. Then his eyes flipped open, and his hand shot out to the wall to steady himself. "I definitely need some sleep."

He shut off the water, and Lady whined. "Oh, be quiet. You can stay in here if you want."

Lady laid her head back down and stretched her legs out.

"Boy, you're one big dog." Jack shook his head. Lady was stretched out across the entire floor. "I think we need a bigger bathroom." He scratched behind her ears.

Jack didn't bother with a shirt; he just pulled on a pair of sweats and opened the bedroom door.

He stopped short.

Oh.

The ceiling light was off, but several candles flickered around the room. His eyes were fixed on Replacement lying in his bed, covered with just a sheet. As his eyes traveled up her body, he knew she was naked beneath the cloth.

Jack swallowed.

Their eyes locked. She smiled, and he saw the flush in her cheeks. She bit her lip and nodded.

He slowly walked forward. Replacement started to pull the sheet back. Quickly, Jack stopped her. The words still echoed in his ears: *Promise me.*

Replacement's eyebrows rose. "Jack?"

Jack exhaled and sat down on the edge of the bed, facing slightly away from her. "Alice." He swallowed.

Her eyes rounded as she pulled the sheet a little tighter around herself. "Are you okay?"

He nodded, then shook his head. "I know we talked about it, but…" He sighed. "I think we should wait."

She scooted over to him and leaned up against his arm. "Thank you for giving me time." She kissed his cheek. "But I'm ready now."

She pressed her lips against his. He moaned. Her fingers ran through his hair. She softly kissed his neck.

Crap.

"Wait." Jack reached for her hands. "We shouldn't."

"No, I'm ready." She clamped both arms around him.

"Not tonight. I just can't right now."

Her lip curled up. "Did you get hurt down there?" She nodded toward his groin.

Jack flushed. "What?"

"Did you get hit in the groin or something?"

"No."

"Why then?" Her eyes widened. "Did I do something?"

"No, it's not you. I just think we should wait."

"For what?"

Jack didn't know how to explain it without actually saying the word he wasn't ready to say: marriage.

"I just think that we should wait until our relationship is more… stable."

"It's unstable?" She sat back.

"No. It's great."

He reached for her; she scooted back. "You just said it's not stable."

"No, I didn't. I said we should wait until it's *more* stable."

"Why?"

"I want to make sure that it's right—special."

"You've slept with other girls." Her lip trembled.

Jack turned toward her. "I don't want to just sleep with you. I want it to be different."

Her eyes began to tear up. "Is it because of what happened to me?"

Jack jumped up. "No." He shook his head vigorously.

Looking confused, her eyes searched the room. "You don't know if this is right?"

"No. I know it's right, but not right." His hands went in all directions. "I just meant I don't want it to be just sex."

"Just sex?"

"That didn't sound right… I think I need to wait."

"Wait? For what?"

Jack stood there with his hands out. He wanted to scoop her up in his arms. *What the hell did I promise?*

"How long do you want to wait, Jack?" Replacement's whole body tensed up.

How long? I didn't think this through. I'm just covering the bills—how the hell can I even think about… I'm not ready to get married.

"How long?" Replacement asked again.

"A couple of years," he blurted out.

She made a face as if she'd drunk spoiled milk. "You're not sure you love me?" She wrapped the sheet around her body.

"That's not what I meant."

As she ran out of the room, she burst into tears.

"No. I do." Jack rushed after her, but she raced into her room and slammed the door. He stood outside the door. "Alice, I love you. I just…" He let his head thump against her door.

"Go away!" she yelled.

Jack stood for a minute, unsure what to say or do.

Lady trotted out of his bedroom.

Jack whispered at Replacement's closed door, "I'm just not ready…"

Lady plopped down beside him and looked at him with her sad pup face.

9

DEAD ISN'T MACHO

The next morning, Jack heard Replacement's bedroom door open and slam shut.

Not good.

When the front door opened and closed shortly thereafter, Jack ran for his shoes. While he pulled on one sneaker, he opened the door and called out, "Alice?"

He heard her hurrying down the stairs. Jack chased after her. As he ran out of the apartment building, he saw her storming down the sidewalk—head up, shoulders square, and her arms straight down with her hands clenched into fists at her sides.

He broke into a jog and quickly caught up.

"You don't have to follow me. I'm fine." She kept her eyes straight ahead.

"I can drive you up to the house," he offered.

"Gerald wants us to meet at U-Do2. We need to pick up cables and stuff."

"Okay. I'll walk with you there." Jack stepped in front of her, and she practically ran right into him.

She stopped and glared at him. "Why?" Her hands snapped up and back down.

"Because I like your company." Jack grinned.

Replacement's face softened, and her dimple popped out.

Jack leaned in and quickly kissed her.

"Why don't you want my company the way I *want* you to want my company?" She pouted.

He took her by the hand and started to walk again. "I do. Let's just slow it down. I did that for you."

"You're talking about stopping."

"Let's talk about it tonight. Are we still on for Antonelli's? I made reservations for seven."

She took in a deep breath. "Okay."

"I'm looking forward to it."

"Where are you heading today?" Replacement asked.

"I have to go see Titus and swing into Patton's Police and Military Supply Depot. I'm out of just about everything. I need mace, Taser refills—"

"What?" She pulled her hand free. "You went out with no gun, no mace, and an unloaded Taser?"

Jack tried to give her a roguish grin, but as her scowl deepened, he knew it wasn't working. "I'm getting them now."

"Now? *Now?*" Her legs kicked back into high gear, and so did her hands. They flew in all directions as she stormed down the sidewalk. "You won't let me come with you because it's *so* dangerous, but then you go out practically buck naked. Seriously? What did you have—nothing? Why? Because you're stubborn."

Her ponytail danced back and forth, and her green eyes flashed. Her body was taut, and he saw the storm of frustration raging in her eyes. But he knew the root cause of her aggravation was her concern for him. She had his back even if it came out as upbraiding him for his own lack of preparedness. She cared about him. Jack had to stop himself trying to kiss her again, because right now he found her irresistible.

"And what about *my* Taser?" she continued. "You could have taken that. It has a cartridge."

Jack rolled his eyes.

She stopped. "It's because it's pink, isn't it?"

He smirked. "Well…"

"Men." She tossed her hands in the air and started speedwalking again. "You'd rather get shot or stabbed or who knows what than be seen with a pink Taser?"

Jack didn't respond.

"Macho? Ha! Dead isn't macho. What if you ended up in the hospital again? Then what? Who would take care of you?"

"You." Jack smiled.

Her eyes narrowed, but then her shoulders slumped. "Seriously, Jack. I love you so much it hurts. Can you please be careful? Let me come with you."

"You have a job to do."

"I'd rather work with you. Let's combine the private investigator business and the bounty hunting."

"Right now the private investigations are bringing in almost nothing, and the bounty hunting is doing less than your computer job. It's too sporadic. That's what I'm going to talk to Titus about."

"Will you promise me you'll be more careful?"

"I'm careful."

"What about the cut above your eyebrow, the huge bruise on your side, your cut lip, and the limp you're trying to hide?" She frowned.

Jack straightened up. "I'm not limping."

"Yes, you are."

"My leg's fine."

Replacement's eyebrow rose.

"It is. Look." Jack jogged in place.

"I can tell it's sore. What happened?"

Jack didn't know whether it had happened when he was fighting with five guys in an alley or when he was jumping off a fire escape, but he didn't want to mention either scenario to her. "It's great. I'll prove it. Race you to U-Do2."

"No. You hurt your leg, and now you want to race me to prove it's not hurt? Are all men perpetually four?"

"Yes. So you admit you're wrong about my leg?"

"I am not."

"I'll wager a piece of garlic bread at Antonelli's that I can beat you."

Jack saw her lips press together. Knowing he'd need an advantage, because his leg did still hurt, he turned and bolted.

"Cheater!" she yelled, and she broke into a sprint too.

Replacement beat Jack to the store by five lengths. She danced in a circle, but frowned as she watched Jack slow to a stop.

"See, my leg's fine." He shook out his leg and tried not to grimace.

She walked over and touched his thigh. "There's no pain?"

"None, but stop. We're on the sidewalk. People are looking."

"I just want to make sure you're okay."

"I'm fine. Seven o'clock for dinner?"

"Of course. I want my garlic bread."

Jack laughed, and she kissed him. "See you soon." He winked.

"Be careful. Love you." She held on to his hand, and his fingers slowly pulled away.

"I will." Jack headed back down the sidewalk. Replacement stood in front of the store and watched him walk away, so he stayed in hide-the-limp mode. When he reached the curb, he looked back and gave her a little wave. She waved back and finally went inside.

He grimaced as he shook his leg out.

10

FROM A DISTANCE

Replacement opened the glass door and forced her eyes open wider to get used to the dim fluorescent lights. U-Do2 hadn't been remodeled since the 1950s. Hard-core, do-it-yourself electronic junkies considered it a bastion of exploration. Shelves were stacked with cables, ties, clamps—everything you could possibly need for any project that had power going to it.

Replacement tipped her head to the side and scanned the aisles for Gerald. She walked along the front of the store, but the aisles were filled with so many different displays it was impossible to see all the way down them.

She turned down the farthest aisle, where a boy and his father scanned a rack. Their heads moved back and forth as they read the tags on the shelf, then they both crouched down at the same time to look at an assortment of clamps. The corner of Replacement's mouth ticked up when she saw them both roll up their sleeves.

Packages and display racks kept pulling at her attention, but she managed to stay focused—until a display for a pet monitoring system got the best of her. Her body kept heading straight, but her eyes scanned the display, looking for something for Lady.

She barreled right into someone, hard.

"I'm so sorry. I wasn't paying attention—" She looked up into a pair of deep green eyes. "Hi… uh…"

"Pierce." He smiled.

"I know."

"Are you okay?"

She nodded and realized he was holding her elbow, steadying her. "Why are you here?"

He let go. "I was driving by and saw you come in here. Then I saw the sign: The Everything Electronics Store. I need to find an adapter, but I'm a little lost." He looked around the large store. "I was hoping to find some help, but I couldn't find the F1 button."

Replacement giggled. "That's a good computer joke."

Pierce smiled.

"I'm looking for Gerald." She glanced around the store. "Have you seen him?"

"No. I didn't know he was here."

"Well," Replacement said, "while I'm looking for Gerald, maybe I can help you find what you're looking for. This place is huge."

"I'd appreciate that. I just need a connector from the TV to my tablet."

"I just saw those." Replacement walked up an aisle, and Pierce followed. They stopped in front of a wall covered with different adapters.

As Pierce scanned the rack, he shrugged. "Right now I'm thinking of another computer nerd joke. Do you want to hear it?"

"Okay."

"How many programmers does it take to change a light bulb?"

Replacement shrugged.

"None. That's a hardware problem."

They both laughed.

When Replacement looked up at him, his laugh trailed off. "I was wondering," he said. "Would you like to—"

"Excuse me," Jack's voice interjected.

Replacement spun around. "Jack! Um… what're you doing here?"

"I had to come back to find you. I forgot to take my keys." Jack was speaking to her, but he kept his eyes on Pierce.

"Oh." Her dimple disappeared. "Pierce, this is Jack."

Jack held out his hand. "Jack Stratton."

Pierce took a small step forward and shook it. "Pierce Weston."

"I'm working at Pierce's house this week." Replacement looked up at Jack with a smile that silently shouted: please be nice. "I was just helping him find something." She handed Jack her keys and then turned back to the display. "Do you know what the TV has for inputs?" she asked.

Pierce shook his head.

"Which TV is it?"

"Do you remember the one next to my bed?" Pierce asked.

Jack stepped forward.

Replacement laughed nervously and took a small step in front of Jack to block him.

Pierce looked at Jack's face. "I'm sorry. Boy, that didn't sound good. I meant she saw it when she was working in my bedroom."

"I was looking for data jacks," Replacement added.

"Uh-huh." Jack kept his eyes fixed on Pierce.

"Hey, there you are," Gerald called out, walking down the aisle toward them. "Hi, Jack. Pierce? What're you doing here?"

Pierce looked relieved. "I was looking for a connector to hook my tablet up to the TV." He quickly grabbed a couple of items off the wall. "One of these should work." He headed toward the checkout. "It was nice to meet you, Jack."

Jack just nodded.

"The car's all packed. You ready?" Gerald asked Replacement.

"Yeah, I'll be right there."

As Gerald headed for the door, Replacement hung back and walked beside Jack. "Is everything really okay? You look upset," she whispered.

"I'm fine." Jack gritted his teeth. "You never mentioned your new boss."

"Oh, well… what's there to mention?" She scooted out of the store.

Pierce, Gerald, and Phillip stood next to the curb, while Bruce sat in the back of Gerald's car, packed in next to a load of boxes.

Replacement pointed a thumb at Jack. "Phillip and Bruce, this is Jack."

Phillip gave a short wave, but Bruce hung out the window and eagerly offered his hand. "It's great to meet you, Jack. I've read about you in the news."

"Nice to meet you too." Jack shook his hand.

Replacement was eyeing the loaded back seat of Gerald's car. "So... where are we all supposed to sit?"

Gerald frowned. "Yeah, I didn't realize how much space all that stuff would take up."

"Maybe I could give Replacement a ride," Jack said.

"No need for you to go out of your way," said Pierce from behind Jack, emerging from the store. "My car's right here. I can take someone."

Replacement's eyes followed where Pierce pointed. Parked two cars away was a shiny blue Porsche. The sleek, expensive car was as out of place on the small-town street as a golf cart would be at the Daytona 500.

But before Replacement could open her mouth, Jack stepped forward. "Phillip," he said quickly. "Have you ever ridden in a Porsche Carrera?"

"Uh... no."

"No?" Jack smiled broadly. "You have to experience it. It's quite the ride." Jack put his hand on Phillip's shoulder and led him over to Pierce's car.

"Really?" Phillip smiled like a kid.

Pierce stood there for a moment and then clicked his tongue. "Sure." Pierce looked at Replacement, then eyed Jack. He tossed his keys up and caught them. "Why don't you ride with me? Phillip, is it?"

"Yeah." Phillip, looking like a kid in a candy store, quickly opened the door and hopped in.

Pierce stared over the top of the car at Jack.

Jack stared right back.

Replacement's head went back and forth between them as if she were watching a tennis match. Neither glared, and their expressions didn't change, but she could almost sense them mentally measuring each other up.

"Great." Gerald waved to Pierce. "We'll meet you at the house. Hop in, Alice."

Jack turned to Replacement. "I'll see you tonight."

Replacement frowned, and her brows knit together. She walked closer to Jack and whispered, "He's just trying to be nice."

Jack leaned in. "Let him be nice from a distance."

He grinned.

She didn't.

11

NEED TO KNOW

Luka sat across the little table from Nicholai and shifted uncomfortably. He wished his Uncle Anatoli had left him in charge rather than this cold-blooded ex-soldier. Trained by the Russian Special Forces, the Spetsnaz, Nicholai was a man whose ruthlessness was feared by his enemies and allies alike.

Nicholai set a scarred forearm on the table and leaned back in his chair. Wrapped around the ragged scar was a tattoo of a coiled snake, its head poised to strike. Even sitting casually, Nicholai still had an air of authority that hovered around him. His gray hair cut short, he looked exactly like what he was—an old soldier who had seen the worst in men. War hadn't broken Nicholai; forged in that fire, he had become stronger.

He looked down at his phone. His fist smacked the table. "чорт." Slowly, a devilish grin spread across his face. "Weston arrived early," he said in a thick accent. "Set up your laptop."

Luka proudly tapped his chest. "I'm ready."

From the living room came a loud scoff. "Он поставил его играть в свои игры."

"What?" Luka asked.

"Speak in English," Nicholai said. "No Russian—no Ukrainian."

The deep voice spoke in a heavy Russian brogue. "He set it up to play his games."

"I had to make sure we had an Internet connection, stupid." Luka glared into the living room at the giant Russian, who was stretched out on the couch with his eyes closed.

"Sure." The man's huge boots, dangling over the end of the couch, shook as he laughed.

"Shut up, Savin," Nicholai snapped.

"Have you heard back from Tolyan and Dima?" Luka asked.

Nicholai leaned back in the chair. "They are on their way back now. Only five guards on a rotating basis at the mansion."

"Only five?" Savin called out. "We could just walk in and take it."

"Idiot," Luka snapped. "It's not that easy. Our informant at Weston—"

Nicholai's hand slammed down on the table.

Luka immediately shut up.

Nicholai eyed Luka. "The men I work for don't like being kept in the dark."

Luka swallowed. "That was Anatoli's decision."

Savin huffed. "Why not just send one of us?"

"You don't blend in, you giant oaf." Luka chuckled until he heard Savin's boots thump on the floor.

"Sit down," Nicholai ordered. "Luka's correct. That's why Anatoli hired someone else."

"Why should Anatoli hire a mole to work the inside and not tell us who it is?" Savin walked into the kitchen. "Even you don't know." He nodded at Nicholai.

"It's need to know." Luka cleared his throat. "If they're compromised, we're safe."

"And if they are caught, what then?" Savin asked.

Nicholai tapped his phone. "We go to Plan B."

"And what might that be?" Savin placed his huge hands down on the table and stared at Nicholai.

"That is also need to know." Nicholai's eyes were cold.

Savin nodded and took a step back.

"What do we do now?" Luka asked.

"We wait." Nicholai flexed his forearm, and the tattooed snake's head rose. "A viper lurks in the shadows as it waits for its prey." His fist slammed down on the table. "And then—it strikes."

12

TOO MUCH FENG

Gerald nervously looked down at his checklist and frowned. The whole job was quickly falling behind schedule. "Bruce?" he called out.

The young man kept his hand in his pocket and stared at the floor. "Hello? Bruce?"

Bruce's head snapped up. "Sorry," he muttered. "I zoned."

"I need you un-zoned. I got the server up yesterday, so you're going to be configuring and hooking up devices. Here's a list."

"Is this everything?" Phillip asked. "I'm having a real hard time keeping the signal steady in the library upstairs with all that glass. If Pierce is using his laptop in there, his results are gonna be a little hit-and-miss."

"We need all hits," Gerald said. "We want to make sure they don't lose signal anywhere. It's going to be a long day." Gerald flipped to the next window on his phone. "A new maid started today. Stay out of her way. Pierce is working in the downstairs study. Let's hold off doing any work there. Other than that, give me a shout-out if you need, all righty?"

"Sure." Bruce nodded. "I'm off to adventure."

"I'll head upstairs," Phillip said.

"Guesthouse for me. Anyone needs help, let me know," Replacement offered before she hurried off.

Gerald watched her go. The young woman was energy in a bottle, and he liked being around her. She was a welcome break from the typical computer techs he worked with. And she was easy to talk to.

He picked up his phone and walked toward the downstairs study. As his shoes clicked on the old wood, he glanced out the window at the pond. He lowered his head, and his pace slowed. He made it a few more feet before he stopped. His hand shook. Slightly at first, then it trembled noticeably.

A wave of dread and panic washed over him. He closed his eyes and took three deep breaths, just like his therapist had told him. Three deep breaths. He opened his eyes and rubbed his chin.

"Deep breaths," he said aloud.

He gripped his phone a little tighter and strode forward with purpose. When he reached the thick oak door of the study, he knocked. He leaned closer but heard only his own heartbeat. He wiped his sweaty palm on his pants and knocked again. Still no answer. He took a deep breath and opened the door.

Inside was a regal study that overlooked a little garden. Filled floor to ceiling with books, and trimmed in dark wood with dark carpeting, the room had a studious feel. Pierce sat at an old desk with his back to the door, huddled over his laptop, his head slowly bobbing back and forth to the rhythm of a silent beat. He started to turn around in his chair, noticed Gerald, and removed his headphones.

"Hi, Pierce. Sorry to interrupt you," Gerald said. "I knocked, but—"

"You're not interrupting, Mr. Mathis." Pierce smiled. "What can I do for you?"

Gerald sighed. "I came to thank you, actually."

Pierce looked puzzled. "Thank me? For what?"

"This job."

"Nonsense. I need—"

Gerald shook his head and let out a nervous chuckle. "Nope. You have a whole IT company at your disposal. They could've swooped in here and set this place up in a day."

Pierce's hand turned out. "I wanted you to do it."

"And I appreciate it, but… I just felt like I needed to say it again."

Pierce looked away.

Gerald could see Pierce's hand nervously opening and closing. He took a step closer.

Pierce's eyes darted around the room. Finally he looked directly at Gerald. Pierce only held his gaze for a moment before his shoulders slumped and he looked at the floor.

Gerald knew Pierce still felt guilty. Gerald tried hard not to let bitterness cloud his judgment, but part of him struggled to let go and not blame anyone for his son's death. "You know," Gerald said, "I was just thinking. Once this job's done, if you have the time…" He sighed. "I thought we'd take a couple of rods down to the dock."

Pierce's face lifted. "Sure. I'd like that. Very much."

Gerald smiled. "Great. We'll stay out of your hair for the rest of the day." His eyes darted around the room and then back to his checklist.

"Do you need to do something in here?" Pierce asked.

"I just noticed Bruce missed marking off the jacks in here. I can get them later."

"No. That's fine." Pierce brushed back his hair as he wound his headphones around his phone. "I should stretch anyway."

"You don't need to go. I'll only be a minute."

"Take your time." Pierce took out his e-cigarette case and headed toward the glass doors that led to the garden. "How's the job going?" he asked.

"Great. Without a hitch. I didn't know you smoked."

"Technically, I quit. Three months."

"That's great. I've been trying to quit myself. Are those e-cigs that good?"

"You want to try one?" Pierce walked over to his laptop case. "I've got two. This one's a spare. I've never used it." Pierce held out a silver case the size of a phone.

"Really?"

Pierce nodded. "You can change the flavor up. Not quite the real deal, but they help take the edge off."

"Thanks," Gerald said. "Actually, before you go, am I correct that there are only two jacks in here? One's on this wall." Gerald gestured and marked his sheet. "And the other should be on that far wall."

"There's a third one here." Pierce pointed.

"Great. That's really all I needed. Sorry to have bothered you." He gave a slight nod and headed toward the door. "I'll go check on the team's progress."

"Mr. Mathis?" Pierce called out.

Gerald turned back around.

"I was wondering if you could tell me where—" Pierce cleared his throat. "The study here isn't doing it for me. Too much feng and not enough shui."

Gerald laughed.

"Where's everyone working today?" Pierce asked.

"Well… Bruce is on the main floor and Phillip is on the top floor. They'll be there for the rest of the day. I'm going to the basement to work in the server room. I need to get the patch panel in."

Pierce nodded.

"And Alice is in the guesthouse."

Pierce grinned. "Okay. Thanks."

Gerald turned and left the room. As he walked down the long hallway, he gulped in air.

It was an accident. It was an accident.

13

SIXTY/FORTY

The little bell above the door jingled as Jack walked in. The lobby of Titus Bail Bonds was empty, and so was the window behind the counter. Jack frowned. Part of him had hoped the place would be crowded so he'd have work, but that also meant more human misery for the people looking to get someone they knew out of jail.

"Jackie!" Shawna called out. The short, very full-figured woman hurried up to the counter window. Her face lit up, but Jack noticed the smile flicker like an overhead light.

He sighed. "Please tell me you have something for me, Shawna."

Shawna's long, jet-black, poufy wig waggled back and forth as her head rocked from side to side. "Well…" Her voice rose higher and so did her hands. "I have the check for the two you just brought in."

"That's good, but do you have something new for me?" Jack leaned against the counter.

Shawna's eyes darted down to a stack of manila folders and then back up to Jack. "I'm sorry, Jack. Maybe next week?"

"Come on, Shawna, you've got five there. Is Titus in?"

Jack had known Shawna since they were kids. He knew she had a habit of closing her eyes when she talked—and that when she got real nervous, her eyes slammed shut. Right now, they were clamped closed. "Titus is really, really busy. He said he was going to steer some work your way, but things have been slow—"

"Shawna," Jack interrupted, "open your eyes and look at me."

Her lips mashed together, and her eyes snapped open.

Jack continued. "I need to talk to Titus. He can give me one of those."

"No," she blurted out. "It's just… you can't have those. They're for Bobbie G."

"Is there a reason Titus is giving all the work to Bobbie?"

Shawna protested, "He's not."

"You've got five folders, and they're all labeled for Bobbie G." Jack pointed. "I know he's been here longer than me, and he's my friend, but I'm talking about throwing me a bone. Should I be talking to Bobbie?"

"No!" Shawna huffed loudly and blew away some strands of wig hair that had fallen in her face. "Bobbie's so mad right now he could spit. Please don't talk to him."

"Why's Bobbie mad? He's getting all the work."

Shawna shook her head and cast a quick look over her shoulder at the closed door. Her eyes searched Jack's face for a second, then she leaned forward.

"Don't tell anyone that I said anything, okay?" she whispered. "Titus had to hire his brother-in-law, Irwin. That's what's going down."

"So those *aren't* going to Bobbie G?" Jack pointed at the folders.

Shawna rolled her eyes. "They are, but Bobbie G is training Irwin. If that's possible. Irwin got fired from selling cars, and Ciella, Titus's big sister—do you remember her?"

Jack nodded. Ciella was the type of woman everyone remembered. Loud and whiny, and she could talk forever without taking a breath. He rolled his eyes at the thought of her rambling on and on about nothing. Her voice alone would wear down anyone, which was probably what had happened to Titus.

Shawna nodded as if she'd read Jack's mind. "Anyway, Ciella's here almost every day, and she's on Titus like white on rice. Now Bobbie G's got to do all the work and split the fee sixty/forty with Irwin."

Jack's face didn't hide his disgust. "He has to split the fee sixty/forty?"

"Shh." Shawna's hands fluttered like a windmill as she stared back at the door. "Don't let Titus hear you. Anyway, that's what's going down."

Jack sighed. "Great. Now I understand at least. I don't like it, but it makes sense."

Shawna patted the back of his hand. "I'm sorry, Jackie. I'll try to work on him."

"Thanks for trying." Jack straightened up and rolled his shoulders. "I appreciate it. Tell Titus I'm here."

"What?"

"I need work. I'm not coming with my hat in my hand. I'm good. I'm fast. He can give me one. I'll talk to Ciella if he wants."

Shawna pouted, but as her lips pressed together, her eyes narrowed. She looked down at the folders and then back up at Jack. "Hold on."

She spun on her heel and marched over to the closed door. She adjusted her wig, straightened her skirt, lifted her hand high, and then timidly tapped on the door.

"Yeah," Titus's baritone rumbled.

Shawna slipped into the office and closed the door behind her.

Jack could hear them talking but not what was being said. From the sound of it, it was a one-way conversation, with Titus doing most of the talking. After only a minute or two, the door whipped open and Shawna hurried out.

Her eyes were open wide. "I got you one." She triumphantly pulled a folder out of the pile. "Here it is."

Jack eagerly took the folder. "I can't thank you enough."

Shawna bit her lip and wiggled her eyes. "Oh, I bet I could think of some way you could."

"Seriously. It means a lot."

Shawna stuck her tongue out. "Don't go getting all mushy. His name's Kayden Wilcox. Twenty-eight. Drug possession with intent to distribute in a school zone. No violent priors. I've got everything in there."

"Anything else?"

"We've only got a week left to catch him."

"Wait, only a week?"

"Yeah. We got his file from Bronson Bail Bonds. He was their bail, but they asked Titus for help. They were on it for two months."

"Trip-B had two months, and I have a week? Come on, it'll take a miracle to pull it off."

"There is one wrinkle. In his family, he's got a—"

"Shawna?" Titus called from his office, and Shawna jumped.

"It's all in the folder." Shawna gave Jack's arm a squeeze and hurriedly disappeared into Titus's office.

Jack grinned as he gripped the manila envelope.

Good deal. I got paid, and I got a new one.

As he walked back to the Charger, he opened the folder and began to study the face of Kayden Wilcox. Kayden had a thin nose, and his eyes were set a little too close together. The mug shot showed an angry man with a tattoo of crossed swords on his neck. Jack made a mental note of the address, and when he got to the car he tossed the folder on the passenger seat.

He headed to Patton's Supply first. He chuckled at the name. The owner, Benny Duggan, was a diehard Patton fan. He even dressed like him and went everywhere in military clothing. Benny was unconventional to say the least, but Jack had come to like the eccentric guy.

As Jack pulled into the parking lot of the strip mall where Patton's was located, he saw Benny trying to set up a new mannequin in the store window. Jack tried not to laugh. Benny was a little guy with a large pot belly, and the mannequin looked like a tall version of him.

"New mannequin?" Jack asked as he walked in.

"Isn't it great?" Benny beamed as he wiped his brow and stepped back to admire his work. "I'm expanding to a big and tall offering."

"Well, that guy's both." Jack chuckled.

"There's more." Benny turned and marched toward the back room like a five-star general.

"I'm just doing a quick pick-up," Jack called after him.

Benny reappeared again through the double doors, carrying a giant, fake police dog. "Check this out. It's like the King Kong of dogs."

Jack took a step back when Benny set the dog next to the mannequin. "It's about as big as my dog," Jack said. "She's a king shepherd." Jack took out his phone and pulled up a photo of Lady. He held it out, and Benny peered at the screen.

"Is that a girl next to the dog? That dog's enormous."

"I told you." Jack grinned. "Big as a bus."

"A bus? Why not make her look like a tank?" Benny reached behind the mannequin and pulled out a huge dog vest with golden stars on both sides.

"It's awesome," Jack said.

"You should get it." Benny held out the vest.

"No way. She's not a police dog."

"What about a bounty hunting dog?"

"A what? They don't have bounty hunting dogs."

Benny's eyes widened. "You can start a trend. Think about it? If you brought that dog with you, I'd surrender in a second."

"Good point." Jack looked at the picture of Lady and then at the vest. "It's a ballistic vest, right?"

"She'd be a Sherman tank with teeth." Benny's heels clicked together as he snapped to attention.

"I bet it'd cost as much as a tank." Jack shook his head.

"What else are you getting?"

"Two cans of mace. Four refills for my Taser, and I was going to pick up another round for my girlfriend just to make her happy."

"Ammo?"

"No. I still don't have my guns."

Benny looked up at the ceiling, and his face contorted. "Tell you what. Five hundred covers everything."

"Benny, I appreciate it, but that vest alone has to run to three times that."

"I got two as floor models, and they're triple large. Someone screwed up at their end. I didn't even think they made dogs that big. Besides, I have my name and number on it too." Benny held up the vest, and Jack noticed the text printed in gold along the side. "It'd be good advertising. Think about it. Jack Stratton, the guy who caught the Giant Killer, and his trusted sidekick shop at Patton's Police and Military Supply Depot."

"I don't know…"

"What's not to know?"

"I can't. I don't have the funds."

"You can. Now it's *free* advertising. You can have it, Jack. The streets are a dangerous place, my friend. You need backup. Even Batman has Robin."

14

YOU'RE BEAUTIFUL

Replacement hustled around the downstairs living room of Pierce Weston's huge guesthouse, peeking behind and under furniture. She checked off the locations of the jacks and tried to work out where they could put the wireless equipment.

She slashed a line through the word JACK and frowned. As she stood in the middle of the room, her eyes burned. Her arms wrapped around her chest protectively, and she worked to hold back tears.

Why doesn't he want me?

Just asking herself the question opened the floodgates. Different answers to her question rattled through her mind like pinballs. But they all led back to one thing: it was her.

She wiped her eyes and headed out the back door. It was fall, but the day was still warm. She took in a deep breath of air and walked toward the lake.

Looking over at the green slope on the far side, she thought about Michelle. Now even more tears ran down her cheeks. How she wished she could talk to her sister right now. Replacement had never had many friends, and now there was only Jack she could go to.

The wind blew the grass, and she sniffled. She knew what Michelle would tell her: *It's not you. You're beautiful.*

Replacement smiled as she remembered Michelle's voice. Michelle, although technically not related, had been the perfect big sister. Teacher, friend, confidante, and protector. While others had shied away from the quirky little newcomer, Michelle hadn't. On Replacement's first day at Aunt Haddie's, they'd become friends.

Replacement squared her shoulders and looked across the lake. "Miss you," she whispered. Then she turned and headed back to the cottage.

She walked into the living room and picked up her phone. Every room was now complete except the den. As she went into the hallway, she saw Pierce with his back to her, peering into the den.

"Hi," she said.

His shoulders popped up, and he spun around, startled. His laptop slipped out of his hands. He grabbed for it, but it landed flat on the floor.

"Oh! I'm so sorry!" Replacement gasped. She rushed forward and scooped up the laptop.

"I'm the one who dropped it. It's okay. It's solid state, and with that case, you could jump on it and it'd be fine." He held his hand out.

Replacement handed him the case. They both entered the den, and Pierce set the case down on a desk in the corner and opened it up.

"The company who designed it said I could drop it down a flight of stairs, though I've never tested that out." Pierce grinned awkwardly. "I didn't hear you behind me."

"Sorry," Replacement said. "I stepped outside for a second. I didn't know you were over here. I'll pack up and go find Gerald."

"No, no need." Pierce opened up the laptop. The machine beeped, and the screen prompted a login. "There you go." Pierce exhaled. "It still works."

"You were worried."

"The case is bulletproof, but… well, you never know."

"I lost a portable hard drive one time, and all that happened to it was it tipped over on a desk. It fell, like, two inches onto its side." Replacement stuck out her tongue.

"When I was in college, I tipped a thirty-two-ounce Slurpee onto my laptop. Fried it," Pierce said.

Replacement chuckled. "Save and save often."

"A creed I live by." Pierce turned to the laptop. "I know you're helping Mr. Mathis, but what's your computer background? Did you go to school?"

Replacement nodded. "I went to the Haddie Williams Military Academy."

Pierce typed his login and took a USB stick out of his pocket. "You? A military academy?"

Replacement laughed and shook her head. "I was homeschooled. My sister and I used to kid and call it that. Aunt Haddie's my foster mother. It was actually a lot of fun."

Pierce looked perplexed. "Did you teach yourself computers?"

"My sister, Michelle, got me started. I took a lot of online classes too. You use double encryption?" She pointed to the USB stick.

"Yeah. It's my development box."

"I read that you wrote VE-Life in your own hybrid of C."

"You did?" Pierce shook his head. "I mean, I did."

"The storage looks fine." Replacement leaned against the desk. "You should still run a diagnostic. It fell hard." She wrinkled her nose. "Sorry."

"Stop apologizing. It was my fault."

Replacement looked back to the door.

Pierce stood up straight. "Are you going to be working over here long?" he asked.

"This is the last room I need to do, then I'll be out of your hair."

"Actually," Pierce stuck his hands in his pockets, "I was hoping I could ask you a few questions."

"What kind of questions?"

"Computer."

"Me?" Replacement's hand went to her chest.

"Well, I'm putting together a presentation about the next version of VE-Life, and I wanted some fresh eyes on it."

"But… why me? I'm like—I mean, you must have tons of Ivy League techs who're better qualified."

"I think you're smarter than you realize."

Replacement lifted her chin a little higher.

"And sometimes execs are so interested in corporate ladder climbing, they're not honest." Pierce stared for a second at the wall. "I mean, it's hard to get an unbiased opinion."

"Well, if you think I can help—fire away."

"Great." Pierce opened the laptop. "I've started this conversion…"

He went on about the modifications he was envisioning. Pierce was like a kid with a shiny new toy. He spoke fast, and his hands danced through the air as he explained.

Replacement smiled. She tried to stay focused on what he was saying, but she had a hard time concentrating on his words and not on him.

15

THERE IS ONE WRINKLE...

Jack decided to swing by Kayden's last known address. Traffic was light, so he stuck to the main drag. He took a right and stopped as the light turned red. The sun was now right in his eyes. He pulled down the visor and grinned. Tucked next to the mirror was Replacement's picture. Jack felt like a fighter pilot whenever he looked at it before going out on a bounty. He wasn't superstitious, but it was a habit now.

He tapped his fingers on the steering wheel as the walk signal came on. An assorted herd of humanity paraded in front of the Charger. Jack scanned their faces. Most turned and looked away. But one of them...

Jack did a double take. He looked once more at the wanted poster on his seat, then back at the man who casually glanced at him as he strolled across the crosswalk.

It was definitely Kayden Wilcox.

Jack looked at the sky. "Thank you!"

A few more stragglers ambled by, then the light changed. Jack cut the wheel and pulled over to the curb. He considered grabbing a can of mace from the trunk, but decided against it. He couldn't take a chance on losing Wilcox.

People moved along both sides of the wide sidewalk. Jack spotted Wilcox only about twenty yards ahead of him. As he hurried after, Jack reminded himself that Wilcox's list of priors included no violent offenses.

Wilcox was four inches shorter than Jack and thinly built. Jack scanned his waist and pockets for any telltale bulges of possible weapons but saw none.

A group of four teenagers jostled one another between him and Wilcox. Jack stayed a few feet behind them. Three of the teens chatted away, while one texted and looked up occasionally.

Wilcox glanced back at the group. His face soured, but he kept walking.

The teens turned into a store, and Jack made his move. He surged forward. "Kayden Wilcox," Jack announced in his police voice as he slapped a cuff on him. "I'm taking you in on an outstanding warrant."

"Wait!" Wilcox blurted out. "You've got the wrong guy."

Jack looked at the tattoo on Wilcox's neck and scowled. "Save it." He clicked the other cuff closed.

"I'm his brother."

"Right."

"My name's Jayden Wilcox. Check my license."

Jack grabbed Wilcox's arm and pulled him back toward the Charger. "You can explain that to the judge."

"When I sue you for false arrest, I will. My name's Jayden Wilcox, and Kayden's my twin brother."

"You both have the same tattoo?"

"Yeah, we do. Call the bail bonds. This happened before, and my lawyer sent them papers."

There is one wrinkle... Shawna's unfinished warning echoed in Jack's mind.

Jack looked at Wilcox, and his eyes narrowed. "You're his twin brother? Where's your license?"

Wilcox huffed. "Inside coat pocket. You'd better take these cuffs off now."

Jack took the man's wallet out of his pocket and flipped it open. He scanned the license and scoffed, "It's a dupe."

"I lost mine. It doesn't matter. Take me in, and I'll sue for false arrest."

Jack rubbed the bridge of his nose. "False imprisonment," he muttered.

"What?" Wilcox glared.

"You'd sue me for false imprisonment or kidnapping. I'm not arresting you."

"Whatever, I'll still sue you."

"Hold on. Walk with me to my car."

"I will not—"

"It's right there," Jack snapped, pointing to the Charger.

"I'll give you two minutes. Take these off first." Wilcox held out his hands.

Jack undid the handcuffs.

Wilcox begrudgingly turned and started to move.

Jack led him over to the Charger, popped open the door, and pulled out the folder. Four pages into the paperwork was a warning page in red. Jack quickly scanned the details. Twin brother, identical, matching tattoos, lawyer contacted office...

Damn.

Wilcox watched Jack's changing expression. "Your time's up." Wilcox's arms flapped up his sides like a chicken squawking. "If you bother me again, I'll sue." He spun on his heel and marched down the sidewalk.

"Do you know where your brother is?" Jack called after him.

Wilcox didn't turn around. He did, however, hold up his middle finger as he scurried away.

Jack tossed the folder onto the seat and closed the door. He watched as Wilcox blended in with the other pedestrians.

"I'm going to nail your brother to the wall," Jack grumbled as he got into the car.

16

CLUNKY

Replacement stood up straighter as Pierce looked directly into her eyes. She nervously rubbed her thumb and index finger together. Normally she was either moving or talking, or both at the same time. Standing there and waiting for him to ask her the big question he'd been leading up to seemed to take forever.

"I was wondering," Pierce began, "do you use VE-Life?"

She waited for a moment to see whether there was more before she answered. "Doesn't everybody?" She smiled.

"What's your favorite part?"

Replacement felt the color rising to the back of her neck. She bit her bottom lip.

Pierce's grin faded. "Wait a second. Do you use it?"

"I… did." Her shoulders crept up and her hands turned out.

Pierce's mouth fell open. "Did? You stopped using it?"

"I really liked it, but… it's sort of for newer users, that's all. It's great. People love it."

"But you don't?"

"It's great. I just don't use it anymore."

"This is humbling." Pierce stuck his tongue in his cheek.

"I'm sorry, but you asked." Replacement shook her head back and forth, and her ponytail danced.

"I did say I wanted to find someone to tell me the truth. I guess I wasn't expecting that. It's a little like a kick in the gut."

"I'm sorry."

"I'm kidding." Pierce smiled. "Sort of. It's more like getting hit a little lower." Replacement chuckled.

"I guess I have people around who 'yes' me to death."

"Well, you want honesty, right?"

"Actually, I kinda like being told it's great," he joked. "Seriously, I've had a lot on my plate lately. A lot of pressure." Pierce took out his e-cigarette case and looked down at it. "Figures. It's not charged." He plugged the case into his laptop and then turned toward Replacement. "What don't you like about VE-Life? Give it to me straight. Brutally honest."

Replacement shook her head. "Most people think my being brutally honest is more 'brutal' than 'honest.' They end up with hurt feelings."

Pierce laughed. "I can take it. Hit me with your best shot."

"VE-Life is… well, it's a little clunky."

"Clunky?" Pierce straightened and cleared his throat. "*High Tech Magazine* called it elegant in its simplicity."

"Their articles are always junk." Replacement rolled her eyes. "Simplicity is the main word. From what I can remember, you had a menu for everything, but no shortcuts. It was like going bowling with bumpers in the gutter."

"We just added a shortcut menu."

"One? Is there a shortcut menu shortage?"

Pierce chuckled. "I see what you mean about brutal."

"Sorry..." She looked down.

"Keep going." Pierce waved her off. "Wait. If you're not using my software, what're you using?"

"I use a few things. Gate-Keeper, My Sched, Go-Go 5—"

"They're open source."

"They're free."

"You still need ten of them to do what VE-Life does."

"I use Organize Me, too." Replacement grinned. "That bundles them. And you can tweak them."

"Then you modded them. Regular users can't do that."

Replacement shrugged. "That's part of your problem. Even a mid-level user can download and install a mod. You aimed for the lowest user level and didn't think about the more advanced users."

"The lowest user is the biggest market base."

Replacement pulled out her phone. "Look at this." She tapped a few things, then held it up. "Look at all these downloads."

"Those are downloads for competitors' programs."

"That's one way to look at it, but you could turn that on its head. Geeks like to mod. If you share some modules, geeks can mod, and they'll use VE-Life for the base. Then everyone will need to buy it in order to use the mod."

"Shared code raises too many security concerns."

Replacement blew a raspberry. "That sounds like something a guy in a suit would say. You're telling me *you* couldn't figure out a way to share some modules and keep it secure?"

Pierce's lips pressed together. "I could take a look at it."

"Check this out." Replacement tapped a couple more buttons, and VE-Life popped up.

Pierce's eyes went wide. "You're using a cracked version?"

Replacement inhaled sharply. "Well, I said I'm not really using it."

He stared at her, and his head moved slowly from side to side. "Okay. I'll forget about you pirating my software, but you know you only get half the features with that crack anyway."

"I was going to show you an example."

"Then can we use my full legal copy?" Pierce pulled out his phone. "Clunky?" He smiled and shook his head.

"Yeah, look at this..."

Replacement stepped in close as she pointed at the screen. Pierce moved a little closer too. As the two began to go through the program, they quickly lost track of time.

17

PATIENCE

Luka walked over to the apartment window and looked down into the street. A few cars drove past, and several people strolled down the sidewalk. He envied them right now. They looked as if they didn't have a care in the world. Meanwhile, he felt as if he could barely breathe. He checked his phone for the umpteenth time—nothing.

"You're worse than an old woman," Savin muttered from the kitchen, where he sat at the table.

"Just do what you do best, Savin. Sit there and do nothing," Luka said.

"Stop." Nicholai was dicing an onion at the kitchen counter. "I don't want to hear you two fighting again. Call Tolyan, Luka. Tell him to pick up more wine."

"We have wine."

"We only have red. I want white. Two bottles, no more."

"There're five of us." Luka shrugged. "Only two?"

Nicholai didn't answer, just continued dicing onions.

"Can we at least get vodka?" Luka held out his hands.

"No." Nicholai's response was a rumbled order.

Luka frowned. He looked out the window. "Can I have him pick up some meat for breakfast? Sausages?"

"Finally you have a good idea." Savin nodded.

Luka glared. He was about to say something when his phone played a cheery tune. Everyone froze.

Luka stared down at the phone. A giant exclamation point was displayed on the screen. The cheery tune played again.

Nicholai stepped over. "Did it work?"

Luka nodded.

"He must have plugged it in!" Nicholai's fist vibrated as he held his hand out triumphantly.

"Yes! It worked!" Savin's deep voice boomed, and he pounded the table.

Nicholai looked at Luka. "How long will it take to copy the data?"

"Fast. Less than half an hour."

Savin grabbed his jacket off the chair.

"Sit down." Nicholai turned back to another onion. "The mole will retrieve it and bring it to us."

"Looks like we may not even need you, Savin." Luka grinned.

"I said I don't want to hear you two fighting." Nicholai pushed the chopped onions into a pan.

"When will you know it is finished?" Savin asked Luka.

"We will get another call."

"This could be finished tonight?" Savin placed his hands above his head. At six foot seven, he could almost touch the ceiling while sitting down. "Good. I want to get back to Volgograd."

"Stop rushing." Nicholai stirred the soup. "Patience. Tonight will be a good evening." He smiled, picked up a spoon, and sipped his soup.

18

A SENSE OF HUMOR

Jack drove down Long Meadow Avenue, looking for his prey. He would still have plenty of time to take Lady out and get dressed for dinner with Replacement. But first he wanted to make one more pass; Wilcox had gotten under his skin.

He took a right and headed over to Grant Street and Kayden's address. Glancing at the clock, he sped up. He wanted to take a long shower before he met Replacement.

He stopped at the light to turn onto Grant Street and watched people stroll down the sidewalk. And then he did his second double take of the day.

What're the odds?

Kayden Wilcox was looking right at him as he walked out of a little convenience store.

Jack pulled over to the curb and hopped out of the car.

"Kayden Wilcox." Jack's voice was low as he ran in front of the man and held up his hand. "You skipped bail—"

"Wait!" Wilcox held up his hand. "You touch me, and I'll sue. I'm Jayden Wilcox. Kayden's brother."

Jack rolled his eyes. "Save it. Your brother just gave me that line."

"Then you're an idiot for believing him. You let Kayden go, and now you try hassling *me*? I'm done with this. I'm going to sue you for false arrest." Wilcox stuck his finger in Jack's face.

Jack scowled.

Wilcox put his hand down.

"Let's get something straight." Jack took a step forward. "I don't have any money, so your threat's a little weak right now. Show me your ID."

"This is harassment." Wilcox pulled out his wallet and held his license up in front of Jack.

"It's a dupe, too. Like your brother's."

"So? It's a legal license, and what you're doing is illegal. I'm calling my lawyer." Wilcox took out his phone and started to walk away.

Jack stepped in front of him.

"Move or I sue!" Wilcox shouted.

People on the sidewalk began to stare.

I've only got a fifty-fifty chance of this being the right guy. Do I roll the dice…?

"Keep being easy to find," Jack growled as he stepped aside.

"Keep being a loser," Wilcox scoffed, and he stomped down the sidewalk.

Jack cracked his neck. He watched Wilcox blend back in with the crowd.

How the heck do I figure out who's who?
He looked up at the sky. "You sure do have a sense of humor," he muttered.

19

THAT'S NOT A THRUWAY

Replacement shook the phone and jokingly choked it. "Nooo!" She stretched the word out as the battery light on Pierce's phone flashed three times and the screen went blank. "But I was right." She tapped the blank screen and looked at Pierce. "See how clunky that was?"

Pierce laughed. "There's that word again—clunky. I'm going to have to establish an Anti-Clunky Department to go through all our software."

Replacement grinned, arched her back, and stretched.

"You know," Pierce said, "we actually do have something like that. It's not called the Anti-Clunky Department, but we have a group that goes over the flow of everything."

"Maybe you need better beta-testers. That was fun. Thanks."

"I can't thank you enough." Pierce leaned against the desk. "You were wrong, though." Replacement raised an eyebrow, and Pierce continued, "You were much more honest than brutal."

Replacement smiled. "Good. And I do like the software, but… if you put half of the stuff in you talked about, it would be unbelievable."

Pierce smiled too.

Replacement grabbed her left elbow with her right hand and looked down at her feet.

Pierce stepped closer.

She hadn't noticed how warm it was in the guesthouse, but she suddenly wanted to open the window and feel a cool breeze.

"You're very good with computers," Pierce said. "It's hard to find someone who likes computers that you can still relate to."

"In that whole company there're no other geeks to talk to?" She smiled.

"That wasn't what I meant." He tilted his head.

Replacement took a step back. "Um…"

"Hello?" Gerald called out from the front door of the guesthouse.

"We're in here, Mr. Mathis," Pierce called back.

Gerald appeared in the doorway of the den. "Hello, Mr. Weston. I was trying to call Alice, but she didn't answer."

Replacement rubbed the back of her neck. "I'm sorry. We've been in here a while and my phone died. What's up?"

"I guess it'd be easier to show you. Do you guys have a second to come to the server room?"

"Sure," Pierce answered.

They followed Gerald back to the mansion. Gerald entered a passcode into the security panel and then held the metal server room door open for them.

The hum from the servers was loud in the small room. Two tall racks filled with computers faced each other. Gerald walked over to a table on the far wall.

"Phillip just installed an AP in the study in the basement." Gerald opened up a blueprint of the house. He set his phone down on the upper-left corner and his e-cigarette case on the bottom while he pointed at the study. "That covers here fine, but we wanted to get the study and the wine cellar with it too. The problem is, the walls are too thick."

"Can we add another access point?" Replacement asked.

Gerald sighed. "Then we'd have to go in through here." When he pointed to the hallway, the right side of the blueprint started to roll up. "Pierce, could you—?"

Pierce put his laptop on the upper-right corner and his e-cigarette case down on the lower-right corner of the blueprint to keep it from curling, then shook his head. "Let's try not to disturb the old house and be as discreet as possible. What if we doubled back through the study?"

Gerald rubbed his beard and leaned back. "That's a great idea. The server room is just down the hall, so it's a short run." He reached out and pointed to the room again.

When Replacement saw Gerald's watch, she gasped. "Gerald, your watch says seven o'clock. Is that right? The clock in the guesthouse said five!"

Gerald gave her an I'm-sorry-to-have-to-tell-you-this look.

"Crap! I have to meet Jack." Replacement bolted to the door and spun around. "Gerald, I need to go!"

Gerald smiled thinly. "Well, I asked Bruce and Phillip if they could work late and—"

"I can't!" Replacement's voice went up. "Please?"

"Sure. Sure." Gerald grabbed his phone and e-cig case and put them in his pocket. He started to quickly roll up the blueprint.

"I really appreciate it, Gerald." Replacement tapped her foot on the floor.

"I just need to get the update started. That'll only take fifteen minutes, tops." Gerald tucked the blueprint under his arm.

Replacement cringed.

"I can give you a ride," Pierce offered.

"Really?" Replacement's face lit up.

"I wanted to take a drive anyway."

"Let's go."

Pierce grabbed his laptop and reached down for the computer lock. "Do you need anything from me, Mr. Mathis?" He clicked the lock shut.

"I don't think so. I'm going to run the updates on the new server and call it a night."

"Thanks, Gerald," Replacement called out before she zipped through the door.

Pierce hurried behind her. "How late are we?" he asked.

"If you start jogging I'll feel better." Replacement quickened her pace.

Pierce broke into a run and chased after her. Dashing into the garage, Pierce headed over to the key cabinet. "We'll take the Porsche."

The door locks clicked, and Replacement jumped into the passenger seat. Pierce slid behind the wheel. Before the garage door was even fully up, the Porsche rolled out.

As they drove down the driveway, the door to the guardhouse flew open, and a guard rushed out.

Pierce skidded to a stop, and the guard ran over to the window. "Nothing to worry about, Manuel," Pierce said. "I'm just giving Alice a ride to dinner."

"I should accompany you, sir. I'll get my car."

"Don't try to keep up. Where am I taking you?" Pierce asked Replacement.

"Antonelli's. It's an Italian restaurant right on Main Street. It's a block after the big courthouse."

Manuel spun on his heel and ran for his car.

Pierce drove out to the main road and sped up. The Porsche's engine purred as it raced along.

Replacement looked at the speedometer and then nervously at Pierce.

"It's okay," he said. "I just started training to race the Sprint Cup."

Replacement swallowed. "How about we slow down a little bit until you finish training?"

Pierce laughed, but let up on the gas. "How fast?"

Replacement breathed normally again. "This is good."

"You don't like driving fast?"

She shook her head. "I was in a car accident when I was little."

Pierce slowed down even more.

"Thank you."

Pierce nodded. "I don't want you to feel uncomfortable."

Replacement smiled. "I'm okay with a *little* fast."

They rode in silence for a few minutes, the Porsche humming along the winding road. When they reached the road that headed straight for Darrington, Replacement glanced at the clock.

"You can speed up a little more."

"Your wish is my command." Pierce pressed on the gas.

Replacement pulled down the visor and looked in the mirror. She saw the flush at the tips of her ears. It spread as she tried to pull her hair down to cover them. "Oh, crud." She groaned. "Look at me." Her business-casual outfit was going to be underdressed for Antonelli's.

"You look great." Pierce smiled.

Replacement felt her chest tighten slightly. The flush spread to her cheeks.

"If you want my opinion," Pierce continued, "you should let your hair down."

Replacement pulled out her clip, and her brown hair fell around her shoulders.

"Beautiful." Pierce's smile widened.

Replacement flipped the visor back up. She turned toward the window, pretending to use the reflection as she fanned out her hair. Mostly she was trying to hide her beet-red cheeks.

"Do you work full time for Mr. Mathis?" Pierce asked.

"No. Odd jobs here and there, mostly." She exhaled and reached into her purse.

"What does your friend Jack do?"

The question hung in the air as she started to put on some light makeup.

"He's a bondsman." She dabbed on some lipstick.

She turned back to Pierce and smiled.

He opened his mouth and held out his right hand to her.

Puzzled, she looked down at his cupped hand.

"Can I have my breath back?" he said. "You took it away." He chuckled.

Replacement blushed even more.

As they entered Darrington, traffic forced Pierce to slow down, and then stop. Replacement rocked in her seat as she tried to peer over the cars ahead of them. She had to clamp her mouth shut to keep from swearing.

"It's an accident." She slapped her knee.

Pierce pressed a couple of buttons on the GPS and took a right.

"Uh..." Replacement frowned as she looked at the map. "That's not a thruway."

Pierce tapped the screen again, and the map changed back to satellite view. "The grid view is wrong. Officially the road ends, but in reality... look."

Replacement looked and saw the connection to another road. "Nice. Thank you." She smiled.

But when the Porsche slipped down the side road, Replacement's grin vanished. Before connecting to the other road, they would have to pass through a dirt parking lot. She felt her fist tighten and forced herself to open her hand. "I don't think you want to take a car like this into the dirt."

Pierce kept going.

"It's okay. We can just turn around," Replacement said.

"You buy a car to drive it, not put it on a shelf," Pierce replied. "Besides, helping a friend's worth it."

The Porsche rocked back and forth as it shot forward. Small rocks pinged off the undercarriage, and Replacement winced.

Pierce looked at her and laughed.

Then the tires hit tar again, and he sped up.

"You really didn't have to do that." She shook her head.

"Yes I did." Pierce flew back up to the main road and took a right onto Main Street.

Replacement beamed. "I'm not that late after all. Jack would have been really bummed. Thank you."

She noticed Pierce's forearm muscles tighten as he gripped the steering wheel. "I'm glad I could help."

20

UPDATES

Gerald was updating the home server, but he still had to give access to the Weston Industries IT department—and the security over there was like dealing with the CIA. Gerald had never seen anything like it.

He looked over his shoulder at the other computer rack. That rack held all the company equipment. Gerald had no access to it. The only thing he had done was unpack it, mount it in the rack, and turn it on. They did everything else to it remotely. Only Pierce could access it.

Gerald pushed his glasses further up his nose. He reached into his pocket for his phone and put it down next to the keyboard. It clinked against Pierce's metallic e-cigarette case. He slid the case to the side and put his phone at an angle so he could read the screen.

He slid the mouse across the mousepad, and a login menu popped up. He entered his credentials and followed the update procedures. He clicked through page after page of screens until another window opened. A little progress window with a green bar popped up.

Gerald sighed and stretched.

Someone tapped on the door.

"Hello?" Gerald opened the door.

Out in the hall stood the new maid with short red hair. "I made some sandwiches for you in the kitchen earlier," she said. Her smile made her freckles stand out. "I wanted to make sure you got some. A lot of guests have arrived."

"Thanks, Sophia." Gerald grinned. "I'll go let the guys know."

"I already did." Sophia started down the hallway. "Roast beef, chicken, and tuna. They're right on the counter."

Gerald hurried down the hallway after her. He had loved the roast beef she had made them yesterday, but Bruce… he had put away three sandwiches and taken a fourth for a snack for later. Gerald wanted to be sure he got there before the big guy.

When he reached the kitchen, he was happy to see the plate of food was still untouched. He snagged two roast beef sandwiches and headed back to the server room, munching on one sandwich as he went.

The list of things he still needed to do scrolled through his mind as he walked. Each room he passed he added to his list as he mentally noted jacks, outlets, and devices.

Gerald reached the server room, typed in his security code, and pulled the door closed behind him. The screen on the computer monitor displayed that the update had finished.

"Finally. Almost done, and I can go home." He reached out for his phone. He ran his finger down the screen to find the final step in the instructions.

While Gerald typed at the server, he was startled by a noise from behind the other server rack—metal scraping against metal. He began to turn around, and everything went black.

21

C LEVEL

Jack paced back and forth on the sidewalk outside Antonelli's. A line of people stretched out the door. He looked down at his phone and hit redial again. Replacement's voicemail kicked in immediately.

"Mr. Stratton?" the maître d' called from the doorway.

Jack tried to smile as he walked toward him. "She'll be here any second."

"I'm sorry, sir, but I've held on to your table for twenty minutes. You can see from the long line that we're very busy tonight. I do apologize." The man's mustache curled down.

"Five minutes?" Jack held up his hand.

The maître d' shook his head. "I'm just doing my job, sir."

Jack exhaled and took a step back. "I know. I understand."

"Thank you, sir." He motioned to another couple, who gave Jack a sympathetic look as they hurried through the door.

Damn it. I'm going out there right now to check on her.

Jack marched over to the valet parking kiosk. Three teenage boys sat huddled on a bench, busily texting on their phones. One looked up, saw the expression on Jack's face, and jumped to his feet. "Yes, sir."

The sound of a car racing down the street toward them made all their heads turn. Electric blue headlights swept the street as a Porsche zoomed down the road and squealed to a stop in front of Jack.

One teenage boy whistled.

"Sweet ride," said another.

Replacement bounded out of the car. "I'm so sorry!" She rushed up to Jack. "I was working in the guesthouse and the clock was totally wrong."

"And your phone?" Jack's voice was low.

"It ran out of juice. I'm super-sorry."

"It's actually my fault," said Pierce. Jack looked over Replacement's shoulder toward the man emerging from the driver's side of the Porsche. "She was helping me, and we just lost track of time. I got her here as fast as I could."

That lit Jack's fuse.

"Fast?" Jack bristled at the word.

"I can assure you, she was safe." Pierce walked around the car. "I told Alice I'm training to drive in the Sprint Cup."

"That's a closed track with just left turns," Jack retorted.

Pierce stopped with one foot on the curb. "That's true, but we're driving at a hundred and ninety miles an hour."

Replacement grabbed Jack's hand and gave it a squeeze. "I'm sorry I was late. Ready?" She gave him a look that screamed please-let-it-go. "Boy, I'm starving."

Jack's scowl softened, and then he clicked his tongue. "We lost the reservation."

"I wasn't *that* late." Replacement glared at the entrance. "Was I? Oh, I'm so sorry, Jack."

"Don't worry about it."

"Let me see what I can do." Pierce shut his door. "After all, it's my fault you're late."

"Really, it's okay." Jack waved him off.

"Just give me one second." Pierce hurried to the entrance of Antonelli's.

Jack watched Pierce go, then he turned to Replacement. "What happened to getting a ride from Gerald?"

"He had to work late."

"You should've called me for a ride instead of riding alone with him."

"There wasn't time. I was already late."

Jack huffed.

Replacement mashed her lips together and closed one eye. "Is someone getting jealous?"

"Jealous—no. Protective—yes. You don't know him from Adam."

"He's a good guy." Replacement pressed up against Jack. "And he didn't drive too fast. I told him to slow down, and he did."

Jack exhaled. "Well…" He ran his hand through his hair to the back of his neck. "Maybe we can go for subs?"

"Sounds good to me." She took his hand.

Pierce walked back out of the restaurant. "They had a cancellation."

Replacement lit up. "Sweet! What're the odds of that?" She grinned up at Jack.

"I'd say a hundred dollars to one," Jack muttered.

"Can I park your car, sir?" One of the teenagers walked up and held his hand out to Pierce.

"No. I'm just leaving."

Replacement squeezed Jack's hand.

What? he mouthed back.

She squeezed his hand again.

Jack rolled his eyes, turned around, and dryly asked Pierce, "Would you like to join us?"

"No, thank you," Pierce replied in a tone that matched Jack's sincerity. "I'll head back to the estate."

"Don't be silly." Replacement waved him back over. "It's late. You and Jack can talk cars over garlic bread."

Jack wanted to tell the man to get lost, but instead he said, "You came all the way out here." Jack knew how hard Replacement was working at this job, and this guy *was* her boss. With a great deal of effort, Jack managed to make the corners of his mouth rise—slightly. "Please. Join us."

Pierce nodded. "Okay. I did see they have sautéed swordfish on the specials board. It sounded delicious. Just one second." Pierce walked back over to the Porsche.

Replacement turned to Jack. "Wow. I'm surprised at you," she whispered.

"Surprised? You wanted me to ask him."

"I didn't."

"You squeezed my hand." Jack looked shocked.

"No, I didn't." Replacement shook her head.

"Right after he said he was leaving, you squeezed my hand—twice."

"Oh, I was just excited about going to dinner with you."

Jack groaned. "I thought you wanted him to come."

"No, but it's still nice of you."

"Me? Nice?" Jack's eyes widened. "Can I *un*-invite him?"

"No." Replacement gave Jack a little elbow in his gut.

Pierce handed the valet the keys and trotted back.

The three of them headed for the door. As they walked in, the maître d' looked at them, and his ever-present smile wavered when he glanced down at Replacement's sneakers. "Mr. Weston. Will you be joining us too?"

"Yes. It seems I will." Pierce moved over to the desk and whispered something to the maître d'. As he did, the maître d's fingers tapped excitedly on the countertop.

The maître d' himself led them to a reserved table in a back corner. The restaurant was filled with diners, and a few conversations stopped as they watched the mismatched set of three get escorted to their table.

Jack pulled out a chair for Replacement.

"I think I should've changed," she muttered as she sat down.

"You look great." Jack smiled at her.

"But I know what you mean," Pierce said. "It's not exactly a jeans and sneakers place."

Jack leaned closer to Replacement and whispered, "You're so beautiful, nobody's looking at your feet."

She blushed.

"So, Jack, Alice told me you're a broker," Pierce said.

Jack cast a quick, puzzled look toward Replacement as the waiter filled their water glasses.

Replacement laughed. "Not *stocks and* bonds." She sat up straighter. "*Bail* bonds."

"Oh." Pierce chuckled. "You're a bounty hunter?"

"Technically I'm a bail enforcement agent, but yeah, you could call it that."

Jack looked at Replacement and tried to guess what she was thinking. *Did she not want to tell him what I do for work?*

"I think I'd write 'Bounty Hunter' on my business card," Pierce added. "You don't get a more bad-ass sounding title than that."

"I think you have me beat." Jack tilted his water glass toward Pierce. "Boy Billionaire sounds better."

Pierce laughed, but Replacement stomped on Jack's foot and said, "Pierce is a CEO."

"Thank you," Pierce replied, "but Boy Billionaire has a nice ring to it. I might change my business cards. The truth is, I'd prefer a job with a little more excitement than sitting behind a desk all day."

"Is that why you're learning to race?" Jack asked.

"Partly. I like to learn. If there's some fear to conquer, it adds to the excitement."

"Fear? About driving?" Replacement asked.

"I had an issue with driving, so I thought if I could learn more about it, I wouldn't be bothered by it."

"That's an interesting way of going at it," Jack said. "I'll give you credit. For most people, driving at a hundred and ninety miles an hour causes fear—it doesn't get rid of it."

Pierce shrugged. "It worked for me. I tackled my triumvirate: driving, skydiving, and scuba diving."

"You dive? So does Jack," Replacement said.

"It was only natural, being a programmer." Pierce leaned toward Replacement. "We like to get below C level."

Replacement giggled.

Pierce grinned.

Jack raised an eyebrow.

"C is a programming language," Replacement explained to Jack. "So... *sea* level?"

"I get it," Jack grumbled. He took a sip of water.

The waiter approached their table. "May I bring you something to drink?"

"Iced tea," Replacement said.

"Do you know what you'll be having for dinner?" Pierce asked her. "We could order a bottle."

"Of what?" Replacement asked.

"No thanks," Jack said.

"I'll have a glass of Coche-Dury Meursault Les Rougeots," Pierce said to the waiter, setting down his menu. "It will go well with the sautéed swordfish with the niçoise vinaigrette."

Jack tried not to make a face as he attempted to unravel Pierce's order.

"Sir?" The waiter leaned closer to Jack.

"Whiskey, neat. It goes great with the T-bone."

Replacement stepped on his foot again. She cocked an eyebrow.

"Actually, water will be fine," Jack said.

Replacement grinned.

Jack closed his menu and held out his hand to Replacement.

"I'll have the house salad with honey mustard and the chicken Marsala," she said.

"I'll have the same salad and a T-bone, rare," Jack said.

Pierce closed his menu and smiled at the waitress. "I'll have the sautéed swordfish with a house salad with Italian on the side."

"Do you want to order for your security?" Jack tipped his head toward Manuel, who blended in with the crowd at the door.

Pierce glanced at Jack. "I'm impressed."

Jack nodded.

"I would, except he'd never eat it. He's all business. Retired Marine."

"Never would have guessed," Jack quipped as he eyed the man's wide physique. "I saw him this morning. Outside U-Do2."

"Very observant," Pierce added. "Perhaps I should suggest he try to be even more invisible?"

"Don't. He's not trying to, and that's good. It puts people on notice that you have security. It also makes people say, 'If I see him, are there other security guys I *don't* see?' Sometimes you want that."

"Where do you scuba dive?" Replacement asked Pierce.

"I'll dive anywhere. I was really fortunate. My last dive was Frégate Island. It's in the Seychelles archipelago. It's a beautiful location. I swam with some giant hawksbill turtles."

Replacement leaned in. "You swam with giant turtles?"

"They're critically endangered. Weston Industries supports a group that's studying them there. Where was your last dive, Jack?"

"In the deep end of my bathtub."

Replacement shot Jack a quick glare, but Pierce laughed. "That's a good one."

Pierce's phone buzzed. "Would you excuse me for a moment?"

As he walked away, Replacement leaned close to Jack. "Be nice."

"I am."

"He was being nice, asking you about diving. That was a snarky answer."

"A snarky answer would've been if I'd said I went diving in Alaska with rare giant sea pandas."

Replacement giggled but then glared again. "Look, he's my new boss. Just go with it. I bet he's trying to find some common ground you two can talk about."

"Common ground? The guy's swimming in the tropics with giant turtles. How am I supposed to 'go with it'?"

"If he asks you again, just tell him where you really went diving last."

"Really?" Jack imitated Pierce. "So, Jack, where was your last dive?" Jack put his elbows down on the table. "Gee, Pierce, it was a cold water dive in a pond when I went looking for the murder weapon used to kill my father." He turned his hands out. "That wouldn't have been a conversation stopper, now would it?"

Replacement whistled low. "Good point. Sorry."

"He's coming back. Am I telling him the truth?"

"Nope." Replacement made a popping sound at the end. "Ask him about his car," she whispered.

As Pierce sat down, the waiter brought the salads.

"Sorry about that," Pierce said. "My assistant was just letting me know that the corporate plane landed. I'm having a bunch of guests at the house for the next couple of days." He turned to Replacement. "Don't worry, they'll all be squirreled away in the conference room—they won't be in your way. And they'll be gone on Monday. I can't wait. Then I can code."

"You still write the code?" Jack asked.

"Not typically, but I have some new ideas that I've been kicking around. At this point, my day-to-day responsibilities make writing code impossible." Pierce put his napkin on his lap. "So... now I have to take a vacation in order to program. How geeky is that?"

"It shows what you love to do." Replacement smiled. "We always say grace."

"Okay." Pierce bowed his head.

"Dear Lord," Replacement said, "thank you for this meal. Please watch over all of us, especially Aunt Haddie. In Jesus's name, Amen."

The waiter set down a plate of garlic bread, and Replacement wiggled in her seat. "You have to have some." She held the plate out to Pierce. "They're the bomb."

"If they get you that excited, then I will. Thank you."

Replacement looked down, and Jack could tell she was counting the slices of bread. He picked up a slice and set it down on her plate. "To the victor go the spoils."

She grinned.

Jack took a sip of his water. "The engine on that Porsche really purrs."

"I'm very pleased with the car. She's a real fun drive."

"I may be mistaken, but I thought I saw that Porsche on a car show. They said it wasn't for sale yet."

"It's not. I have a weakness for things I can't have," Pierce said.

Jack leaned forward.

"Jack has a Charger," Replacement said.

"That's a powerful car." Pierce tipped his glass. "I bet she's fast."

"She is."

"Have you ever raced?" Pierce asked.

"Technically, when I drive fast, it's called a chase. I'd like to race some time and not have to PIT someone at the end."

Pierce laughed. "I heard you used to be a police officer."

Jack nodded.

"PIT? Is that where you hit the other car and make it fishtail?" Replacement asked Jack.

"Yeah. Replacement's working on her police acronyms," Jack explained to Pierce. "If you like driving, you should take a TEVOC class. They're a blast."

"Replacement?" Pierce looked confused.

"It's my nickname." Replacement shot Jack a sideways look. "So you skydive too?"

"I love it. My next jump's going to be in a flying suit."

"I've seen those. They have the fabric on the arms." Replacement held her arms out.

"Have you skydived?" Pierce asked Jack.

Jack nodded.

Pierce leaned in. "When you were standing there, ready to take that leap, what made you step out into the void? What drove you?"

"What drove me?" Jack repeated, trying not to smirk.

Pierce nodded. "It's an interview question that I always use. I think it tells a lot about someone. Why someone would jump out of a perfectly good airplane."

"In my case, I don't think it'll tell you much."

"I think it will. Try me." Pierce settled back in his chair.

"I jumped out of the plane because the guy ordering me to had a gun."

Pierce's mouth dropped open.

Jack smirked. "I was in the Army."

Pierce's laugh was a mixture of relief and understanding.

"Did you ever jump into any action?" Pierce asked, fascinated.

Jack blinked. In that fraction of a second, he could still almost feel himself slowly floating to the ground. Watching the flashes below him. Listening to the bullets that streaked up unseen, knowing they were aimed at him. As he remembered that sensation of drifting, helpless, while the seconds seemed like days, his heart thumped in his chest.

Jack looked down at his glass, and it took all his will to force his hand not to shake as he finished the drink. "I don't really talk about it."

***

After dinner, Replacement headed to the ladies' room. The waiter brought out coffees and the bill. Pierce went to pay, but Jack waved him off and handed the waiter his own card.

A minute later, the maître d' walked over. "I'm terribly sorry, sir," he whispered, "but there seems to be an issue with your credit card."

Damn.

Jack's stomach tightened. "Could you run it again?"

"We have, sir. Do you have another?"

Jack's hand turned into a fist. He had another credit card, but he knew it was already maxed out too.

Replacement returned to her seat. She looked at Jack's stern face and whispered, "Is there a problem?"

"I'm afraid there is," the maître d' said.

Jack cleared his throat.

"Oh, it's my fault." Pierce reached for his wallet. "When I reserved the table, I used my old card. I'm terribly sorry." He handed a credit card to the maître d'.

Replacement exhaled and settled back into her chair. A big smile spread across her face.

Jack looked at Pierce.

Pierce gave the slightest wink.

Jack nodded.

22

IT'S BAD

While Replacement sipped her coffee and talked with Pierce about work, Jack was watching Manuel, who still stood by the restaurant's front door. After answering his phone, the ex-Marine's head tilted slightly to the side, and his shoulders squared. Something about how he reacted to the call put Jack on alert.

Manuel approached the table. "I'm sorry to bother you, sir. But there's an urgent phone call."

"Excuse me," Pierce said. He and Manuel walked toward the restrooms and stopped in an alcove.

Jack looked over his shoulder and frowned.

"I think he just got some bad news," Replacement whispered.

Manuel stood at attention as he spoke to Pierce. Pierce's face grew noticeably paler. He nodded twice, then hurried back over to the table.

Pierce paused before addressing Replacement. "Alice, there's been an accident at the house. Mr. Mathis was hurt."

"What? What happened?" Replacement stood up, and so did Jack.

"He was in the server room, and one of the server racks fell on top of him. They've taken him to the hospital here in Darrington."

"It's bad," Replacement said. She grabbed Jack's hand.

"I know the way," Jack said. "Why don't you two follow me?"

And all four of them, including Manuel, headed for the door.

***

Jack leaned against the wall outside the hospital waiting room while Replacement paced back and forth. Bruce and Phillip had followed the ambulance to the hospital, driving Gerald's car, but they'd gone home an hour ago. Pierce was speaking with Manuel and two other people at the end of the hall. Jack had never seen the man in the dark-gray suit or the older woman before.

"He wasn't trapped there long, was he?" Replacement asked Jack again.

He shook his head. "Pierce said the maid heard a crash and called security, so it can't have been long. And the ambulance got there quickly."

Pierce, the man in the suit, the woman, and Manuel walked toward them.

"Alice, Jack," Pierce began, "this is my executive assistant, Mrs. Lydia Maier."

The older woman tipped her head. "It's a pleasure to meet you."

Her eyes scanned both Jack and Replacement up and down. Jack smiled, but he had the distinct impression the woman was summing them both up, categorizing them, and filing that information away.

The man in the suit took Replacement's hand and shook it firmly. "I'm Roger Braxton, an old college roommate of Pierce's. You know Mr. Mathis?"

Replacement nodded.

"I'm sure he'll be fine," Roger continued. "It looks like you've got a great hospital here, and I'm certain he's getting the best care."

Jack looked at Roger's pearly-white teeth, dirty-blond manicured hair, and expensive suit. He looked like a sharp salesman.

A doctor came through the door and motioned Pierce over. The two spoke briefly. All three listened intently.

After the doctor walked away, Pierce came back. "There's still no word. Mr. Mathis is in X-ray." He turned to Lydia and Roger. "There's no reason for you both to remain here. Roger, would you please give Lydia a ride home?"

"Mr. Weston," Lydia said, "may I have a quick word?"

The three retreated back down the hallway. Jack watched the animated conversation. Pierce stood straight while Roger paced back and forth. After several minutes, Lydia and Roger both left, and Pierce came back to Jack and Replacement.

He sighed and sat down hard on the bench outside the hospital room.

Replacement moved next to him and put her hand on his back. "He'll be okay."

The hours ticked slowly by. The hospital shifts changed, and still they waited. Finally, as they wheeled Gerald on a gurney back into the room, a doctor approached them.

"Alice Campbell?" he asked.

"Yes?"

"Mr. Mathis requested to see you."

"Me?" Replacement swallowed.

The doctor spoke softly. "Mr. Mathis has a hairline skull fracture and a concussion. He keeps asking if he can speak with you. You should try to keep it light and brief."

The three of them followed the doctor into the room. Replacement winced when she saw Gerald's swollen face. Around him, machines hummed and beeped. Monitors flashed charts and numbers. A nurse adjusted a drip tube.

"Alice?" Gerald's voice was just above a whisper.

She hurried over to stand next to the bed. "Yes, Gerald."

He tried to sit up.

"Just lie back down, Gerald. You need to take it easy."

"No. I need to finish the job." His voice rose and fell like a wave as he spoke.

"It'll wait." Replacement put her hand on his arm.

"No." He shook his head and winced. "Please. It's important. Can you do it?"

"Me? Finish the job?"

"Please?" Gerald's eyes opened wider. His pupils were dilated and couldn't seem to lock on to her.

"Sure. I'll do it. Just don't worry about it, okay?"

"Thanks," he mumbled.

"I'm so sorry you got hurt."

Gerald's leg pressed against the rail of the bed. "I don't know what happened. They said," he grimaced, "they said the rack fell on me."

Jack stepped forward. "Who told you the rack fell on you?"

"I don't remember. The ambulance people… or someone." Gerald's voice faded off. His eyelids drooped and then closed.

The nurse put a hand on Replacement's shoulder. "We should let him quiet down."

Replacement nodded. "We'll be back," she whispered. But Jack could tell that Gerald had already fallen asleep.

"Before you go—" The nurse picked up a manila envelope from the table beside the bed and handed it to Replacement. "Mr. Mathis asked if you would hold on to his things. He thought you may need them for a job you're working on."

Replacement looked into the envelope. It contained some network plugs, cabinet keys, and a metal case. She closed it and looked at Gerald.

"Thank you. I'll hang on to them."

23

BAD TO THE BONE

The next morning, Jack woke before dawn and slipped out before Replacement was up. He brought Lady along, loading her in the back seat of the Charger. He intended to find Kayden *today*. He had a plan—he glanced down at the orange prisoner jumpsuit he'd bought at Patton's Supply—but it would require a lot of things going his way.

As he drove away from their apartment, he glanced back up at Replacement's window.

What would Alice's life be like with me? I mean, what do I have to offer? Maxed-out credit cards, a dinky apartment, and no good job prospects on the horizon. I'm a hell of a catch.

Jack wanted what was best for her—and when he looked at the facts, he questioned whether he could provide that.

Traffic was almost nonexistent as he made the trip to Fairfield. He got on the highway and stayed in the high-speed lane the whole way. Replacement needed his help later, so he had to move fast.

After exiting the highway, he weaved down side streets until he reached his destination. Gripping the steering wheel hard, he pulled over to the curb. The blue duplex that Kayden called home was in the middle of Grant Street. Today must be trash day, because green bins and bags lined the curb.

Jack flipped Kayden's folder open and scanned the letter from Kayden's lawyer. It stated that Jayden frequently stayed at the residence, too. The bounty hunter from Trip-B had tried to arrest a man he *thought* was Kayden at home. But Jayden called the police, and the police almost arrested the bounty hunter.

"How convenient," Jack grumbled. "The perfect excuse to walk around free while you skip bail."

The duplex door next to Kayden's opened, and an older woman came out carrying a small trash bag. Jack watched her as she came down the walk. He got out of the car.

"Hello," he called. He gave her a small wave and walked over to her.

The woman eyed him suspiciously as she pulled back the trash lid and tossed in the bag.

"I'm looking for Kayden Wilcox."

"He lives there." She pointed to the right side of the duplex.

"Have you seen him this morning?"

"I ain't seen nothin'."

Jack nodded. "Thank you anyway. Can I leave you my card?"

"Nope. I don't need him thinking I helped you, and I didn't help anyway." She walked to the driveway and opened her car door.

Jack walked back to the Charger.

The woman pulled the car to the end of the driveway and stopped. She eyed Jack up and down, then rolled down her window. "Are you a cop?"

Jack walked closer to her car. "Bail bondsman."

"He left an hour ago. I heard him go out. There's a breakfast place on Ellis. Sunnyside Café. I may have overheard that he's meeting his brother there for breakfast."

Jack grinned. "Thank you."

"I didn't do nothin' or say nothin', so don't thank me." The woman waved her hand and drove off.

Jack got in his car. The old woman had given him the best news he could have hoped for. His plan depended on finding the two brothers together.

Maybe his fortunes had turned.

***

Lady stood up in the backseat. It seemed like she was eager for a chase too. She stuck her head out the window and barked.

Not wanting to take a chance on missing this golden opportunity, Jack sped down back roads in order to avoid traffic.

He was glad he did.

As he drove down Windsor Street, not far from the Sunnyside Café, he spotted Kayden and Jayden strolling down the sidewalk on his left.

This really is my lucky day.

Jack scrunched up his shoulder and looked to his right to shield his face as he drove by. He pulled into the deserted parking lot of an out-of-business auto parts store.

Jack grabbed the bright-orange jumpsuit, rolled down the rear window of the Charger, and got out. Then he walked over to the middle of the parking lot and waited.

A minute later, both Jayden and Kayden strolled into view. One of the brothers elbowed the other and pointed to Jack. Smirks crossed both of their faces.

"You got a second?" Jack called out as he waved them over.

"Screw you," the one on the left yelled back.

The one on the right piped up, "You don't get it, do you? There's nothing you can do to us." He strolled over to Jack, and his brother followed. "Arrest me. Arrest him. Arrest us both. Roll the dice. We'll sue your sorry ass."

"That's the thing, Jay-Kay. I'm not going to guess. I don't make suckers' bets. But I'm taking Kayden in today."

They both laughed. "You don't bet, huh? Then go ahead. How do you know which one of us is Kayden?"

"I *don't* know." Jack grinned. "But my partner does. And she's never wrong."

"What the hell are you talking about?"

Jack reached back and opened the back door of the Charger. The car rocked back and forth on its chassis, and Lady leapt out. With the ballistic vest on, she did look like a tank with teeth.

The two brothers backed away. "Don't move!" Jack warned. "I don't know how she'll react."

Both men froze.

Lady's claws clicked on the asphalt as she strode over and stood next to Jack. Her mouth was closed, and her brown eyes stared at the two men. Her chest swelled as she pressed up against Jack's leg.

Jack leaned close to her and whispered, "Meanie face."

Lady's teeth flashed and her ears lay flat on her head as she barked.

The brothers' eyes went wide.

Jack held up his hand, and Lady stopped barking.

"Now, Jay-Kay, just to let you know, American police dogs are trained to take down a suspect by grabbing their arm. But my partner here was a German police dog. They don't have all the laws we have here in the good old US of A."

The two men nodded, their eyes wide as saucers.

"She's trained to go for the groin." Jack said.

Both men gulped.

"Wait a second." The guy on the left held up one hand while he kept the other one low and in front of himself. "How's she going to tell us apart? Even our DNA's the same."

"But not your scent." Jack's mouth curled into a broad smile. He held up the bright-orange jumpsuit. "Recognize this, Kayden?"

"Wait. Where'd you get that?"

"They bag them for DNA now." Jack held the shirt down in front of Lady and whispered, "Crazy bark."

Lady's barking boomed across the deserted parking lot and echoed off the building. Her head rolled back and forth. She reared up, clawed at the sky, and let out an enormous roar.

"I'm Jayden," the one on the left squealed, pointing at his brother. "*He's* Kayden!"

Kayden turned and bolted.

Lady took off after him.

"LADY!" Jack bellowed. "Stay! Halt! Kayden, stop! I don't know what she'll do to you! Honestly!"

Kayden didn't even make it out of the parking lot. Lady bounded by him, turned, and barked ferociously in his face. Kayden dropped to the ground and curled up in the fetal position.

"Keep it off me! Keep it off me!"

Jack ran over and grabbed Lady's collar.

Lady looked up at Jack expectantly. Her brown eyes were bright. A huge grin burst across Jack's face. He patted Lady, and she pranced a little in place.

"Who's the best bounty hunting dog, huh? It's you, girl. Stay." Jack frisked Kayden, then he pulled the man to his feet.

Lady barked again.

"Quiet down, girl." Jack grinned as he clicked the cuffs on. "We've got him now."

"Keep it away, man. Please!" Kayden pulled away, but Jack held on to the cuffs.

"Shut up, Kayden." Jack pulled him over to the Charger. Lady walked just behind them, growling the whole way to the car.

"Thanks for nothing, Jay," Kayden spat toward his brother, who still hadn't moved.

"I told you it was a stupid idea," Jayden yelled back.

Jack put Kayden in the back seat, and Lady jumped in after him. Kayden wiggled himself up against the far door. "This ain't safe. It's going to eat me."

Jack got into the driver's seat and closed the door. "No she won't. She won't bite you—unless you keep talking."

Kayden pressed his body harder against the door.

Jack pulled down the rearview mirror. "Sit back and relax."

Kayden whimpered.

Lady rubbed her head against Jack's shoulder. "This song's for you, girl," he said.

Jack pushed in a CD. "Bad to the Bone" blared over the speakers as the Charger sped out of the parking lot, with Jack grinning all the way.

24

SHE'S A GIRL

As Jack and Lady walked through the apartment door, Lady took off into Replacement's room—but returned a second later. She came to stand in front of Jack and whimpered.

Jack could hear the shower running. "It's okay, girl. You can brag about what an awesome bounty hunter you are when she gets out of the shower."

Jack took Lady's vest off and set it on the floor, then took out his phone to check for messages. But after a moment, a sound made him turn around.

Lady had snagged her vest in her mouth and was dragging it into his bedroom.

Jack smiled. "You liked that? Feels good getting the bad guys, huh?" Jack went over and rubbed her head before heading for the kitchen.

A minute later, Replacement came hurrying into the living room wearing a cream blouse and tan slacks. She grinned when she saw him. "I'm so late. Does Lady need to go out?"

"No. She's good."

"Are you coming with me?" Her eyebrows arched. "Please?"

"I have to do something but... are you okay?"

"Yeah." She darted into her bedroom. "I'm just worried. The list of stuff that needs to get done is long." She called out, "Did you get a lead on the guy you're after?"

"I did better than that—I got him."

"Got him? This morning? That's awesome."

Jack's chest puffed up. "Thanks."

"That's really great." She came out holding a notebook, her laptop, and assorted papers. "I'd really appreciate if you could help me. It's so much work. Phillip's going to be running a cable to the guesthouse, and he needs help. It needs to be underground."

Jack did a double take. "What? You want me to be a ditch digger?"

"The trench isn't that far. Do you want me to do it?"

Jack held up his hand. "Yeah, like I'm gonna let a girl—" He stopped himself right after he said the word.

"That sounded sexist."

"No." He shook his head and hoped she'd just let it go. "It's just that I still have to see Titus."

"This is more important than seeing Titus."

"I need to pick up that check and deposit it. There's a bunch of bills coming due."

She waved her hand as she looked through her papers. "I'm making more money. I'll just get an advance from Pierce."

Jack's jaw clenched.

She let the papers go and moved over to him. "Sorry. That came out wrong."

"Don't worry about it."

"I do worry about it. I'm sorry." She clasped her hands together and batted her eyes. "Can you go see Titus later? Will you please help me?"

"Fine."

"Is that an I-love-you-and-I'll-help-you fine?" She grinned.

He nodded and kissed her. He went to pull away, but her fingers grabbed the lip of his jean's pocket. She pulled him closer. Her lips were soft. Jack could taste cherry. The warmth from the shower still heated her skin as his hand stroked her arm.

She stopped kissing him and put her head against his chest. "I'm glad you caught the bad guy, but... you know I could have gone with you. I'd really like to go with you when I can."

He smiled and stroked her silky hair. When he touched it, he always found himself running his fingers through it. The brown strands glided over his skin, and his chest felt warm.

"You're helping out Gerald and making us some money. You're doing plenty already."

"Why won't you let me help you with the bounty hunting? We could be a team." Her green eyes grew larger as she gazed up at him.

"It's too dangerous."

"But I could help."

"No."

She laid her head back against his chest.

The sound of Lady dragging the vest back out of Jack's bedroom made them both turn.

Jack grinned. "There's my girl."

"What does she have?" Replacement asked.

Lady dropped the vest with a loud thud and raised her head proudly.

Replacement walked over and picked up the vest. Her arched eyebrows slowly inverted into a glare as she read the text on the side. "Is this a bulletproof vest for a dog?" Her muscles strained as she held it toward Jack.

"Uh... yeah." Jack grinned crookedly.

"You bought this for Lady?"

Jack exhaled. "I didn't buy it." He smiled. "Benny let me have it."

"The point isn't whether you paid for it or not!" She stomped her foot. "Did you take Lady with you? Bounty hunting?"

"Yeah."

"You won't take me, but you take her?"

Jack's shoulders slowly rose.

Replacement's eyes narrowed.

"She's good," Jack said quickly. "You would have been so proud—"

Replacement's hands vibrated at the sides of her head. "Without even talking to me first?"

Jack rubbed the back of his head. "I told you the guy I was going after was a cakewalk. She wasn't in any danger. I just needed her to smell the guy."

"What?"

"You see, there were these twins. I couldn't tell them apart—"

"I don't care why. It's not about that. I want to be your partner, but you don't want me." Her lip trembled.

"Alice, don't."

He took a step forward, and Replacement held up a hand.

"I got you some more Taser cartridges," Jack said.

She glared. "Seriously, Jack? I can help, but you can't see that, and that's *wrong*. You treat me differently because I'm a girl."

"I do not."

"You do too."

"I took Lady. She's a girl."

"Not funny, Jack." Replacement's nostrils flared and she stood up tall. "Fine. You don't want me to help you? You don't have to help me, either." She leveled her glare at him. "I'll have Pierce help me."

"You didn't just go there."

She turned and stomped into the kitchen.

Jack rubbed the back of his neck. "You're blowing this whole thing out of proportion, and now you're trying to make me jealous."

"I am not. If you're jealous, that's on you. I need the help, and Pierce *wants* to help me."

"Okay. I'll call your bluff. Have the boy billionaire dig a ditch."

"He would. He *likes* being around me."

"He likes being around you a little too much. Listen, I want you to be safe. How am I supposed to watch out for both of us while we're running down crackheads?"

"You won't even try! You'll bring Lady but not me. What's wrong with me?"

"It's not you." Jack took a step forward, and Replacement backed up.

She shook her head. "No. It is. You don't want me as a partner, and you don't want me as a lover."

"Now you're kitchen sinking it. One has nothing to do with the other."

"Don't they?"

I can't win.

"Look, I just need to slow down this freight train—"

"Call it what it is, Jack. You want to stop. Not slow."

"No, that's not true. I don't want to stop. I just want to *slow*."

"Fine."

"Fine."

They both glared at each other for the rest of the morning. Neither of them spoke on the drive over to the estate.

25

RIGHT AWAY, BOSS

Jack watched as Replacement punched in her passcode to enter the server room in the basement. He could tell she was tired when she got it wrong the first two times; neither of them had gotten much sleep last night, having stayed so late at the hospital.

"Are you okay?"

"Sorry," Replacement muttered. "Pierce just gave it to me. It's a high security room. Only Gerald and Pierce had access."

The keypad light turned green, and Replacement opened the door. Immediately she gasped. There was dried blood on the floor.

Jack instinctively wrapped his arm around her and pulled her back. "Why don't you let me get some of this cleaned up first?" he said.

"Do you mind?" She turned her head away.

"Of course not. Can you get me some cleaner?"

As Replacement hurried off, Jack looked into the small room. It was clear that two tall metal racks had once faced each other, but now, the one on the right lay on its side. A patch panel had been pulled halfway off the wall, and wires hung down.

Jack grabbed the top of the fallen rack and lifted. It was quite heavy, but he managed to stand it back in place.

Replacement reappeared in the doorway with some cleaning supplies, but she kept her head turned away. "Jack?"

"Thanks," Jack said, taking the supplies from her. "It'll just take me a couple of minutes, if you want to wait outside…"

She nodded. "Sure."

Jack set to work cleaning the dried blood off the floor. After a few minutes, he called out, "Alice? It's all set in here."

She peeked in, then smiled up at him. "Thank you."

"It's still a mess. I don't know where anything goes."

Replacement looked behind the rack and made a face. "Yeah, it's a mess all right. Looks like a lot of the plugs were ripped out of the wires. I'll have to make new ones."

"You know how to make cables?" Jack asked.

"They're easy. I should use new cable, though. Can you hand me that spool?" she said, pointing.

"Right away, boss."

Replacement flashed him an I'm-so-glad-you're-here grin.

Jack smiled as the memory of their fight dissolved away.

"Once I get everything hooked back up," Replacement said, "we'll both need to cross our fingers before I turn it on."

For the next hour, Replacement crimped cable while Jack either handed her plugs or worked on pulling the broken ones out of the patch panel. Finally, as Replacement was restoring the last patch cable, Jack surveyed their work.

"What're those two black things in the bottom of the rack?" he asked.

"UPSs. They're a backup power supply if the house loses power. They last long enough so everything shuts down nicely."

"They're heavy."

"They're super-heavy."

Jack walked to the front of the rack and grabbed the rails. He slowly tilted the rack toward him.

"Hello!" Replacement darted out from behind the rack. "We just got it back together, and I haven't even turned it on. Can you try not to knock it back down?"

"How did this tip over?" Jack asked.

"It's tall. Maybe Gerald pulled out the top server?"

"Pulled it out? How?"

Replacement reached up, grabbed both sides of the flat server, and pulled. Like a kitchen drawer, the server slid forward. "It slides out, see? Maybe he was working on it?"

"Pull on it more."

"It's out as far as it can go," Replacement said.

"I know, but… try. Humor me, okay?"

Replacement raised an eyebrow. "Just make sure it doesn't tip. I'm not putting it back together all over again." Shaking her head, she grabbed both sides of the server.

Jack saw the muscles in her arms tense as she pulled. At first she was gentle, but then she put all her weight into it.

The rack stayed where it was.

Replacement exhaled. "Huh. Well… he's a guy."

"Yeah."

The lock on the door clicked, and the server room door opened.

"Hi, Alice." Pierce stepped into the room with a huge smile for Replacement—and then he saw Jack. Like switching channels, his smile clicked off and then on again—but the new polite smile to Jack was thin and strained. "Oh, Jack. You're here too."

"Morning, Pierce."

"I came to see if I could help." Pierce looked to Replacement.

Jack was about to say his help wasn't needed, but Replacement answered first.

"Sure. But do you have time? I thought you had a big company meeting."

"Under the circumstances, I've asked Lydia to push it back a few days."

"Well, I was about to go over Gerald's plan, and I do have a few questions." She picked up Gerald's notebook.

"Sure," Pierce said. "But first, I wanted to let you know, I called the hospital about Mr. Mathis. All they'd tell me is that he's resting comfortably."

"That's what they told me too," Replacement said.

"Well, it's a good sign, I guess. So—how can I help?"

Replacement opened the notebook, clicked her pen, and began going through her list of outstanding tasks. Then she added all the things they needed to do to test anything that might have gotten damaged in the server room. When her list filled a page, she started another.

They were interrupted by a knock at the door—Bruce and Phillip. Replacement, Pierce, and Jack joined them out in the hallway.

"Perfect timing, guys," Replacement said.

"Sorry we're late," Bruce said. "I couldn't sleep. Seeing them load Gerald into the ambulance last night freaked me out."

"Any news on Gerald?" Phillip asked.

"He's pretty bad. But he'll be okay. I know he appreciates everyone's hard work. He asked us to finish the job, so that's what we're going to do." Replacement looked down at her to-do list. "Bruce, you were snaking the cable in the basement yesterday?"

"Yeah. Sorry I left everything out. When Gerald got hurt, it was just pandemonium."

"Don't worry, I haven't even seen it—I'm just trying to figure out where everyone left off."

"Oh, then yeah. I got about a quarter of it done."

"Phillip, you were running the lines for the APs?"

"I only got one done," Phillip said. "They're really long runs. I was trying to hustle, but I kept having to snake some and then go back to the spool."

"Well, Jack can help you with that. Pierce and I will power up the server and check everything. Once that's done, we still have to configure it."

Jack slapped a thin smile on his face and looked at Replacement with a slightly raised eyebrow.

Phillip turned to Jack. "I'm working on the living room upstairs. Ready?"

"Just give me one sec," Jack said. "I'll meet you there."

"Sure." Phillip headed off.

"And I guess I'm back to the dungeon," Bruce added, and he disappeared as well.

Pierce looked between Jack and Replacement. "Um… I'll just go check the connections on the server before we power it on." He tipped his head and went into the server room.

Jack frowned. "I thought I was going to help you today."

"You are." Replacement looked puzzled.

"I mean work with you. I don't even know what an AP is."

"It's an access point. But that doesn't matter. Phillip is running cables for it. I just thought you could help with that."

"I'd rather work with you."

"But I have to configure the server and…" She looked apologetic. "I need Pierce's help."

Jack smiled, but not with his eyes. "Fine. I'll go help Phillip." He made a popping sound on the last *P*.

Replacement pulled him down and kissed him. "Thank you, thank you."

He let out his breath. "You're welcome, welcome."

Replacement headed off to the computer room while Jack started up the stairs to the first floor. He had no idea where the living room was, but at the top of the stairs, he guessed left.

Every room he passed was immaculate. Every piece of furniture screamed expensive. He started to total up the cost but quickly gave up.

A woman in her late thirties wearing a dark-blue business suit came walking down the hallway toward him. "Morning." She brushed back an errant strand of her short sandy-brown hair.

Jack smiled. "Good morning. I was wondering if you could help me. I'm looking for the living room."

"I'm not sure. I just arrived here myself yesterday evening."

"I'm thinking I should've worn my jogging shoes. What is it? A 5K to get from one end of the house to the other?"

The woman laughed. "It's a big house." She held out her hand. "I'm Nancy Bell."

"Jack Stratton."

"Are you new at corporate?" She eyed him up and down.

"No. I'm here helping out a friend."

"Oh, well. It was nice meeting you, Mr. Stratton."

Jack nodded politely and continued on his way. At the end of the hall, he reached a huge stainless-steel kitchen where a woman with short red hair, dressed in a black and white maid outfit, was busy washing coffee pots.

"Hi." Jack looked around. "I'm sort of lost."

She looked him up and down and smiled. "Where're you heading?"

"The living room?"

"Which one?" She winked.

"Seriously?" Jack chuckled. "All Phillip said was it's upstairs."

She laughed. "There's a living room on the first and second floors. But Phillip's right through that door." She pointed to the back of the kitchen.

"Thanks. I'm Jack."

"Sophia." She held up a soapy hand. "Can I get you a cup of coffee?"

"Really? Yes. Thank you."

"How do you like it?"

"Black."

"I'll just be a few minutes."

"Take your time, and thanks."

Jack walked through the doorway into the living room and stopped. The entire back wall was glass, providing a breathtaking view of the lake.

"Awesome view, huh?" Phillip climbed down a stepladder.

Jack just stared.

"Waking up to that every morning has to be tough, huh?" Phillip held his arms out. "Who wouldn't love living this life?"

"Yeah."

Phillip pointed at the table and chairs out on the patio. "If it were me, I'd take my laptop outside."

Jack scanned the living room. "Okay, well, what do you need me to do?"

Jack helped Phillip all morning. At first Phillip seemed a little uneasy around Jack, but once Jack asked the young man some computer geek questions, he warmed right up. In fact, he started to talk and he didn't stop. He went on about everything: news, movies, sports, you name it.

It was a little after one when Sophia came in with a tray of sandwiches and soda. Bruce followed closely behind her.

"I made an assortment," Sophia said as she set the tray down.

Bruce grabbed a roast beef with each hand and grinned.

"My girlfriend's downstairs and—" Jack started to say.

"Alice? I already took food to them."

"Oh. Thanks," Jack muttered.

He took out his phone and dialed Replacement's number.

"Did you get your sandwich?" she asked when she answered.

"Yeah. Aren't you coming up to eat with me?"

"Ah… Pierce and I were going to eat while we worked. The configuration's going slowly. I had to make some new cables, and that set us back an hour. Do you mind?"

Jack exhaled. "No. Do what you have to do. I've got it covered here."

"Are they coming up?" Bruce asked.

"Nope," Jack grumbled. "It's just us."

"Great. More sandwiches for me." Bruce grabbed a tuna fish and another soda.

Jack looked at the food, then walked over to the tool bag.

"Aren't you taking lunch?" Phillip asked.

Jack gestured to the AP that was hanging by wires from the ceiling. "I just want to finish putting the plate in. I have to trim back the wood around it."

"Use the Dremel," Phillip said.

"It can wait until after lunch," Bruce mumbled through a mouthful of food.

"Can you imagine living like this?" Phillip sat down on the couch and faced the pond.

Bruce flopped down next to him and put his feet up on the coffee table. "Pierce is beyond loaded. This place is a palace."

"If it were my house, I'd put in a movie theater." Phillip sipped his soda.

"Totally. If this place were mine, I'd live in the bathroom. Did you see the whirlpool tub?" Bruce took a huge bite of his sandwich. "What would you do, Jack?"

"I'd tell you to get your feet off my table."

Bruce frowned, but he put his feet on the floor.

Jack held up the Dremel. "This thing has a European connector. It doesn't fit the extension cord."

"There's a converter in the bag," Phillip said. "Really, Jack, come eat. That can wait."

"I'm good." Jack found the converter, plugged in the Dremel, and hurried up the ladder.

"Seriously, what a life," Bruce said. "Pierce has it made. Money, this house. I'm surprised he doesn't have a wife."

"He has to have his pick of girls," Phillip said. "Any girl he wants. He could just snap his fingers."

The Dremel whirled up and sawdust fell like snow as Jack cut the slot for the plate.

Bruce whistled. "They'd come running. And look." He thrust a hand toward the window. "Look at that yard."

Phillip sat up straighter and peered out. "I'd have, like, a dozen kids."

Bruce laughed. "I'd have a dozen wives."

Jack forced the plate into place. "How long do you think this job will take?"

"We have six more after that one," said Phillip. "This place is huge. It's like wiring up a whole office building."

Jack interlaced his fingers behind his head and stretched his back.

Bruce was apparently still daydreaming about the easy life. "Man, Pierce never has to work. I mean yeah, he has a company, but he doesn't have to *do* anything. I'd be on vacation all the time. Think about it. You could wake up and just say, 'Where do I want to go?'"

"I'd go to Hawaii," Phillip said.

"No way. Tahiti. Or Fiji." Bruce held up a water bottle. "Have you ever been?"

Phillip shook his head. "I've never been out of the States. What about you, Jack?"

"Right now I'm only thinking about wrapping up this job and putting a bow on it. Let me know when you're ready to start again."

Phillip and Bruce continued to talk about extravagant lifestyles and exotic getaways during lunch. Then Bruce went back to the basement, and Phillip helped Jack finish with that AP.

After that, they did three more. And through it all, Phillip's talking never ebbed. He was still going strong at six when they finished the third one.

"I'm going to talk to Alice," Jack said suddenly.

"Are we calling it a day?" Phillip asked.

"No. I'm just… I'll be back."

As Jack headed downstairs, he rubbed his face and wished he had a cup of coffee. At the server room door, he knocked and waited.

No response.

Jack huffed and knocked louder.

Sophia came walking down the hallway toward him with an empty tray. "Are you looking for Alice?"

"Have you seen her?"

"I just brought her and Pierce some drinks. They're in the small study." She pointed down the hall.

Jack marched down the hallway. He heard laughter ahead of him. The door to the study was partly open, and he looked in.

Replacement and Pierce sat together on a couch—too close together, in Jack's opinion—with a laptop set out on a coffee table in front of Replacement. She was typing while Pierce looked over her shoulder. Then she pointed at something on the screen, and when Pierce put his hand on her shoulder, her face lit up.

Jack knocked loudly.

Replacement jumped up, and her smile broadened. "Hey!"

Jack tipped his head to the side. "Hey. I was just checking on how you're holding up."

"Great." She squeezed her body tightly like a cheerleader getting ready to jump. "We're getting so much done."

"Great. I, uh… Do you need a hand?"

"Nope. Are you and Phillip done?"

"We just finished another one, but we still have a couple to go."

"Pierce invited us all to stay for dinner."

"Okay." Jack looked around the stately library. Deep mahogany bookshelves circled the room, and thick carpet covered the floor. The small windows and dark wood created a private, almost intimate atmosphere. "I thought you were configuring the server?"

"We are." She pointed back to the laptop. "Remotely. We can't drink in the server room."

Jack's jaw tightened. He wanted to ask her where she'd had lunch while she worked on the server, but he held his tongue.

Sophia appeared in the doorway. "Dinner is being served on the pool deck."

Pierce stood up. "Thank you." He smiled at Replacement. "Shall we?"

26

HE'S MY GUY

A catered dinner with silver chafing trays and candlelit tables had been expertly arranged on the blue slate patio. White tablecloths reflected the orange hue of the sunset. Jack, Replacement, Bruce, and Phillip sat at one table, while Pierce, Leon, Lydia, Nancy, and Roger took another. Manuel stood guard at the gate.

Pierce stood up, and the conversations stopped. "I thought I'd take a moment to make introductions. Lydia is my executive assistant. She's been with Weston since the company began."

Lydia nodded and smiled.

"Roger Braxton is the assistant vice president of marketing. He's the creator of our new campaign, 'VE-Life is now.'"

Roger held up his drink. Jack expected to see fumes coming from the cup given how strong the smell of gin was. "Thank you, Mr. Weston," Roger said, "for inviting us all to your absolutely breathtaking new home." He smiled to each and every person present in turn.

Pierce continued with the introductions. He nodded to a tall man in his mid-fifties who wore a black suit. "Leon Bagwell here is the head of Weston security." With gray, buzzed-cut hair, a square jaw, and steel eyes, Leon sat at the table, but his upper body remained at attention. His feet were planted flat on the floor, his back ramrod straight, his hands in his lap, and his elbows close to his sides.

"Nancy Bell is our vice president of human resources. She recently came to us from Rutland Systems."

"Nice to meet you all." Nancy gave one of those waves where you hold up your hand and bend your fingers rapidly.

"Spearheading the re-networking of the estate is Alice Campbell." Pierce looked at Replacement. "She's been invaluable in keeping things moving." He held out his hand to Replacement, giving her the floor, and took his seat.

Jack saw Replacement's eyes go wide. He gave her leg a little squeeze under the table.

Replacement stood up and cleared her throat. "Hi. Uh… This is Bruce Atwood. He's our… wireless guy. And this is Phillip Miller. He's our AP guy. And this is Jack Stratton." Replacement grinned. "He's *my* guy."

Everyone laughed.

Replacement sat back down, and conversation resumed.

"What do you think they have for us?" Bruce whispered to Jack. He was hungrily eyeing the steaming chafing dishes.

Jack shrugged.

"Whatever it is," Bruce continued, "it smells great, and they have lots of it." He grabbed a hunk of bread.

"Mr. Weston." Leon's voice was low and gravelly. "My apologies, sir, but do you have a moment?"

Pierce rose, and the two men walked over to the corner of the patio.

Replacement, Bruce, and Phillip soon fell into tech talk, and Jack found himself staring at his water glass. It was impossible not to overhear the conversation at the next table even if he didn't want to.

"So the meeting's Tuesday now? We're stuck here for days?" Nancy was saying. "I have to get back to the office. I have work to do."

Lydia stirred her coffee. "It's not that bad. You can work remotely. Besides, a man was nearly killed."

"Think of it as a mini-vacation." Roger grinned.

Lydia scowled. "Just be sure you don't disturb Mr. Weston with your 'mini-vacation.' He needs to relax."

"That's what I'm good at—helping people relaaax." He drew out the last word and flashed his white teeth.

Nancy pulled out her phone. "I'm going to need to reschedule my entire week," she grumbled.

Roger took a long swig of his drink. "Just do what I do, Nancy."

"And what's that?"

"Have my secretary do it." He laughed.

Lydia's eyes narrowed. "Roger, do try to apply a filter."

Roger tipped his head toward Pierce and Leon. "What's that all about?"

"I'm sure it's nothing," Lydia said.

Sophia set a cup of tea down in front of Nancy.

"Thank you," Nancy said with a smile. To Lydia she said, "Why is the head of security here in the first place?"

"Mr. Weston requested he be at the meeting too," Lydia said. "The security group's part of the testing."

Roger sat back. "Yeah, but something else is going on. I bet Leon's looking for whoever leaked the fact that we blew by our earning estimates."

"It's a good thing it's not our job to speculate." Lydia glowered.

Jack was surprised that Lydia's words didn't freeze her tea before she took a sip.

Jack's attention drifted back to his own table, where Phillip was pulling out his cigarettes. But when he started to light one, Replacement's eyes went wide and she shook her head.

Phillip's shoulders slumped.

"C'mon," Bruce said, pulling out his own cigarettes. "We'll go smoke over by the pool."

"I'm sure the food will be right out," Replacement whispered.

Pierce appeared behind Bruce and pointed at the cigarettes. "Do you mind if I...?"

"I thought you quit." Replacement shook her hand over the cigarettes as if she were warding Pierce away.

Pierce cleared his throat. "I'm in the process of quitting. But I can't find my e-cigarette case."

"Have you lost something, sir?" Sophia asked.

Pierce's smile seemed forced as all eyes turned to him. "My e-cigarette case. It's a silver metal case about as big as a cell phone. Have you seen it?"

Sophia shook her head. "No, sir."

Pierce drummed his fingers on the table while he looked at Bruce's pack. "I really could use one. I don't remember where I left it."

Bruce quietly slid the pack back into his pocket.

"Why quit?" Roger strolled over and handed Pierce a drink.

"Roger," Lydia piped up. "It's good he wants to break that nasty habit."

"It's silver?" Replacement asked. "Does it have a USB plug?"

"It does. So you can recharge it. Have you seen it?"

Replacement made a face. "It's at my house."

Roger raised his eyebrows and smirked.

Jack scowled.

"Gerald must have picked it up," Replacement added. "It was in his things. They gave it to me at the hospital with everything else."

"Ah. That's my backup. I gave it to him yesterday, thinking I wouldn't need it. Wouldn't you know it, I lose mine right after."

"I can bring it tomorrow."

"No, no, it's Gerald's now. I'll buy another one."

The servers walked out to the patio and moved behind the table with the chafing dishes.

Pierce held up his hand. "Well, shall we eat?"

27

DID YOU LEAVE THE LIGHTS ON?

As Jack turned onto his street, police lights reflected off the trees in the back parking lot. His training immediately kicked in, and the familiar surge of adrenaline washed through him. His eyes scanned the area as he pulled in. Two police cruisers were parked at odd angles out back. Their lights flashed, but no one was inside them.

Replacement sat up straighter. She spoke slowly when she asked, "Did you leave the lights on in the apartment?"

Jack's throat tightened. He threw the Charger into park and then ran to the rear entrance of the building.

On the wall along the stairs was a long blood smear. Jack took the steps three at a time, with Replacement right on his heels. At the top of the landing, they both froze. Their apartment door was open, and Jack could hear someone walking around inside. His hand instinctively went for his gun, but clutched empty air.

Damn.

Jack looked back at Replacement and held up his palm.

She nodded and crouched low.

Jack knew it was probably the police who were now in his apartment, but he also knew it only took letting your guard down once to get yourself killed. He pressed his back against the wall and moved toward the door.

"This is Jack Stratton." His voice boomed in the narrow hallway. "You are in my apartment. Identify yourself."

"Jack, it's me, Kendra." Kendra stepped out of the apartment with her hands out to the sides, her shotgun in her right hand. "You made me jump a mile. You should've been a drill instructor."

"Oh no. Lady!" Jack rushed by her.

"Jack, you shouldn't come in."

"Lady! Lady!" Replacement called, racing after him.

"Guys, your dog's okay. She's fine. She's downstairs with your landlady."

Jack looked around the apartment and ran his hand through his hair. The little hall table lay on its side. Broken glass and change covered the floor. Blood was smeared on a broken lamp.

Replacement groaned. "What a mess."

Jack exhaled and turned to Kendra. "What happened?"

"We got two calls fifteen minutes ago. One was from your landlady, who said that someone was breaking into your apartment. Another was from a man who said a werewolf was chasing a car down the street."

"He had to mean Lady," Replacement said. "I have to go see her."

She dashed downstairs, and Jack and Kendra followed. The door to Mrs. Stevens's apartment was open.

As Jack walked in, Kendra blurted out, "Wait. I need to tell you—"

"Murphy." Jack's eyes narrowed when he saw Officer Billy Murphy.

Murphy nodded. "Stratton."

"Alice!" Mrs. Stevens hurried over to her as fast as her large frame allowed. "I'm so glad to see you."

Replacement gave her a quick hug.

Mrs. Stevens looked over Replacement's shoulder at Jack. "It was terrifying." Her mane of red hair wobbled back and forth. "Simply terrifying."

Lady jumped off the couch. As she trotted over to Replacement, she kept her front right paw in the air.

"No, no, no." Mrs. Stevens turned and intercepted the dog. "Sit back down, little Lady."

"Is she okay?" Replacement knelt down. "What happened to her paw?"

Lady licked Replacement's face.

"I'm guessing she stepped on some glass." Mrs. Stevens patted Lady's head.

Lady pressed hard against Replacement. Jack crouched down and tried to examine the dog's paw, but she growled.

"She won't let me look either," Mrs. Stevens said. "But it can't be too bad. And other than her foot, she seems okay."

Lady limped back to the couch.

"What happened?" Jack asked.

Mrs. Stevens sat down on the couch next to Lady. "I was watching TV, and I heard a scream upstairs. It being your apartment, I almost didn't think much of it, but then Lady just started barking nonstop, and there were some crashing sounds. I went to my door, and I heard someone tearing down the steps. Then I opened the door and saw Lady charging after him."

"Did you get a look at him?" Jack asked.

Mrs. Stevens's trembling finger tapped her chin. "Not a good one. Only from behind. He had short hair. Broad shoulders, like a bodybuilder. He seemed to be rather thick, but not fat. I'd think… he was around six feet tall. He wore black boots, jeans, and a light tan jacket."

"You saw a lot." Murphy wrote in his notebook.

"I'd never forgive myself if something happened to this precious dog." Mrs. Stevens stroked Lady's head, and the dog stretched out on the couch. "So I went after them. The man must have been parked right outside. He took off like a rocket."

"Did you see the car?"

"No, it was gone in a second. I'm sure Lady would've caught him if she wasn't running on three legs. Oh, my poor little girl." Mrs. Stevens rubbed her face in Lady's neck.

"It looks like Lady took a bite out of the guy," Kendra said.

Jack froze. "No. I don't see where you get that."

"The blood on the wall." Kendra gestured with her thumb toward the staircase. "And the blood around her mouth."

"I think that guy may have cut his feet on all the glass upstairs," Murphy said.

"What? Who do you think he is, the barefoot bandit?" Kendra's face scrunched up. "That makes no sense. Think it through. The guy breaks in. Lady goes for his arm. They struggle. He breaks free, and on the way down, his injured arm rubs against the wall. Lady bit the guy."

"Without the guy, we don't know that." Jack stood up. "I'm agreeing with Murphy."

Kendra's eyebrows went up. "I never thought I'd hear you say *that*." She stared at Jack, then at Murphy.

"Kendra." Murphy leaned in. "Do you know what the procedure is if a dog bites a human?"

Kendra's mouth twisted. "She'd have to go to the animal shelter for two weeks of observation."

"That's not happening." Replacement moved protectively in front of Lady.

"No, it's definitely not." Murphy reached down and patted Lady's back. "This dog saved my life. No way am I saying she bit anyone." He glanced at Jack. "But I still hate you, Stratton."

"I sort of had a hand in saving your sorry butt, too. But thanks." Jack nodded in appreciation.

Kendra smiled. "You're right. Perp cut himself on glass." She turned to Jack. "I need you to take a look upstairs and tell me if anything is missing."

"Let's do it fast. I want to get Lady to the vet."

"I'll wait with Lady." Replacement stroked the dog's head.

Jack went upstairs with Kendra and Murphy. Glass crunched and metal plinked as they stepped into the apartment.

"Obviously, the table got knocked over." Jack pointed down. "I bet that's how Lady cut her paw. The computer's still here." He walked over to Replacement's bedroom. "So is Alice's TV."

"Undoubtedly Lady scared him away before he took anything," Murphy said. "Who wouldn't run from that dog?"

"I really have to get her to the vet," Jack said. "Can you guys process this without me here?"

"Sure." Kendra nodded.

"Yeah, great. Thanks, Kendra."

Jack went back to the Charger and pulled it right up to the door to the building, so Lady wouldn't have to walk far. Then he returned to Mrs. Stevens's apartment.

"Okay," he said to Lady in a quiet voice, "I'm trying to help, so don't bite my face off."

Mrs. Stevens rubbed Lady's head. "My snookums would never."

"Just be careful of her foot." Replacement pouted.

As Jack started to pick up Lady, a deep rumble in her belly shook his chest. He froze.

"You be a good girl, baby," Replacement cooed.

"Do you have any dog biscuits?" Jack asked.

Mrs. Stevens frowned at him. "Of course I do." She leaned over to a container next to the table.

Boy, she sure likes this dog.

"Why don't you get some biscuits and walk in front of us?"

Jack then took a deep breath and lifted Lady up. Lady didn't struggle, but her low growl made Jack's back tense.

Mrs. Stevens grabbed some biscuits and walked into the hallway, and Jack followed, with Replacement right behind him. The huge dog pressed her face against Jack's as he walked.

"Cut it out, dog," Jack grumbled. "I'll trip and drop you."

"You'll do no such thing," Mrs. Stevens said as she held up a cookie, "or my little baby will eat you."

Replacement giggled.

Outside, Jack managed to get Lady into the back seat of the Charger. After he closed the door, Mrs. Stevens reached through the window and rewarded the big dog with a couple of biscuits.

"You'll call me and let me know how she is?" Mrs. Stevens said, wringing her hands.

"I will. Thank you."

28

YOU'RE BOTH SCARY

As Jack got out of the car in front of the Darrington Animal Shelter, a long one-story building set back from the road, he paused. "Do you think they have a dog stretcher of some kind?"

"I don't think so." Replacement made a face.

Jack debated about going in to see, but Lady whimpered from the back seat. She didn't want to wait.

"It's okay, baby." Replacement rubbed Lady's chin and coaxed her, still limping, out of the car. Jack lifted her up again. This time she didn't growl.

As he was carrying her up the ramp to the shelter, a familiar face appeared at the door and held it open for them. Lacie. Jack and Replacement had gotten to know Lacie a few weeks ago, during their pursuit of the Giant Killer.

"What happened?" Lacie asked.

"We think she might have glass in her foot," Replacement said.

"Follow me."

They followed the petite girl as she headed through a set of double doors to an exam room. Lacie was in her mid-twenties. Her dress was retro punk—high-top sneakers, black skirt, silver nose ring, and a short-sleeved, paint-splattered shirt revealing arms covered in tattoos. The last time Jack had seen her, she'd had a pink streak running down the middle of her jet-black hair; that streak had now been changed to a bright blue.

"Put her up on the table." Lacie pressed a foot pump and raised the metal table up. "I'll get Ryan."

Lady whimpered and pressed against Jack's chest.

"Shh." Replacement stroked her head.

The door swung open only a moment later, and Lacie led Ryan in. Ryan ran the animal shelter. He was medium height and had a thin build, with round glasses and a wavy brown ponytail. And although he was in his early thirties, his khaki pants and blue T-shirt gave him a youthful appearance.

"Hi, Ryan." Jack stuck out his hand, but Ryan's focus was on the dog.

"What happened?" Ryan asked.

Lady lifted her hurt paw and held it out to Ryan. Jack's mouth fell open. "I guess I should let her tell you."

"She hurt her foot," Replacement said. "We think she might have broken glass in there."

Ryan pulled down a light and examined Lady's paw. "I can see the glass," he said. He adjusted the light. "It looks like just one piece. I should be able to remove it and bandage her up. Lacie?"

Lacie nodded and got some supplies from a cabinet.

"I'll need you to hold her," Ryan said to Jack.

Jack swallowed.

Lacie frowned. "Don't be scared."

"Holding on to a grizzly bear while he operates on her foot doesn't seem like a great plan," Jack muttered.

Replacement rolled her eyes. "I'll help."

"Lady weighs more than you," Jack said. "Seriously, Ryan, can you give her an anesthetic or something?"

"She'll be fine." Ryan spoke softly. "Won't you, girl?"

Jack wrapped his arms around Lady and kept his face behind her head.

Lacie handed Ryan some rubber-tipped mini vise grips. He lifted them toward Lady's paw and hesitated. Then he exhaled and looked up at Jack. "Okay, a dog this large makes me a little nervous too," he admitted. "But let's try it without sedation first."

Replacement stroked Lady's back as Ryan reached in with the grips.

"Wow," Ryan muttered as a large piece of glass emerged.

Lady whimpered, but held still.

The glass pulled free, and Ryan grinned. "Kind of a big piece of glass, but the wound itself isn't bad. She'll be fine."

He cleaned the wound and applied an antiseptic, then wrapped the paw in a bandage. "See if you can keep her from chewing the bandage off, but if she insists, don't worry too much about it. It's mostly to keep her from getting blood on your carpets." He stepped back. "You can let her go now."

Jack did, and Lady shook. Jack smiled until she licked his face. "Gross."

Ryan chuckled. But as he looked at Lady, his eyes narrowed. "Wait a second."

Jack looked from Ryan to Lacie for an answer. Lacie shrugged.

Ryan put his hand on Lady's back and moved it slowly down Lady's side. A low rumble started in Lady's chest and grew steadily into a growl. "She has a large bruise on her side," Ryan said.

Jack snarled.

Lacie leaned away from Jack. "Wow. They say people start to look like their dogs, and it's definitely true in your case. You're both scary."

"What happened? Was she in a fight?" Ryan asked.

"Someone broke into our apartment when Jack and I weren't home," Replacement explained. "Lady was." She pouted.

"Did she fight with them?" Ryan asked.

Jack gave him a sideways look. "Hypothetically, what would happen if a dog may have bitten a guy?"

"Did Lady bite him?"

"I'm not saying until you answer." Jack rubbed Lady's head.

"Well, Lady's had all her shots. If she did bite someone, besides the wound, I don't think there's anything to worry about."

"Wait—could she catch something from the scumbag?" Jack's voice rose.

Ryan frowned. "That definitely answers my question about whether she bit someone or not." He examined Lady's mouth. "Dog and human systems are very different. It'd be very rare if she caught something from him. But I want to check her teeth." Ryan held open Lady's mouth and peered in. "And I'm concerned about that bruise. It looks like she was punched or kicked."

Jack's fist came down hard against the cabinet, and everyone jumped.

"How about you don't startle her when my fingers are in her mouth?" Ryan said. He looked a little pale.

"Sorry."

"You won't have to keep her for observation, right?" Replacement asked.

"Not my little Lady." Ryan scratched behind her ears. "Just try to keep her resting while that bruise heals. No more fighting bad guys, okay?"

"She'll be good," Replacement promised.

As Jack and Replacement left the animal shelter, with Lady once again in Jack's arms, Lady whimpered. Jack shoved the door open with his foot.

"When I find the guy who hurt my dog…"

29

LIKE AN IMPERIAL PROBE DROID?

On the way home, Jack got a call from Kendra.

"Did you get any lead on the guy?" he asked.

"We canvassed the area and got next to zip. Not even a good description of the car. On the plus side, we did get that there was more than one guy. He had a driver. Morrison asked if you'd do another check for anything missing."

"We're heading back to do that now."

"Have you had any run-ins lately? Maybe a bounty that broke bad?"

Jack almost laughed, but he didn't want to hurt Kendra's feelings. "No bounty ends well, from their point of view. So yeah, I haven't been making friends. That's another reason I need Collins to give me my guns back."

"Morrison's working on that too. I gotta run. When are we going to go for a beer?"

"Let the dust settle. But I do want to know how you ended up working with Murphy."

"He's getting better. Maybe almost getting killed did something good for him."

***

Back at the apartment, Jack was relieved to see that Mrs. Stevens had already cleaned up the blood on the wall.

Best not to have any evidence of a dog bite.

When Jack opened the apartment door, Lady started to head in. But then she turned back around and planted her feet in the middle of the doorway. A deep rumble started in her chest, and out came three sharp, challenging barks.

"I think she's letting the world know the queen has returned to her castle," Jack said.

"Bad guy beware." Replacement led Lady over to the couch. "I thought we could give her the couch until her foot gets better."

"Bye, couch," Jack said.

"She'll give it back."

Lady stretched out on the couch. Her body extended the whole length of it. She let out a satisfied huff and closed her eyes.

"Or maybe she won't." Replacement's nose crinkled.

Jack and Replacement started cleaning up. They set the hall table upright, threw the lamp in the trash, and swept up the remains of the change jar. Jack was reaching for the key holder on the floor when he noticed a silver case smeared with blood.

He picked it up by holding the corners.

"What's this thing covered in blood? I've never seen it before." Jack turned it over. "I think it's one of your computer things."

Replacement turned away. "I'm not looking at it if it's all bloody."

Jack carried it into the kitchen to get a better look. He set it on the counter.

Replacement yelled into the kitchen, "You just said there's blood on it. Don't put it on the counter!"

"Sorry," Jack muttered as he looked closer. "What *is* this thing? Lady, is this yours?"

Lady opened an eye.

Replacement walked over and gave Jack a playful smack on his backside. "Fine, I'll look at it." Peering through her fingers, she eyed the bloody case. "Oh. That's the e-cigarette case that Gerald had, that Pierce gave him. Is that a fingerprint? Can the police use it?"

"No, it's way too smudged for ID. But the fact that there is a fingerprint means the guy who broke in either had this in his hand when Lady bit him, or picked it up after she bit him. Either way, he had some interest in it. Can you check what's on it?"

"Touch it? Gross, it's all bloody." She made a face. "Besides, there's nothing *on* it. It's just a charger." She scanned the apartment and shivered as if she had just stepped into ice-cold water. "I think I'm just going to disinfect everything." She walked to the bathroom.

"Are you worried the guy who broke in here had a bad cold?" Jack asked.

Replacement's voice came from the bathroom. "Very funny. I just don't like the idea of someone else having been in here." She came back out with a bucket of cleaning supplies, yellow gloves on her hands, and a determined look on her face. "I'm not going to let some creep, creep out my home."

She pulled out a spray bottle and held it up to the bedroom doorknob, but her finger hesitated on the trigger. "Crud." She straightened up and her lip curled like Elvis. "Can I clean? Did they dust for prints?"

"You can clean. They don't dust for prints."

"They don't? I thought they always did."

"On TV. Every police department is different. For most, the crime needs to rise to a certain level. This is a low-level break-in."

Replacement huffed. "It's not low level. It's *my apartment.* I want them to catch the jerk."

Jack was still eyeing the e-cigarette case. He took it over to Replacement's computer and plugged it in. "I just meant they didn't steal anything. The police budget's limited. We do—*they* do the best they can."

"Why are you charging that case?" Replacement asked.

"I wanted to see what's on it."

"It's not a hard drive. It—*CRAP!*"

Replacement dashed over and yanked the computer's network cable out of the wall. Its plastic end snapped across the room and pinged off the opposite wall.

Jack's mouth dropped open. "What the hell?"

Replacement sat down at the computer, ripped her gloves off, and began typing furiously. Her fingers flew across the keyboard.

"Care to clue me in?" Jack put his hands on the back of her chair.

"Hold on." She continued to type. "I need to take some snapshots. That thing tried transmitting."

"Transmitting? Like an Imperial Probe Droid? What're you talking about?"

"One second." She leaned closer to the screen.

Jack couldn't believe it, but it seemed as if her flying fingers got even faster. "Wow, can you type."

"Got it." Replacement sat back and smiled triumphantly.

"Great. Explain it to me. What is 'it'?"

"I don't know. I got the log."

"Does the log tell us who it was calling?"

"It might."

Jack shook his head. "Might?"

"I have to go through it. I need to run traces and…" She sighed. "Technical stuff."

"Can you explain what just happened?"

Replacement tilted her head and looked up at him. "Well, you know the websites I sometimes have to go to?"

"You mean the hacker sites." Jack frowned.

She rolled her eyes. "They're computer sites, but… anyway. If you go to places like that, you better wrap your PC in a digital condom. Seriously, there's no honor among thieves or hackers, and even the guys helping you may try to give you something. Know what I mean?"

"I do, but the imagery in my head is grossing me out."

"I have layers of protection. One went off when you plugged the case in. The case was trying to transmit."

"Trying? Did it?"

"I don't think so. Unless I let it, my computer doesn't send jack." She grinned.

"*What* was it trying to transmit? To who?"

Replacement shrugged. "I don't know." She turned back around in her chair. "But I'm going to find out."

Jack put his hands on her shoulders. "You go, geek girl."

He rubbed while she typed. After a minute, she began to purr.

"That explains why someone tried to steal it," Jack mused aloud.

"Wait. You're saying that this was the *reason* someone broke in? For this e-cigarette case?"

"Look." Jack pointed to the kitchen counter. "I left the checkbook on the counter. Your laptop is right here. He didn't touch any of it. But he grabbed a cigarette charger. Yeah, he came here for this."

"What do you think it all means?"

"I don't know. But I hope whatever you find on that thing will help." Jack walked over to the window. "I need to think. I'm going to take a shower."

"Okay. While you 'think,' I'll *work*." She gave him a big wink.

Jack pulled the curtain on the window closed too soon to see the green sedan that drove slowly down the street.

***

Jack squinted as the morning light peeked from behind the shade. Lady climbed up on the bed, and Jack's eyes fluttered open.

"Get off," he mumbled.

She put her head behind his back and pushed.

"Stop."

She placed her nose close to his ear and huffed.

"Gross!" Jack rolled out of bed and shook his head. "Fine. Okay. I'm up." He headed for the bathroom.

Lady scratched at the door.

He patted her head as he came out a minute later. "Sorry to keep you waiting. I had to go, too." He grabbed her leash off the bureau, rubbed his eyes, and trudged out to the living room.

Replacement was still at the computer.

"Hold up." Jack stopped. "Have you been up all night?"

"I got a couple of hours' sleep, but then I had another idea." She stood up and stretched. "Crud, is it morning already? Double crud."

"I have to take Lady out."

"I'll come with you. I need some fresh air."

Replacement bounded after them as they headed out the door.

"So, did you find anything?" Jack asked. "Do you know who it was transmitting to?"

"It sent an email message. The message was just a number one and a space, and then fourteen-slash-nine-slash-fifteen. Maybe that's a code."

"Or a date," Jack said as they made it outside and Lady started sniffing.

Replacement made a face. "There's no month fourteen."

"Sometimes people write the month first. It drove me crazy when I was stationed in Germany. September fourteenth was two days ago. The day of Gerald's accident."

"It's a date then. Maybe the number one is binary. Like one is on, and zero is off."

"Anything else?" Jack asked. "Who was the email to?"

"That I don't know yet. But there is something else. The case has files on it."

"Files? So it *is* a hard drive." Jack grinned. "I was right."

"Whatever."

"No 'whatever.' Give credit where credit's due." Jack leaned close to her with a big smile on his face.

She kissed him. "You're brilliant. But what it means is, someone modified that e-cigarette case. They turned it into a hard drive to copy files."

"Copy them?"

Replacement nodded. "I need to talk to Pierce."

"Why?"

"The files on the case are his. He showed me some of the code for VE-Life. The directory structure on the case is identical. I'm sure of it."

"I'm the last guy to argue with you about computers. But wait—is there any way that case could transmit its location? Like a phone?"

"No. The memory stick takes up almost all the space in it."

"What time did you say you were going out to the mega-mansion?"

"In an hour." Replacement groaned. "Great. I hardly got any sleep."

"Let's put you to bed for an hour, and then we'll go there. I'll drive. You can sleep on the way."

"What do you think all this means?" Replacement asked.

"I don't know. But I think we need to have a chat with the boy billionaire."

30

THE BOY BILLIONAIRE

"Wait a minute." Pierce paced the floor of the upstairs study. "You're saying someone modified my e-cigarette case in order to steal my files?" He held up the still-bloody case.

Replacement nodded. "Don't plug it in unless you've disconnected everything. I brought my laptop if you want to use that." Replacement set her laptop down on the desk and turned it on.

Pierce nodded but didn't move. He turned the case over in his hands, then looked up at Jack. "I need your help to find out who's behind this."

"Mine?" Jack leaned against the doorframe. "Why not go to your security?"

"I would, but… I don't know who to trust." Pierce walked over to the window. "We've had security issues at the home office. Corporate spying. And now this." He studied Jack for a moment. "I've been reading up on you, Jack Stratton. I'd value your opinion."

Jack picked up a notebook off the desk and fanned the empty pages. "Do you mind if I use this?"

Pierce nodded. "Sure."

"When did you get that case?" Jack asked.

"A couple of months ago."

"You bought two?"

"Yes. They're identical."

"Where?"

"You can buy them anywhere. Lydia picked them up for me."

"Who knows you have it?"

Pierce ran his hand through his hair. "About a million people."

Replacement's mouth fell open.

"I mentioned it during an interview in *Tech Talk Magazine.*"

"Well, someone went to great lengths to get the files off your laptop. What's so valuable on there?"

"It's my development machine," Pierce said. "The raw code for VE-Life, both the old and the new version, is on there. Another corporation could leak the features, or copy it for their own program."

"And hackers would love to get their hands on it, so they can exploit the code," Replacement added.

Jack jotted that down. "I'm assuming whoever switched the e-cigarette cases did it since you came to Darrington—or close to it."

"Why would you assume that?"

"Because we know they're here now. Besides, you come to your summer palace, and there's less security. So they switch the case. You plug it in. It phones home and lets someone know it's ready for pickup. None of the cameras in the house work?"

"Nope," Replacement said. "That's the next thing we were going to hook up."

"That's not entirely true," Pierce said.

Replacement's neck lengthened.

"There are perimeter cameras for security. They feed into the guardhouse."

"They're on, working? Monitored?"

Pierce nodded.

"You said you had two cases," Jack said. "Where's the second one now?"

Pierce shrugged. "I have no idea. You remember me begging for cigarettes last night? I'd love to smoke one right now, as a matter of fact."

"So you lost your case, and later that same day, someone tried to steal your backup case," Jack said.

"Oh—no. I mean yes, but—this case is mine. I don't know why Gerald had it. I gave him my backup. That's the case that's still missing."

"I thought the cases were identical," Jack said.

"They are, but see"—he held up the case—"this one's got a ding in the corner where I dropped it. It's mine. I gave Gerald the backup, which was brand new. I'm sure of it."

Replacement jumped up. "The cases must have gotten mixed up. Remember? Gerald was showing us that blueprint in the server room. It kept curling up, and both of you put your cases down to hold down the corners. And then we had to leave in a hurry, because I was late—" She glanced sheepishly at Jack. "You must have picked up the wrong case."

Jack turned to Replacement. "The hospital only gave you one case?"

She nodded.

Jack crossed his arms. "Someone at dinner last night is involved in this."

"You can't be sure of that," Pierce said.

"I am."

"How?"

"Alice told them where it was. There's no other way anyone could have known that."

"What?" Replacement gasped. "I didn't… Oh, no. I did." She pointed at Pierce. "You said you wanted to smoke. I said I had the case."

"Leon, Roger, Nancy, and Lydia," Pierce muttered. "And Manuel. They were all there."

"Eight people heard, not counting us," Jack said. "Bruce and Phillip were there, too. So was the maid."

Replacement shook her head. "There were a bunch of servers there too."

"Not when you said you had the case," Jack said. "All the servers had gone inside the house to get instructions for the dinner service."

Replacement's eyes lit up. "We might be able to narrow the list down. Have you noticed if anyone has a wound? Most likely on their arm. My dog bit whoever broke into the apartment."

"I saw Lydia and Sophia this morning. They both looked okay."

"Everyone at dinner is fine," Jack said. "The robbery occurred while we were all here. Someone has an accomplice."

Replacement nodded. "So even if someone doesn't have a chunk taken out of their arm, they could still be involved."

Pierce looked at Replacement. "Is your dog okay?"

Replacement's eyes rounded. "She's fine now. Our landlady is watching her."

Jack changed the subject. "What's happening in your company?" he asked.

Pierce looked up at the ceiling. "Why would you ask?"

"You told me there have been security issues, corporate spying. You already suspect this was an inside job."

Pierce rubbed both hands down his face. "We've had a number of leaks. Two have been very big ones. We've been investigating. We attributed them to corporate spying—it happens all the time—but lately they've been… painful."

"Has your investigation turned up anything?"

Pierce shook his head. "No."

"Is that why you brought these particular employees out? They seem like a mixed group."

Pierce gave Jack an appraising nod. "You're very insightful. Yes. Only a handful of people could've known the information that was leaked. So I came up with this meeting idea. Basically, I intended to plant a false story and see if someone took the bait."

"That's brilliant." Replacement grinned.

"And do you have reason not to trust your security team?" Jack asked.

Pierce's shoulders slumped. He suddenly looked tired. "Nothing specific. I really don't think Leon has anything to do with it, but I can't be a hundred percent sure. *Someone* in the company's responsible. I don't know if I'm being paranoid, but…"

Jack walked to the window and looked out at the lake.

"So," Pierce said, "do you have any idea how you can find out who's behind this?"

Jack turned back around. "Yeah. When Alice gives you the case back, they'll come and get it."

"What?" Replacement looked confused, but before Jack could answer, her phone buzzed. "It's Bruce," she said.

"Answer it. Act normal."

"Hey, Bruce." She nodded a few times. "Okay, I'll be down." She hung up. "Bruce and Phillip are here. What did you mean, I'm giving the case back to Pierce?"

"You offered to give it back to Pierce last night, and that's exactly what you're going to do. We need to go back to business as usual. If we're going to draw them out, we first have to get them to relax," Jack said.

"But what do I tell people?" Replacement asked.

"The truth." He looked back and forth between Replacement and Pierce. "We're all going to tell everyone everything—except about the e-cigarette case. Don't mention it. You can talk about the cops, the mess at the apartment, Lady going to the vet—everything but the case. We want them to think everything's fine."

"Data was copied off my laptop. I need to report the data breach to someone," Pierce said.

Replacement made a face. "Well, *was* it a data breach? They copied data off your hard drive but never saw it. The data was never transmitted."

"That's technically true," Jack said.

Pierce nodded.

Jack turned to Replacement. "Okay. You need to get Bruce and Phillip working. Then I need you to start looking at everyone who was here when you told Pierce you found the case."

"Can I get access to Weston's databases?" she asked Pierce.

"Sure. That won't take long." He turned to Jack. "But Jack, what about the case? I understand you want to draw them out, but I can't take a chance on this data getting out. It's far too valuable."

"Replacement can clear your data off the case," Jack said. "You and I will take a ride and get another one. We'll use the new one as bait."

"I want in on that," Replacement said.

Jack shook his head. "We need to act normal—and that means you're at work today. You'll get Bruce and Phillip started and go to the server room. You can do your research there. Don't let anyone in."

"The server room?" Replacement's hands went to her hips. "You're trying to lock me away."

Jack smiled. "Exactly." She opened her mouth and he held up his hand. "Look, we need background on everyone who was here. And you're the best at doing the background checks. Can you work in the server room until I'm back?"

"Fine." Replacement crossed her arms.

31

STABLE

In the garage, Pierce grabbed the keys off the rack while Jack stood back and admired the cars.

"We'll take the Porsche," Pierce announced.

Jack whistled. "You do have good taste in cars. She's beautiful."

Pierce tossed him the keys.

Jack's eyebrow rose. "You're going to let me drive?"

"I think some things need to be experienced to be appreciated."

Jack didn't argue. He hopped in and started up the engine. He couldn't help the boyish smile that spread across his face.

He drove the Porsche out onto the road and got the car going thirty. Pierce studied him for a second and then clicked his tongue.

"What?" Jack scanned the dashboard.

"I forgot. You used to be a policeman. I bet you're a stickler for traffic laws."

Jack nodded. "I am. For everyone else." He pushed his foot down.

Pierce was pressed back into the seat as the Porsche took off toward the reservoir.

The Onopiquite Reservoir was a lake that sat at the bottom of a natural basin, shaped like a long serving dish. Reservoir Road circled the lake on the lower side of the basin, closest to the water, and Pine Ridge ran along the eastern ridge on the lip of the bowl.

Jack turned onto Reservoir. Reservoir Road was windy, but it was wide. It was used by tourists in foliage season, so when the city put in the new road twenty years ago, they made it a little extra wide in anticipation of people pulling off to the side to appreciate the view.

The car hummed as it hugged the curves. Jack looked at the dials on the dashboard, and the corners of his mouth ticked up. "She's not even breaking a sweat."

"I've been very impressed with this car. But did you bring me out here to talk about her, or the plan?"

Jack pressed his foot down, and the Porsche shot down a long straightaway. "First we get the case."

"Do you mind if I ask you a question?" Pierce asked.

Jack gave Pierce a sideways glance as the Porsche slipped into a turn. He kept speeding up until the tires just started to slip, then he slowed down.

"She's got great grip," Jack said. Then he added, "Usually when someone asks permission to ask a question, it's not one I want to answer."

Pierce shrugged. "Why'd you leave the police force? With everything I found out about you, I'd assume that you'd have been promoted to detective. But you quit?"

Jack's hand choked the steering wheel. "I didn't quit."

Pierce waited, but Jack kept driving. Reservoir Road ended, and Jack had to slow down when they hit the main road.

"I apologize for pushing the subject, but I'm putting a lot of faith in you," Pierce continued. "I read the piece about you in the Hope Falls newspaper. That reporter did some digging into your past."

"And?"

"The article raised some questions. I need to know: Why did you leave the police force?"

"Why I left the force doesn't matter."

"It does." Pierce's voice was clipped. "I need to know why you left because I need to make sure you're… stable."

"Stable?"

"Yes. It's the only explanation I can come up with. You're a vet. You've been through a lot in your life. I don't believe you just 'walked away' from being a policeman to become a bounty hunter. Which means you were *asked* to leave. I need to know if it was for mental health reasons."

"It wasn't."

"They also took away your license to carry."

"How do you know that?"

"Alice told me."

The Porsche's engine revved louder.

Pierce held up a hand. "We were talking about security, and I said I wanted to get a gun. She mentioned it then. It just came up; she didn't mean anything by it. And I didn't think anything about it until after I decided to hire you."

Jack didn't say anything.

Pierce crossed his arms.

"You're in business." Jack slowed down. "If you had an employee who did what was right but didn't do what you said, would you fire him?"

"I wouldn't be happy."

Jack clicked his tongue. "Law enforcement's a hard business. The sheriff asked me to let someone else handle things. I'm not that type of guy. I kept coloring outside the lines. The sheriff couldn't figure out what else to do with me, so I was asked to go. Simple as that."

"And your license to carry?"

"After I left the force, Alice and I caught the Giant Killer and the sheriff didn't. It didn't make him look good. The only thing he could really do to get back at me was pull my license. So that's what he did."

Pierce stared out the windshield for a moment, then turned to look at Jack. "I had to ask."

"I would've asked too." Jack stopped at a red light. "I just would've done it *before* I hired you."

32

AN UNANSWERED QUESTION

Replacement's fingers flew over the keyboard. Pierce had set her up in Weston's systems, and she was printing out the HR files; Jack preferred paper, and it drove her crazy.

She started separate folders for Leon, Roger, Lydia, Nancy, Sophia, Bruce, and Phillip. She was surprised when she found résumés for Bruce, Phillip, and herself. Gerald must have had to provide them to corporate. She was even more surprised to find notes on them; security had done a very thorough background check.

Everyone had been cleared. All Weston employees had passed drug tests too.

She connected to the web and headed to her online background checkers. Since she'd started the private investigator business, she had gotten even more adept than before at discovering secrets hiding in the virtual cloud. In fact, discovering secrets was what the bulk of her cases had been about. Especially when it came to cheating spouses—it seemed every other case she got was one of those.

Replacement's shoulders slumped as she thought of those cases. She usually found evidence of infidelity in less than a day, but she never celebrated. She knew marriages were destroyed. She remembered her last case when she had told a man about his wife's trysts. She shook her head and tried to drive the sound of the man's sobs out of her head.

Choosing more or less at random, she decided to start her searches with Bruce. She only knew a little about him. He was thirty-two and had worked technical support for fifteen years at the university. He left to start his own support company, but it never took off.

But once she started looking at him on the web, things got interesting fast. He had an online dating profile that made him sound like the CEO of a tech company, along with a poorly Photoshopped picture that made him look thinner. He was also very vocal online. From computer forums to political groups, he let his opinions be known. His biggest beef, apparently, was open source code. Replacement wasn't surprised by that—a lot of computer geeks were big on open source—but Bruce was exceptionally opinionated about it. She gathered up some of the main links and moved them to Bruce's folder.

Phillip was next. His résumé listed his most recent employment as a hospital in California, working at their help desk. His social media was by invite only. He had a blog, with tech entries posted only every couple of months or so, mostly reviews and how-to guides. Nothing very interesting.

Replacement tied her hair in a ponytail and forced herself to move on. She could dig deeper later; right now she wanted to make a first pass at everyone and get the thirty-thousand-foot view.

Finishing up the tech team, she tackled Gerald next. She pulled over his folder and frowned when she saw his smiling picture at the top of his résumé. She forced herself not to look at the floor of the server room, but an image of him lying there, injured, flashed in her mind. She bowed her head and said a quick prayer.

She hastily flipped past the résumé. The next document she'd printed out from Weston's database was a system access form. Replacement started to flip right past it, but her hand hesitated. She scanned the form again. It was a request for an access code for Gerald to the server room.

She looked at the server room door. "Who else has access to this room?" she muttered.

Her fingers glided over the keyboard. She opened the program that controlled the access to the server room door. She clicked on the events tab.

Dates, times, and names filled the screen.

She scrolled to the bottom of the log and reviewed the latest entries.

PASSCODE – SECURITY
OPEN DOOR
OPEN DOOR
PASSCODE – CAMPBELL
OPEN DOOR

There was a line item for every time the door opened, and a line item for whenever someone typed in their passcode. For security purposes, each user had been given a different passcode, so that the system could keep track of who came and went. Gerald had requested codes only for himself and Pierce had just got Replacement hers. Besides security, no one else had access.

She scrolled up through the log. The past couple of days were just a repeating pattern of Gerald entering and leaving:

PASSCODE – MATHIS
DOOR OPEN
DOOR OPEN

That made sense. Gerald punched in his code, opened the door to enter, and later he opened the door to leave. Then he would come back and do it again.

But something bothered her. She scrolled back once again to the end of the log:

PASSCODE – MATHIS
DOOR OPEN
PASSCODE – MATHIS
DOOR OPEN
DOOR OPEN
PASSCODE – SECURITY
OPEN DOOR

OPEN DOOR
PASSCODE – CAMPBELL
OPEN DOOR

Mathis, Door Open, Mathis.

How could Gerald punch in his code, enter the room, and then punch in his code again? From inside the room?

Just to be certain she understood what she was looking at, she highlighted the lines and checked the date.

As expected, this was from the night Gerald was hurt.

Replacement blinked at the screen. She read the entries again. The hairs on the back of her neck tingled, and her skin grew cold. She tried to picture what happened in her mind.

Gerald entered his passcode and came into the server room. But Gerald couldn't enter his passcode again without leaving the room unless...

Someone else entered Gerald's passcode.

Did they enter while Gerald was already in here? No—then Gerald would have identified them when he awoke at the hospital. Which meant the impostor must have entered the room *first.*

Someone used Gerald's passcode, entered the server room, then hid in here, waiting for Gerald. Or Gerald surprised him...

Replacement's heart sped up and her mouth went dry. Gazing up and down the server rack, she remembered Jack's unanswered question: *How did this thing fall over?*

"It didn't fall," she whispered. "Someone pushed it. It wasn't an accident."

Replacement looked at the door. She suddenly realized that whoever had hurt Gerald could come in right now. Could hurt *her.*

She turned back to the server and disabled Gerald's code. Her fingers shook as she then took out her phone and called Jack.

33

HE'S BUYING

Jack compared the two silver cases. The one in the package was identical to the original. He gave the original back to Pierce and took the other one to the register.

"He's buying," he told the teenager behind the counter.

Pierce paid for the case, and they headed back to the Porsche. Jack held his hands out for the keys.

"Don't you think it's my turn to drive?" Pierce said.

Jack smirked. "It would look odd if we switched now."

Pierce shook his head and tossed Jack the keys.

Traffic was light, and they made quick time getting to the lake. Once Jack hit the long straightaway, he sped up. "Why did you hire Gerald for this job?" he asked.

"I've know Mr. Mathis since I was a kid."

"But why hire him? You have an IT company. Why not use them?"

"He's a friend. And I knew he could do the job."

Jack was approaching a turn, but he didn't let off the gas. Pierce looked back and forth between him and the turn. Finally Jack took his foot off the gas, came halfway around the turn, and pressed the pedal down. The dials on the dash all started to rise.

"Did anyone vet Gerald?" Jack asked.

"What? Yeah, Leon did. He vets everyone. Why do you ask?"

"It's what you want me to do. Turn over every rock. What happened to his son?"

Pierce stared out the windshield. "He died."

"When?"

"Seven years ago."

"How?"

"Why is that important?"

Jack flew into the next turn. The tires gripped the road, but the tail end shimmied.

"You really *do* like to drive fast," Pierce said.

"But not unsafe. I can see the whole road here because of the curve of the lake, and there's no traffic," Jack explained. "So. What happened to Gerald's son?"

"He died in an accident."

Jack took his foot off the gas. They approached the spillway, and Jack put his window down. Above the wind and engine noise, he could hear the water rushing under the road and into a waterfall on the other side.

"Take a left up here," Pierce said.

Jack slowed and turned down the small road that Pierce had indicated. They rounded a bend, and a pond appeared, marked with a small wooden sign that read: SOUTH POND.

South Pond sat nestled at the bottom of two hills, and was about the size of three football fields side by side. All around the bank were little cottage homes. A sandy beach area to the left had a horseshoe dock, but the beach was closed, and no one was around.

"Pull over and park there," Pierce said.

Jack did, and they got out. Jack followed Pierce toward the beach. Pierce walked all the way to the end of the dock before stopping.

Jack stood beside him and looked across the pond. The water was clear, and he could see small fish swimming along the sandy bottom.

"Tyler lived there." Pierce pointed to a little cottage house. "And that"—he pointed to a two-story colonial—"that one was mine."

Jack looked at the second house with a bit of surprise. He would have expected Pierce's summer home to be a lot larger.

"Why do you keep asking about Mr. Mathis?" Pierce asked. "There's no way he had something to do with this."

"I don't think he did."

The muscles in Pierce's neck stood out. "Then why do you keep asking?"

"Because you keep giving me half the story."

Pierce looked down at the water. "It has nothing to do with anything."

"Look. I'm not asking just to ask. You hired Gerald. He ended up with that e-cig case in his pocket. And right now, that case is what everything's revolving around. I need to know everything, even if it's just to rule it out."

Pierce sighed and shuffled his feet. "I've known Mr. Mathis since I was six. My parents used to come here for summers. My father was an accountant, and my mother's a biologist. They both had hard upbringings. The Mathises, on the other hand... they were laidback. Every summer for me was a trip to normal."

He nodded to the colonial. "That was officially my house, but"—he pointed again at the Mathises' cottage—"I lived over there."

A cold wind blew across the pond. Jack looked up at the gray clouds rolling in.

"Tyler was like my brother. He was into sports, but I was into computers. Mr. Mathis was too. He made me my first computer. During the school year, computers... that was all I did. I wrote code. And every summer when I came back, Mr. Mathis helped me.

"My parents thought I was some protégé, so they put me in college early. I was fifteen years old. It sucked. I didn't know anyone, and no one wants to be around a geek, let alone a *young* geek. But Mr. Mathis let Tyler come out to visit me."

Jack looked down at the water, but it had clouded up like the sky overhead. He watched the little waves while he waited for Pierce to continue.

"So one time, Tyler was with me, and we were hanging out. And this lady's car got stuck in the snow. Just an ordinary thing. So Tyler and I went to help her. But as we were pushing the car out, this truck came skidding right at us. Tyler shoved me out of the way. But... he died."

He took a deep breath. "After that, I lost touch with Mr. Mathis. Until recently. Six months ago, I found out he had cancer. It's in remission now, but I wanted to do something. He refused. He said he couldn't take charity."

"That's why you gave him the job, networking the house?"

Pierce leaned against the post. "I didn't think he'd take it."

"Does Gerald blame you?"

Pierce looked down at his reflection and scowled. "No. He doesn't, but... I owe him. I really do. I don't know if you can understand that."

"Yeah," Jack said. "I can."

Somewhere a fish jumped. Jack gazed up at the sky. The hills now felt too close. Pierce's pain reminded Jack of his own.

"When did the leaks start happening?" Jack asked.

"We've had little ones in the past, but nothing like this. It's making me crazy. Everything's virtual. It's all about data, Jack. Information about what Weston is doing makes stocks rise and fall. Someone's making a fortune, but they're hurting my company. And I can't stop them."

"You must have hired someone to look into the leaks."

"I have. A few different investigators, but they came up with nothing. Although their investigations did at least narrow down the list of which employees knew what. Which was how I knew who to invite to this meeting."

"So you gathered your suspects. What exactly was your plan?" Jack asked. "How was it going to work?"

Pierce crossed his arms. "I was going to find an opportunity to pull each person aside, tell each of them a different story. All of them false. Then I'd wait and see which false story got leaked."

"When is this meeting scheduled?"

"Well, it was supposed to be yesterday and today. But after what happened with Gerald, I had Lydia move it to Tuesday."

Jack frowned. "That's the day after tomorrow. We'll need to hurry then. I have an idea, but the more information we have, the better. The biggest thing we need is for whoever it is to not get freaked. So when we go back to the mansion, I'm just going to go back and work with Bruce and Phillip."

"What should I do?"

"You've been working with Alice in the server room, right? Go back in there. We need her to look for everything she can find on the people who were at dinner last night."

Jack's phone rang. He saw it was Replacement and answered. "Hey. What's up?"

Replacement's voice sounded worried. "You need to get back here right away."

34

DOUBLE-SCUMBAG

As Jack pulled the Porsche into the garage, Leon and Lydia hurried in. "Mr. Weston." Leon's voice echoed off the cement as he came to attention. "We had an eleven o'clock."

"My apologies." Pierce shut the door.

Lydia frowned at Leon. "Mr. Weston, the hospital just called. Mr. Mathis is more alert. They've upgraded his condition, and he can have visitors."

"That's great news." Pierce turned to Leon. "I'm sorry again, but we'll need to reschedule. I'd like to go see Mr. Mathis right away."

Leon nodded, expressionless. "Of course."

Pierce turned to Jack. "I assume that Alice will want to come?"

"I'm sure of it. I'll go get her."

Jack went inside and made his way to the server room. He knocked on the door.

"Who is it?"

"It's Jack."

Replacement whipped the door open. "I'm so glad you're here." She eyed him. "Is something wrong?"

"No, it's just that we found out Gerald can have visitors and—"

"I'll get my stuff." She zipped back into the server room and then hurried back into the hallway. "Is he okay?"

"They upgraded his condition, and he's alert. That's all I know."

Jack picked up his pace as he followed her to the garage.

"I have to talk to you and Pierce. I found something," Replacement said.

"Wait until we're in the car."

"Should we asked Bruce and Phillip if they want to come to the hospital?" Replacement asked.

"No. I want to talk to Gerald alone."

Replacement pulled out her phone and started texting. "I'll let Bruce and Phillip know that we're leaving then."

When they entered the spacious garage, Leon and Lydia were gone, and Pierce was standing next to the key rack. Pierce looked at Replacement and gestured to the selection of cars. "Do you have a preference?"

Jack looked around. "You have quite the showroom."

"I like cars."

Replacement raised herself up on her toes, her hands clasped together behind her back. "How about the red convertible?"

"It's a two-seater."

Replacement hopped over to a silver Maserati Quattroporte. "This has a back seat." She opened the rear door.

"The Maserati it is." Pierce took the keys off the rack.

This time Jack headed for the passenger side, and Pierce got behind the wheel.

Just past the guardhouse, Manuel was already waiting for them behind the wheel of a dark sedan. As they drove past, he pulled in behind them.

Pierce headed for Darrington. Jack rolled down the passenger window and glanced back at Replacement. "What did you want to tell us?"

Replacement grabbed the back of the seat and pulled herself forward. "I got totally freaked out. I was pulling background on everyone and remembered the server records passcodes and door events."

"Door events?" Jack asked.

"When the door opens, if it stays propped open, stuff like that." She undid her seat belt, and both Jack and Pierce frowned at her. "It's just for a second. I need to explain."

"And you can't explain one foot back?" Jack asked.

"Shh, listen. The night Gerald was hurt, someone used his passcode."

"How can you be sure it was someone else and not him?" Pierce asked.

"Because they entered in his code, came in the server room, and *then* Gerald came in. He can't have entered the room twice."

"You're sure?" Jack asked.

"One hundred percent. When Gerald entered the server room, someone else was inside. The pattern should go you enter your passcode, open the door, do what you've got to do, then open the door again. But what the log shows from that night is that someone entered Gerald's passcode and opened the door—and then someone entered Gerald's passcode again, and the door opened again."

"Wait a second." Pierce pulled down the rearview mirror so he could see her. "That doesn't mean someone was in the server room. What if Mr. Mathis opened the door and didn't go in? He closed it, and then he had to enter his passcode again."

Replacement's lips mashed together. "When have you ever entered your passcode, opened the door, and then not walked through?"

"He could've forgotten something," Pierce said.

"Well, maybe, but there's another thing. After the second time Gerald's passcode was entered, the door opened two times before Security entered their passcode."

Jack understood immediately. "Meaning whoever entered that passcode opened the door to enter the room—and then, someone opened the door to *leave*."

Replacement nodded. "Exactly. And we know Gerald didn't leave."

Jack made a fist. "Someone was waiting for Gerald. That's who left."

"You can't be sure." Pierce shook his head.

"Oh, I'm sure. That server rack falling over never made sense to me," Jack said. "The rack's bottom heavy. It doesn't want to fall. Someone had to push it over."

"That's why you had me tug on it!" Replacement whacked Jack's shoulder.

Jack nodded. "I should've listened to my gut. The whole scenario didn't feel right."

"Maybe Gerald surprised him!" Replacement sat bolt upright. "The guy was already in the computer room, trying to get the cigarette case."

"Slow down." Pierce waved his hand. "You think that the case and Gerald getting hurt are somehow linked?"

"They are," Replacement insisted.

Pierce shook his head. "You're making a huge leap. Corporate espionage is one thing. That rack falling on Mr. Mathis could've killed him."

Replacement's lips pressed into a hard line.

Jack gave the slightest shake of his head.

Replacement sat back in her seat with a huff.

"How does someone get a passcode?" Jack asked.

"Corporate assigns them," Pierce said.

"Who has access to open that door?"

"Just Mr. Mathis, Alice, me, and security. Even Bruce and Phillip weren't granted access."

Jack looked into the side mirror at the dark sedan that followed them. "No one else?"

Pierce shook his head.

"Someone could've watched Gerald enter his code." Replacement crossed her arms.

"That's not the easiest thing to do." Pierce sped up. "I saw a security demonstration of people trying to look over someone's shoulder and steal their code. No one could do it."

"Alice does it all the time," Jack said. "Never let her see you put in a password."

"Really?" Pierce's eyes darted between the road and Replacement.

"People also use their phones to record video now," Jack added. "And that keypad is in a bad spot. It's high on the wall so someone short like Gerald has to raise his hand to enter the code. It gives people a clear view."

"I'll have it moved," Pierce said. "But I still don't think the case has anything to do with Mr. Mathis's accident."

Jack looked back at Replacement. "How are you coming along with the background checks?"

Replacement reached down to the seat beside her and held up the files.

"You got all that already?" Pierce asked.

"She's a machine," Jack said.

Replacement grinned. "I went through the employee database in fifteen minutes. I'm running background checks on everyone now. Social media data, school records, blog posts—everything I can get my hands on."

"Can you give me a rundown?" Jack asked.

Replacement looked at her files. "As for my research, right now the big look-at-me flags go off on Roger and Bruce. Roger has some major money issues."

"He just came out of a nasty divorce," Pierce said.

"Yeah," Replacement continued, "and the wife creamed him. I had to stop myself reading the whole thing. It was like a soap opera. His wife went for the jugular in the divorce and posted online about everything she got—like trophies. House, cars, jewelry. It was nasty. But then, get this, the mistress sued him."

Pierce shook his head. "I know. And she won. She got a bundle. But I'm not worried about Roger's loyalty; I've known him since school."

"He's a scumbag." Replacement scowled.

Pierce shrugged. "He's a lovable scumbag. He just needs to try to control it."

"He cheated on his mistress. That makes him a double-scumbag."

"I don't think Roger had anything to do with this."

"But you're not sure," Jack said. "You did invite him to this meeting, after all."

Pierce opened and closed his mouth. He tapped the steering wheel and then shook his head. "Roger knew about the new mapping feature in VE-Life—which was one of the things that was leaked. I don't think he'd ever *intentionally* say something, but maybe he's confiding in someone who is. I don't know what to call it—pillow talk on the wrong pillow?"

Replacement leaned forward. "Like one of those World War Two things where he's talking about stuff to his mistress but she's really a German spy?"

"Not as dramatic as that, but…" Pierce's head wobbled from side to side as he struggled with the words. "Yes. Roger has always had a big mouth."

"Well, he's tops on my list." Replacement grabbed another folder. "Then there's Bruce. Bruce is… odd."

Jack shrugged. "That was a given."

"I mean, he's all over the Net. He blogs, and he's even mentioned VE-Life. He's an open source type. You know? All code should be free, and we should all share."

"And he doesn't get that it can't work that way." Pierce scowled. "Does he have any idea how much it costs to bring software to production? Or how many jobs we create?"

"But what about the people who can't afford it?" Replacement shot back.

"We have student versions and discounts for—" Pierce started, but Jack whistled and cut him off.

"Time out. How odd? Does he rail against VE-Life in particular?"

"Not really," Replacement said. "He seems to hate all software companies equally."

"Well, that's very fair of him," Pierce quipped.

"Anything on anyone else?" Jack asked.

"Just boring stuff. I'm looking for additional links, but not everyone posts their life online."

Pierce slowed down. "Well, there's the hospital. And I think we're going to find out that Mr. Mathis's accident was just that—an accident."

35

SELLING NORMAL

"You'll only have a few minutes," the nurse explained. "But he kept asking to see you."

Replacement followed the nurse into Gerald's hospital room, with Jack and Pierce following. The big bag in Replacement's hand swung like a pendulum. It had been her idea to stop by the little gift shop, but Pierce had bought out half the store.

"Hey, guys." Gerald sat propped up slightly in the bed.

"Hi, Gerald." Replacement scooted right next to the bed and set the bag down. "We brought you some things."

Gerald started to shake his head, but winced. "You didn't need to do that."

Replacement gently took his hand and leaned over so he didn't have to turn his head. "How are you feeling? Do you need anything?"

"A bigger bottle of aspirin. I'm much better, but I still have a headache fit for an elephant. How's the job?"

"It's going great. Don't worry about a thing. I'm following your plan. You laid it all out."

Gerald turned to Pierce. "I'm sorry. I don't know what happened."

Pierce put his hand on the rail of the bed. "It's okay, Mr. Mathis. It was an accident."

"Gerald." Jack tried to soften his voice. "Do you remember anything about what happened?"

Gerald swallowed. "Not really. I was upgrading the server. Then everything went black."

Jack moved closer. "Did you leave at any time?"

Gerald shut his eyes. "Roast beef." His eyes snapped back open. "Sophia came by and told me she made roast beef sandwiches."

"Did you go with her?" Pierce asked.

"Oh yeah." Gerald stared up at the ceiling, and his eyes moved as though he was watching a TV. "I wanted to get one before Bruce ate them all."

Replacement chuckled. "Then what?"

Gerald's voice got a little stronger. "I went back and saw that the update had completed." Gerald's lips pursed together.

Replacement leaned closer.

Gerald sighed. "Then everything went black."

"Did Sophia go with you to supper?" Jack asked.

"No. She went to tell Bruce the sandwiches were ready. Why?"

The nurse cleared her throat. "I'm sorry, but we need to keep this brief."

Replacement squeezed Gerald's hand. "One last question. You didn't give your passcode to anyone to use, right?"

"Of course not." Gerald grimaced as he shook his head. "That would be a huge security breach."

Pierce patted Gerald's arm. "We know you never would. We'll stop by again soon, Mr. Mathis."

***

Jack sat in the passenger seat and stared at the road as they drove back to the mansion.

Replacement wrinkled her nose. "I hate hospitals. I just want to go home and take a shower."

Jack looked back at her. "We can't yet. You and Pierce need to get the two security cameras working in that big living room. Can you get them going without anyone knowing?"

Pierce nodded. "It should just be a matter of connecting the feed."

"Why do you need the cameras going?" Replacement asked, pulling herself forward.

"We need to draw the guy out, and we need a controlled environment."

"A controlled environment?" Pierce repeated. "Do you mean you want to try to get everyone together? Like a sting?"

"Something like that."

"That's a lot of people," Pierce said. "And I can't think of a good excuse to invite Bruce and Phillip, or Sophia, to a meeting with my business associates."

"You already did it once. We do the same thing again: dinner. A way to say thank you to everyone."

"Sweet." Replacement squeezed Jack's shoulder.

"Okay," Pierce said, "that works to get them together. How do we let them know that I have the case?"

Replacement's hands shot up. "At dinner, I can get up and hand it to you."

Pierce grinned. "I'll say something like," he cleared his throat, "'Thank you for finding it, Alice. I'm really dying for a cigarette.'"

Jack cringed. "Noooo." Jack stretched the word out. "That sounded like a middle-school play. We need to keep it simple. After dinner is over, we lead everyone into the living room. Have Sophia serve desserts. Pierce makes a thank-you-for-coming speech and smokes an e-cigarette. You'll leave the case on the table."

"And we use the cameras to see who goes after it!" Replacement beamed.

"Can your secretary put together a dinner this fast?" Jack asked.

Pierce nodded. "Oh, sure. Lydia's a pro. She's done it a thousand times."

"Great." Jack looked back and forth between them. "The name of the game is normal. We do what we've been doing and stick to the plan. Keep it simple."

36

CRUMBS TO THE PEASANTS

Jack stood outside with Phillip and Bruce while they smoked. They all watched as a catering truck pulled up to the mansion. The lettering on its side read "Antonelli's."

"They're bringing in food from Antonelli's?" Phillip's voice rose.

"Oh, man." Smoke poured out of Bruce's nose and clung to his beard. "Alice was just talking about that place. She said it's her favorite restaurant."

"What are the odds?" Jack muttered.

"That's the super-expensive one on Main Street," Phillip said.

"I guess his guests will be eating well," Bruce grumbled. "No surprise there."

"I really wanted to try the food there," Phillip said.

Bruce's eyes lit up. "Hey, I bet we'll get leftovers. Rich people always do that. It makes them feel better to throw the crumbs to the peasants."

"Dogs. It's 'throw the crumbs to the dogs,' not peasants," Phillip corrected him.

"Whatever." Bruce shrugged and tossed his cigarette on the ground. "They'll give us a bowl, and we can eat outside."

A woman cleared her throat behind them. Lydia held the door open for the caterers. "Actually, Mr. Weston is doing this for everyone, to say thank you, and all three of you are invited to join us in the dining room. Alice too. Dinner will be at eight."

"Thank you." Jack nodded.

Lydia cleared her throat and gave Bruce's discarded cigarette a cold look. "I don't believe you saw the cigarette can."

"Sorry," Bruce muttered. He picked up the butt and threw it away.

After the last of the line of caterers disappeared inside, Lydia followed them and shut the door.

"Sweet." Bruce licked his lips. "Free food from Antonelli's."

"We're still going to have to work till eight," Phillip said.

"Food and more money? It just keeps getting better. I have to thank—hey, how's Gerald?"

"He's doing much better," Jack said.

"Man. Gerald must have a thick skull. That rack had to 've weighed a ton. You've gotta wonder how it didn't kill him. You'd figure it'd be like when some dumbass rocks a candy machine and it falls on them, you know? It crushes them. And they die because they can't breathe." Bruce made a face as if he was doing bench presses.

"Maybe it just knocked him backward, and he hit his head on the other server rack," Phillip suggested.

"We should probably go see him," Bruce said.

"No more visiting today," Jack said. "They may allow it tomorrow though."

"You guys want to go with me?" Bruce asked as they headed for the guesthouse. "Or we could send flowers."

"Flowers?" Phillip rolled his eyes. "What guy wants flowers?"

"What am I *supposed* to send him? A *Playboy*?" Bruce shot back.

***

They worked into the early evening. Bruce went on about food so much that Jack's stomach was loudly grumbling. Finally, at seven forty-five, Sophia came out to the guesthouse to summon them to dinner.

Bruce practically jumped off the ladder. "I'm starving. Is it really Antonelli's?"

Sophia nodded. "The kitchen smells incredible."

"Now you're making me hungry." Phillip tossed his screwdriver into his bag, and they all headed for the door.

As they walked down the path, Phillip and Bruce hurried ahead, but Jack stayed next to Sophia.

"You have to be tired," Jack said. "You're working around the clock."

"I'm exhausted." Sophia stuck her tongue out. "But it's not that bad."

"It's just you for all that?" Jack gestured to the length of the house.

"The guests were only supposed to be here for one weekend, and then it was just going to be Mr. Weston. That wouldn't have been so bad. Now that they're staying an extra three days, I've got my work cut out for me."

"What did you do before this?"

"Secretary, waitress, hostess, and unemployed." Sophia laughed. "Now I'm all of that rolled into one." Her arms twirled, and she pretended to hold a ball.

Jack admired the graceful way she moved. "Do you dance?"

"Not here," she joked.

Jack laughed. "Seriously."

She nodded. "I do enjoy dancing. I wouldn't call myself a serious dancer or anything, but I did have a part in *Rent* earlier this summer, for the Northbank Players in Connecticut. But you know how that goes: I was in *Rent*, so now I can't pay it. I had to get a real job."

Jack chuckled. "At least it looks like you have an easygoing boss."

She frowned and tossed back her head. Her red hair shook. "I did until his assistant, Mrs. Maier, showed up. She's all over me. She has a list of what Mr. Weston likes. No, not a list—a *book*. Seriously." She fumbled for her phone. "Look." She scrolled down a long document. "It's my 'do and don't list,' as she calls it."

The phone buzzed, and a picture of Lydia Maier appeared.

Sophia's eyes went huge, and she stifled a laugh before answering. "Hello?" she said, then paused. "Yes. I just informed them. I'm heading back now." She rolled her eyes at Jack. "Yes, I will try to hurry." She hung up and laughed.

"That was kinda creepy." Jack chuckled.

"Kind of?" Sophia pointed to her phone. "This thing is like an electric leash. I have to keep it strapped to the side of my head."

Try wearing a police body camera, Jack wanted to say, but he held his tongue.

"She'll be gone soon." Sophia hung her arms low and then grinned. "And then I can breathe again, whenever I like."

Jack laughed.

Sophia smiled back. "So… you and Alice?" She walked closer to him. "Are you two an exclusive thing?"

Jack nodded. "Yeah. Monogamous."

She clicked her tongue. "Traditional."

As they came toward the entrance, Replacement bounded out the door.

"Two in a row," Sophia whispered. "I'd better watch out for lightning. See you inside, Jack." She went on in.

"Hey," Replacement called out as she came over to Jack.

"How's it going?" he asked.

"I called Mrs. Stevens. She said Lady is doing great." Replacement looked around to make sure no one could hear. "We're not getting much on Leon or Lydia. Leon's records are in a vault in the Pentagon, I think." She stuck her tongue out. "He doesn't have anything to do with social media either. And Lydia? Work is her life."

"Is she married?"

"Thirty years. No kids."

"What about her husband?"

"Eagle Scout and referee. He subbed on a couple of NFL games, but he refs everything."

"Well, keep looking. Did you get the cameras set up?"

She nodded. "I had a hard time with the feed, but Pierce showed me this little trick." She snapped her fingers. She took Jack's arm, and they continued on inside. "I can't believe he picked Antonelli's," she said. Her shoulders squeezed together, and she vibrated. "He must've really liked it."

Jack scowled. "A little too much," he muttered.

***

Caterers dressed all in black hurried back and forth, bringing out dishes to a long table in the dining room. Most of the guests were already seated and were chatting quietly. Jack looked at the huge room and realized they'd moved the furniture around so the table ran horizontal to make the room smaller for the limited party. On the interior wall was a mural that ran the complete length. It was a scene of the countryside with colonial Americans picnicking during the summer.

"If this were my house," Replacement said, "I'd have Christmas in here. Can you imagine the size of tree we could have?"

Replacement continued to talk about her dreams for Christmas, but Jack stopped listening. He had to turn his head to block out the image of Replacement standing in front of a Christmas tree with Pierce. His hand clenched into a fist, and he fought back a wave of jealousy.

As he turned his head to crack his neck, Jack noticed Leon just outside the doorway, speaking with Manuel. Leon was doing all the talking, while Manuel gave curt nods. Then Manuel came to attention and marched away, and Leon strolled into the room and over to the table.

"Have you been listening to me?" Replacement asked.

Jack nodded and gave her a brief smile.

Pierce stood up and held out a hand to Replacement. She sat on Pierce's left, and Jack sat next to her. Going around the table from Pierce's right were Lydia, Leon, Roger, Nancy, Phillip, and finally Bruce, who was on Jack's left.

A server came over and stood near Pierce. She leaned down and whispered. While they spoke, another server brought out trays of cheese, fruit, prosciutto, and warm garlic bread.

After a moment, the server speaking with Pierce stood up and smiled. "Good evening. Tonight you'll have your choice of a house or Caesar salad. For soup, toasted pumpkin seed or allspice crème fraiche. Entrees include conchiglie with sausage, pan-roasted salmon, chicken confit with wild mushrooms, and New York sirloin."

Pierce motioned to the waitress, and she leaned down.

"What's conchiglie with sausage?" Bruce quietly asked Jack.

"Baked pasta."

"My apologies." The server stood up and placed her hands behind her back. "There is also a chicken Marsala."

Replacement clapped her hands together silently under the table.

Pierce grinned.

Jack fiddled with his steak knife.

Once dinner was served, Jack observed that Nancy was quite the adept conversationalist. She, Pierce, and Replacement kept the conversation moving throughout dinner. The three went back and forth on a number of topics while steering clear of politics and sports.

In situations like this, Jack felt observation was far more important than interaction. He was like a lie detector technician getting a baseline reading. He observed how someone normally acted, and anything else set off alarms.

It seemed as if everyone present was more relaxed tonight than they had been at the earlier dinner. Nancy wore a loose coffee blouse and stretch pants. Roger had traded his business suit for khaki pants and a pullover top. Even Lydia had let her hair down with a flowered dress.

Jack noticed, surprisingly, that Roger was the quietest of the group. He'd never known a salesman to be an introvert. The beverage of choice at the table was wine, and Roger was tossing them back.

Jack ate his steak as he watched everyone. From Leon's formality to Phillip's awkward social skills, Jack built his mental database of movements, patterns, and rhythms. Lydia spoke on occasion but mostly watched over Pierce like a hawk. Nancy seemed to gel with Replacement, but Jack could see how Nancy's eyes lingered on Pierce and how she leaned in whenever he spoke. Bruce appeared to be self-conscious of his eating, but he still packed it away.

Jack answered an occasional question or made a small joke. He caught himself several times fighting down pangs of jealousy. The favorite topic of the night seemed to be technology, and every point was batted back and forth between Pierce and Replacement like they were tennis pros. The longer the night wore on, the more they talked.

On any other occasion, Jack would have put a stop to it, and he might have done so tonight as well. But each time he was about to interject, Replacement would surprise him by asking someone a question, digging for information. From the subtle way she got Lydia to open up about her work for Pierce or got Leon to talk about how technology aids security, he knew she was fishing for answers.

Still, the more she and Pierce interacted, the more the uneasiness grew inside him. Jack was a man who trusted his gut, and his instincts were making him crazy. On one hand, she was looking for information; on the other…

Jack drained his water and set his glass down on the table a little too hard. On the outside, Jack looked as calm as ever, but underneath the surface, he was aching to get the meal over with.

Pierce put his turned-over fork on his plate. "I thought we could have dessert in the living room. The lake is beautiful at night." As he stood, he removed the e-cigarette case from his pocket.

Jack reached out for Replacement's chair, and his hand bumped Pierce's, who had reached out too. Replacement cleared her throat, lowered her head, and slipped by Jack.

"Be right back." Phillip headed for the door and motioned for Bruce to follow him.

Bruce looked toward the living room. "I just want to see what they have."

Phillip took a step closer. "This isn't the type of crowd to rush the dessert table. They'll leave you some. I need a smoke. Come on."

Bruce frowned, but he followed Phillip.

The rest of them moved to the living room, where a long table had been transformed into a dessert counter. Replacement oohed as she scanned the pastries.

Roger headed straight to the bar, and Jack followed. "What's your poison?" Roger asked Jack as he poured himself a bourbon.

"Just a water." Jack filled a tall glass with ice.

"That was as much fun as a board meeting," Roger huffed before taking a long sip. He breathed out through his teeth and took another. "You sure you don't want one?"

"I'm fine. It may not have been fun, but the steak was great," Jack said.

"Should be. Cooked fresh in the kitchen."

Jack raised an eyebrow.

Roger chuckled. "Pierce doesn't do simple catering. He had them send out a chef."

Jack looked at the bottle of whiskey. He wanted to pour himself a real shot. He looked back for Replacement. She and Nancy stood on either side of Pierce, who was pointing to the lake. Jack followed their gaze and saw the lights sparkling on the water.

"Crappy view, huh?" Roger finished his drink and started to pour another. "I'm not up for puffed pastries. Have you seen the game room?"

"No."

"Second floor. Pool, table tennis, darts, and more TVs than a sports bar. Do you shoot pool?"

Jack heard Nancy and Replacement laugh at something Pierce had said. Doing his best to ignore them, he replied, "I play a little."

"Well, if you want to catch a game, second floor. There's a full bar up there too." Roger took out his phone and walked to the corner of the room.

As Phillip and Bruce came in, Pierce moved to the dessert table. He picked up a plate and put the e-cigarette case on the table.

Pierce looked at Bruce and held up a cannoli. "You have to try these."

Bruce nodded eagerly and put two on his own plate.

Jack stayed by the bar and scanned the room. Pierce had waited until everyone was present, including Sophia, before taking the case out. The bait was set.

Replacement walked over to Jack. "Did you see Pierce? He was very smooth," she said.

Jack gripped his water glass. "Is there a way to monitor the camera from here, or do we have to go to the server room?"

Replacement held up her phone, and Jack saw himself on the screen. He almost looked up.

"That's nice, kid."

She grinned. "Give me your phone. I'll install the AP and stream the feed."

Replacement worked on his phone while Jack headed for the dessert table. Lydia and Leon stood in front of it now. Leon held his plate in his hands at a crisp forty-five degree angle, and one hand pressed against his hip.

Lydia, on the other hand, was watching Pierce. When he moved, her eyes followed. Jack nodded at Leon as he approached.

Leon nodded back.

Lydia folded her hands in front of herself. "Hello, Jack. Did you enjoy your dinner?"

"It was very nice, thank you."

Leon nodded approvingly. "The steak was exceptional." He set down his plate.

Lydia's eyes went back to Pierce. "Excuse me." She moved to Pierce's side.

"You're working on the computer systems?" Leon asked Jack.

"I'm more like helping Alice." Jack inclined his head her way.

"She took over for Mr. Mathis after the incident?"

Jack nodded.

"You served?"

"I did. Army."

"You went into law enforcement after." Leon wasn't asking; he was stating a fact.

Jack picked out a hard Italian cookie. "I did. Local."

Leon looked directly at him. "A number of the men in my crew are ex-military and ex-police. You'd be surprised how many former soldiers find the confines of law enforcement aren't for them."

"I met one of your men—Manuel. He was a Marine."

"Manuel's new. You two have a lot in common. He served two tours in Afghanistan. He opted out and took a police job in Connecticut."

"Now he works for you?"

"Weston Industries security is a small force because I keep an eye out for men like you." As he said the words, his eyes hardened, and he scanned Jack up and down. "We run checks on all the workers—even ones helping their girlfriends," he explained. "You don't belong running cables. Excuse my forwardness, but you don't belong chasing down junkies either." The muscle in his jaw pulsed.

Jack took a bite of his cookie. He took his time chewing while Leon waited for some response. "No offense taken."

"Well, if you're interested, I'd like to talk with you further. It's an opportunity. Or you can go back to working with him."

Leon pointed at Bruce.

Bruce had just taken a bite of a cannoli, and it broke. White filling trailed down his belly and landed on the carpet in a small mound. "Son of a—oops!" Bruce laughed awkwardly. Powdered sugar puffed off his beard.

Lydia hurried to the kitchen and came back, dragging Sophia with her. Sophia cleaned up the mess while Lydia stood there tsking.

"Well. Think it over," Leon said. He marched over to Pierce, exchanged a few words, and walked out of the room.

As soon as Leon left, Roger held up his hands. "What say we take this get-together upstairs to the game room?" he asked loudly.

Lydia frowned.

Pierce shot Roger a look.

Bruce started to move, but Phillip grabbed his elbow. "I'm sorry, but I need to go," Phillip said.

"It's still early," Bruce replied.

"I'm helping a friend, and I'm already late."

Bruce looked longingly back at the dessert table, then rolled his eyes. "Okay. You're my ride—what else am I going to do?"

"So, any takers?" Roger asked from the doorway. "We can put the game on." Roger's voice took on a singsong tone.

Bruce moved back to the dessert table. He rubbed his hand on his trousers, and his eyes darted around the room. The e-cigarette case was almost in the middle of the table.

Jack forced himself to try to remain looking natural. He was turned toward Roger, but he could see Bruce out of the corner of his eye.

Bruce's hand darted out. He grabbed a handful of cookies, stuck them in his pocket, then grabbed another.

Jack exhaled.

"I'm in," Nancy said to Roger.

Replacement looked at Jack, and he nodded.

"Me too," Replacement called out. "Eight ball?"

"You play?" Pierce asked. "I'll give you a game."

As the others headed out of the room, Jack hung back. Phillip and Bruce went out the left door while Roger, Nancy, Replacement, and Pierce headed right.

Lydia hadn't moved. She watched Pierce with her hands clasped together in front of herself. Jack casually followed the group.

Lydia walked over to the dessert table.

Replacement looked back at Jack, and he tipped his chin up. She kept walking toward the door.

Jack glanced back just as Lydia reached down and picked up the case. She palmed it in her hand and walked after the group.

Pierce turned around toward Jack.

Jack tried to give Pierce a look that screamed *Keep going,* but Pierce stopped.

"Mr. Weston." Lydia hurried over to Pierce. She held the e-cigarette case out to him and smiled. "You almost forgot this."

"Thank you." Pierce took the case.

Damn.

37

NAUGHTY CINDERELLA

Pierce's game room was larger than some bars Jack had been to. Its centerpiece was a pool table, and at the far end stood a ping-pong table and foosball table as well. A full mahogany and brass bar stood to one side, and Roger was already behind it.

Roger hammed it up as he put an elbow on the bar and gestured to the bottles behind him. "Step right up and pick your poison."

"He's got to get some new material," Jack muttered.

Replacement stepped close to him and whispered, "Pierce had to take it back."

"I saw. Just go with it for now."

"What should I do?"

"Act normal." He looked down at her for a second, then smirked.

She shot him a playful cross look. "Should I play pool?"

"You take that side of the room, and I'll take the bar."

She frowned at the ladies who had gathered next to the booze. "We should switch."

"I'll be good." Jack headed over to the bar with Nancy and Lydia.

"Seven and seven," Nancy said, hopping up on a stool.

"And for the young lady?" Roger winked at Lydia, and for the first time, Jack saw the hint of an actual smile on her face.

"Wine. Anything red."

"Jack?"

"I'll stick to water." Jack looked over at Replacement and Pierce, who were getting ready for a game of pool.

"What about you, Alice?" Roger asked loudly.

"She's driving," Jack said.

Roger thought for a second. "Then a Cinderella it is. Orange juice, pineapple juice, Grenadine, club soda, sweet and sour, with a cherry garnish."

"That sounds good," Lydia said.

"Me too. But can you spice it up?" Nancy asked.

Roger's grin spread like the Cheshire cat's. "Two Naughty Cinderellas with a twist, coming up."

While Roger mixed his ingredients, Jack grabbed a glass and packed it with ice.

Pool balls clacked together. Jack looked over at the game. Pierce had broken, but nothing dropped.

Replacement picked up her cue and eyed the table. She dropped three balls while Roger finished making her drink. Roger put a little flowered umbrella in it and slid it down to Jack.

Jack walked over to Replacement and set her drink down on the table.

"Oh, man." Pierce leaned on his pool cue. "I think I'm getting hustled."

"By little ol' me?" Replacement feigned innocence and placed her hand on her chest. She grinned before she shot another ball across the table and straight into the pocket.

She took a big sip of her drink, and her eyes lit up. "That's good."

"I accept tips," Roger called from the bar.

Replacement grinned. "Put out your glass. You deserve them for this." She held up the drink. "It's great."

She shot at the three ball and missed.

"At least I get a chance." Pierce picked up his cue.

Replacement stood close to Jack. "What's our next move?"

"I need to talk to Pierce. Take your time on the next shots."

Pierce's ball stopped a half inch from the pocket.

The tip of Replacement's tongue appeared on her lips as she pranced to the front of the table. "I'm up three. But you left me a tough shot." As she walked around the table, Jack caught Pierce's attention.

Pierce walked over to the window and stood next to Jack. "What now?"

"Just go with it. Have a smoke."

Pierce took out his e-cigarette, left his case on the windowsill, then strolled casually back over to the pool table.

"Four in the side." Replacement dropped it. "Six all the way." The cue ball knocked the six in and came right back to Replacement. "Seven cross sides." She chipped the seven, and it caught the side of the pocket and hung on the edge.

Pierce took his turn. "Thirteen." He slammed the cue ball into the thirteen. Balls scattered around the table, but the only one that dropped was the eight.

"My game!" Replacement said. "Sweet. I'm up one."

"I should have warned you, she's not a good winner," Jack said.

Replacement stuck out her tongue.

Jack walked over to Lydia. "Are you up for some darts?"

Lydia looked from side to side, then sat bolt upright. "Me?" She chuckled. "No, but… I'll keep score."

"Well I'm in." Nancy hopped off the stool.

"Me too." Roger slapped the bar. "Right after I make another drink."

Replacement started to rack another game while Jack and Nancy walked over to the dartboard.

"We'll keep it simple," Jack said. "Do you know Call Three?"

"It's been a while." Nancy grinned.

"Three people. You go first," Jack explained. "I call three numbers, and you need to hit them. One point if you hit the number. Two if you hit the number in the first ring, and it's three for the second ring."

"Bull's-eye?" Roger asked, joining them.

"Two for the outer ring of the bull's-eye, three for the inner. We do ten rounds. Most points wins."

The games began, and Roger soon started boasting. The more he drank, the louder he became. Jack was doing his best to throw the game, but Roger wasn't making it easy on him.

Replacement continued to play pool with Pierce, slaughtering him every game.

Finally, Roger scored five points in the final round and made a big show out of it.

"Yeah, baby!" Roger cheered. "Pulled it out. Winner." He grinned broadly while Lydia, who had been watching from the bar, gave a consolation smile Jack's way.

"You did very well, Jack."

"What say I take on the pool shark next?" Roger headed back to the bar. "But first, Naughty Cinderellas all around. On me!"

"I'd like a go at darts, if I could." Lydia rolled up her sleeves.

Nancy smiled. "You're on. Jack?"

"Sure." Jack looked away from the e-cigarette case still on the windowsill.

"Do you want a pointer?" Nancy asked Jack. Her voice had softened. She took another sip of her drink and smiled up at him.

"Sure."

"Relax." She mimed throwing a dart and gave him a wink. "The trick's in a nice soft touch. But not too soft."

The games started back up, and Replacement coughed as she sipped her drink.

"Did I make it too strong?" Roger asked, just as he sank another ball.

She shook her head.

Jack caught Replacement's eye. She gave him a quick wink.

Replacement mopped the floor with Roger. Jack would've loved to throw the dart game again, but neither of the women played darts well at all. Lydia had a hard time even hitting the board. In the end, Jack won. Lydia stomped her foot and giggled.

"Now we're talking." Nancy lightly pushed up against Jack. "See what happens when you relax?"

"I'd like another game," Lydia said. "Right after I come back from the restroom. Excuse me."

Nancy tossed a dart at the board. "You want to practice?" She grinned at Jack.

"I'd better."

"You're a local, right?" Nancy asked.

"Born and raised." Jack hit the seven. "You?"

"A little dot in the Midwest." Nancy's dart just made the board.

"Weston's out in California. What brought you there?"

"I floated on the tech bubble." She laughed. Jack caught a light sigh at the end. It was the kind of sigh that told of a story without a happy ending.

"I guess the wind was pushing west?"

She laughed again. "It blew east first. I went to college in New York." She shrugged. "Then the winds changed."

"You're the VP of human resources?"

"I am." Her eyes darted over to Pierce, and she held her finger in front of her mouth. "But I make it a point to never talk about work with my boss in the room."

"That's a good rule to follow."

Nancy pulled the darts from the board. "So, you don't look like the typical computer geek," she said. "What's your story?" As she gave Jack the darts, her fingers brushed his hand.

"I should probably follow your rule." Jack nodded over to Replacement. "I shouldn't talk about work with my boss in the room."

Nancy took a long sip of her drink. "Is she your boss or your girlfriend?"

"Both."

"I give you credit. Most men would be intimidated having a girlfriend with power over them. But you like that arrangement?" Nancy's grin warmed into a leer.

Jack was rescued by Lydia's reappearance. "You didn't start without me, did you?"

Jack shook his head. "How could we?"

Lydia smiled and rolled up her sleeves.

Pierce moved over to the bar, and Jack followed.

"What are you drinking?" Jack asked.

"Roger goaded me into one of those Cinderellas." Pierce reached over the bar and grabbed a water. "Only one gave me a huge buzz. I'm trying to slow down."

"We need to stay the night. Invite Alice and me to stay."

Replacement hopped over to the bar, her drink in her hand. It was almost empty. Jack smelled vodka on her breath.

"Don't have another one," he said.

"Why? It's so good." She smacked her lips. "I think he may have given me a naughty one."

"I think so too." Jack grabbed a water bottle. "Here."

Roger walked over, whacked his hand against his head, and laughed. His laugh had an edge to it. He leaned down so he was nose to nose with Replacement. "Sorry. I forgot you're the virgin."

Replacement turned beet red.

Jack shot forward. He was four inches taller than Roger, and it looked like more as he glared down at the man.

Roger stepped back. "Bad joke. Stupid joke. Sorry."

Jack felt Replacement's hand on his forearm.

"Apology accepted." Replacement gave Jack's arm a squeeze. "Now I'll really mop the floor with you in the next game."

Roger took another step back and looked back and forth between Jack and Replacement. "Sure. Sorry again. I'll rack." The ice cubes in his drink clinked against his glass as his hand shook.

"Easy, Jack," Replacement whispered.

Lydia strolled up, swigging the last of her drink. "Jack, I'm going to have to pass on that second game after all. I just realized how late it is. We've got our big meeting tomorrow." She looked at Pierce and angled her head toward Roger. "I think it would be best if we all called it a night."

Pierce nodded. "That sounds like a plan."

Roger tossed the pool cue on the table and grabbed his drink. He looked at Pierce and frowned, and his hands went out.

Pierce turned to Replacement. "It's late. Why don't you stay here?"

Jack stepped forward. "No. It's too much trouble."

"No trouble." Pierce nodded. "I'll just get Sophia to set up a room."

Jack looked at Replacement, and she nodded. "If you don't mind. We could get an early start that way."

"Well, I guess I'll go watch TV." Roger took his drink and headed for the door. Jack caught the wink he gave Pierce as he passed.

"Me, too." Nancy walked over to Pierce. "Thank you for dinner."

"Thank you, Nancy."

They were all heading for the door when Lydia called out. "Oh, Mr. Weston."

Jack held his breath but didn't turn around.

"You forgot your case again." She hurried over to the window and picked it up. Jack saw Replacement grimace.

"Ready for bed?" Jack put a restraining hand on her shoulder.

38

SHE'S SWEET

Pierce held the bedroom door open for Jack and Replacement. The bedroom he had led them to was on the top floor, separated from his by a long study.

When they were all inside, Pierce shut the door and tossed his hands up. "At least we can take Lydia off the list." He chuckled. "She gave it back twice. I was just about ready to strangle her."

"It was making me crazy, but she's so sweet." Replacement sighed.

Pierce laughed. "You're one of the few people I've ever heard refer to Lydia that way—but I agree. Maddening, but it is nice to have someone watching your back."

Jack shrugged and looked out the window.

"Don't tell me you still suspect her?" Pierce leaned against the doorway.

"Don't take it the wrong way," Replacement said, rubbing her eyes. "He suspects everybody." She squeezed her eyelids shut. "Wow, Roger makes a strong drink."

"First thing tomorrow, we need to pull the full backgrounds on everyone," Jack said. "Can I get printouts?"

"We can send them to your phone," Pierce offered.

Replacement shook her head. "He's old-fashioned. He likes hard copies."

"Does your bedroom door lock?" Jack asked.

"Yes," Pierce said. "I actually have two doors. There's a side door that leads to a little staircase. But both of them lock."

"Good. Lock them both."

"Do you think someone would be that brash? Is that why you're here tonight?"

"Someone wants that case badly. I do think they could make a play for it."

"Well, I know we can rule out Lydia," Pierce said.

"We don't rule out anyone yet. Alice, I need you to set up your laptop."

"Sure. Why?" She walked over to her bag and took it out.

"I need to look up someone tonight. Can you get me online?"

Replacement nodded. She set her laptop on the desk and turned it on.

"Did you get a lead on someone?" Replacement asked as she got her background check program up and running.

Pierce made a face. "Who are you looking up?"

Jack ignored the questions. "I think we're all set here tonight, Pierce. Thanks again for your hospitality."

Pierce stared at Jack for a moment and nodded. "Sure. Should I go put on a pot of coffee for you?"

"No. We won't be up too long. That meeting's at two?"

Pierce nodded.

"We'll get an early start tomorrow then," Jack said.

Pierce opened the door. "Well, let me know if you need anything."

Replacement gave a little wave. "'Night."

Pierce shut the door.

"Okay…" Replacement frowned. "That was a little rude. He was just trying to help."

"I know he was, but…" Jack looked at her for a minute and shook his head. "Look, we're going to be looking at people Pierce works with every day. People he trusts— or used to, anyway. Just in case I'm wrong, I don't want to get him going one way or another. If I told him I wanted to look closer at someone, and it turns out to be nothing, he could still hold a grudge."

"He's not like that."

Jack frowned. He wanted to say she didn't know that, but he wasn't sure whether she did.

"I need you right now," Jack said instead.

"What do you need me to do?"

"Pierce said he has a tablet, right?"

"What? When?"

"At U-Do2. He was getting a connector for his tablet."

"You're right."

"Does it have a camera?"

She nodded. "It should."

"Can you stream a feed to your phone? It sure beats me staying in his room all night."

"You really think someone would try to take it from his bedroom?"

"Something really bothers me about this. Look, the guy who hit Gerald hit him *hard*. He could have easily killed him. Whoever wants this data wants it badly enough to kill."

"I'm sure I can get the camera going. Do you want me to do it now?"

"In a minute. First, did you find out anything at dinner?"

"Not really, but you're the one who reads people, not me. If I were looking at money as a motive, it would be Roger, hands down. He's got to have cash problems, and he gives me the creeps. I think Pierce has blinders on with him anyway."

"How so?"

"They went to college together. Pierce seems real loyal." She grabbed her left arm with her right hand. "I think that's why…" Her mouth clicked shut.

"Why what?"

"Pierce is taking what happened to Gerald hard. Really hard. He doesn't really say it, but I can tell."

Jack nodded.

"Did he say anything to you?" she asked.

"Enough. He's watching out for his friend's father. He needs to find the guy who hurt Gerald. I understand that."

Replacement paced. "But do you get the feeling that somehow Pierce…" She exhaled and looked at the ceiling. "I think he feels guilty about Tyler. How he died. Did he say anything to you?"

Jack nodded. "He does. Tyler pushed Pierce out of the way of a truck. Tyler died. Pierce lived. That can do a number on anyone's head."

Replacement wrapped her arms around herself. "That's horrible." She turned to look at the door. "That must've been so hard on him. I should go... I'll go get the camera set up."

"Sure, let's go do that."

Replacement hesitated. "Oh—you're going with me? I was thinking—I mean, if I go and anyone sees me, I can say I'm talking to him about work."

Jack frowned. He didn't like the idea of Replacement going alone to Pierce's bedroom, but...

"Okay. I need to call Mrs. Stevens anyway, ask her to look after Lady."

"I already did." Replacement smiled. "She said she'd have a girls' night with Lady. They're going to watch TV. *Wheel of Fortune, Murder, She Wrote,* and *Downton Abbey.*"

Jack chuckled. "I'm glad she loves that dog. I need to pick up some buffet coupons for her, to thank her."

"She'd like that." Replacement headed for the door.

"Make sure the camera gets both doors," Jack said.

"I will. I'll be right back." Replacement hurried out of the room.

Jack sighed. He rubbed his eyes as he walked over to the desk and sat down. Lights sparkled on the lake. He looked around the immaculate room with the polished wood furniture and huge bed.

"This stupid guest room's nicer than my apartment."

He leaned his head against his hand and checked out Replacement's laptop. Her background check program was running, but he switched out of that and pulled up Google. Something had bothered him tonight, and he wanted to check it out.

39

BABY ON BOARD

Replacement tapped on Pierce's bedroom door and waited. After a moment, Pierce opened it a crack, saw Replacement, then opened the door wide and got out of the way.

"What's going on?" he asked.

Replacement's eyes darted away from his shirtless chest to the floor. "I need your tablet. Jack wants me to feed your camera to my phone."

"Sure. One sec." He walked over and took a shirt out of a drawer. "Sorry, I hope I didn't make you uncomfortable."

"You didn't." She shook her head.

"Then I'll leave it off." He set the shirt back down.

She inhaled and felt her neck flush. "I meant... I didn't..."

"I was kidding." He pulled the shirt on, then walked over and picked up the tablet. "Here you go."

Replacement bit her lip and closed an eye. She opened the program selection on the tablet, and her finger hesitated over the screen. "Boy, I can see how that Naughty Cinderella got its name. I can't think straight."

"Here." Pierce moved next to her and his hands flew across the screen. "We can use this camera AP and just treat it like a video chat."

"Thanks." She pulled out her phone. "So I can just connect here and..." She looked down at the screen, and the video appeared.

"Do we need volume? I might snore." Pierce grinned.

Replacement laughed.

"If it's going to be on all night, I should plug it in." Pierce grabbed a power cord. "Where should we focus it?"

"You said there was another door?"

Pierce pointed to a panel next to the bookshelf. The second door almost blended with the wall.

"That's a weird door." She moved to the far corner of the room so the camera could get the front door, the bed, and the side door.

"It was put in so people could come and go from the master bedroom without being seen," Pierce said.

"That's dumb. Why would someone want to get out of the bedroom without..." Her voice trailed off. "Oh, I get it."

Pierce sat down on the bed and waved at the tablet. "Does my baby monitor work?"

She laughed. "It's not a baby monitor. We're just worried about you. You should turn off your screensaver and power settings."

"Thanks." Pierce walked over to her. "You're... worried about me?" He stepped closer.

Replacement swallowed. She felt light-headed. She never drank, and that Naughty Cinderella had gone straight to her head. Heat rose up from her chest. Her eyes darted around the room, because she now found herself unsure where to look.

"Alice?" Pierce's voice was low.

Her eyes met his, and the heat rose straight to her cheeks. She blinked twice.

"It's all set." She darted for the door.

"Wait," Pierce said.

She stopped. Her heart pounded, and she rubbed her hands on her pants.

"Can you turn around?"

She hesitated. The warmth in her chest was growing, but in a way that didn't feel good. Slowly, she turned to face him.

When their eyes met, his smile faded.

"Pierce..."

He held up a hand and shook his head. "Don't say anything. We both had a little to drink."

She nodded and turned back around. When her hand landed on the doorknob, he spoke. "Alice. Thank you for helping me."

She slipped out the door and pulled it closed behind her. She shut her eyes and tried to catch her breath. The stout hardwood felt good against her back. Her mouth felt dry.

After a minute, she opened her eyes and saw that the light in the study was now on. She hesitantly approached the door. Roger sat in a chair that was turned so he could keep an eye on the hallway.

A leer spread across his face, and he held up an almost empty drink. "I had a feeling it would be you."

"We had to go over tomorrow's workload," Replacement explained.

Roger chuckled and took a gulp of his drink. "Sure."

Replacement's eyes narrowed.

"Sorry." Roger rose unsteadily to his feet. "Don't go getting all upset again. I get what you're doing."

"Me?"

Roger chuckled. "I've seen it before. Little girl from a little town. You see your ticket to the big leagues, so even with your boyfriend in the next room you sneak—"

"You're wrong, and you're drunk."

"I'm not drunk." He shook his head. "I mean, I *am* drunk, but I'm not wrong. Hell, who am I to judge? If I were you, I'd trade up."

Replacement's lip curled into a snarl.

Roger stumbled toward her. "It's not a hard decision. A billionaire or your local yokel boyfriend?" His hands tipped back and forth as he held them out. "Gee, which one will she pick?" He laughed.

Replacement turned to leave.

Roger grabbed her arm and pulled her back. "Don't run away." His voice had changed. There was an edge to it.

"Get your hands off me." Replacement tried to fight down the fear that seized her.

"I know your type. You're just after his money. He may not see through you, but I do."

"Get your hands off me now or I'll scream. You'll be getting your unemployment check in the hospital."

"Just leave him alone. Stop messing with his head. He's a good guy." Roger let go and staggered sideways.

Replacement backed into the hallway and bolted for the bedroom.

Jack looked up as she came in. He jumped up and rushed over. "What's wrong?"

She shook her head. "Nothing. It's nothing."

"Alice, look at me."

She exhaled. She didn't know what Jack would do if she told him. "I'm okay. The drink must've gone to my head."

"Are you sure you're all right?"

She nodded. "I got it working." Her hand trembled slightly as she handed her phone to Jack.

He looked at the screen, and his eyebrow rose. "What is that?" Jack pointed and squinted. "Is that a note for us?"

Replacement looked at the screen. Pierce had put a Post-It note on the frame of the bed. She could just make out the words: *Baby on board.* But she didn't want to explain that to Jack. "I don't know. It's nothing," she said.

"Why don't you go to sleep?" Jack suggested. "I'll take first watch."

Replacement didn't argue. All she wanted to do was crawl under the covers. She got into the big, comfy bed and curled into a ball. She knew she hadn't done anything to feel guilty about, but her chest still ached.

40

I'M A MACHINE

Replacement's eyes fluttered open, but she tried not to move. She felt Jack sitting beside her. He stroked her hair. She lay there as his fingers glided over her with the softness of a breath.

After a few moments, she rolled over to face him. He was looking down at her with the phone in his hand. His eyes looked exhausted, but he grinned the roguish smile that melted her heart.

"This has to be the most boring show I've ever seen," he said, tapping the screen.

She laughed and put her hand on the phone, and her fingers touched his. "I bet it gets canceled after one season." She pulled him down and kissed him.

Jack let go of the phone and wrapped his arms around her. She inhaled as he rolled her partway onto her back. His left hand slid up her side and caressed her face.

Fierce. That was the word she'd use to describe how he became. He seized her, and she loved that. His touch was tender, but there was a need in his muscles. His need for her set her ablaze. He leaned back, and his chest heaved. She could see it in his eyes. He wanted her, and he was fighting with himself over taking her now.

She kissed him quickly, then buried her face in his chest. "I'm sorry I gave you a hard time. We can wait. I'm sorry."

Jack exhaled loudly and put his head back.

She sat up and watched him. His eyes were closed. When they opened, that fire was gone.

"You're exhausted," she said. "It's almost five. You let me sleep all night."

"I don't need sleep. I'm a machine." But even as he said it, Jack's eyes closed again.

"I'm unplugging you. Two hours."

Jack sighed. "One."

"Sure."

"You agreed too quickly. Seriously, one or I won't fall asleep."

"Okay."

Replacement pulled back the covers so he could get under them. Then she took her phone and sat next to him.

Jack lay on his back and stared at the ceiling. Replacement softly traced her fingers on his face. With just the tips of her fingers brushing his skin, she moved her hand over his eyebrows and down to his cheekbones. As she caressed him, his breathing deepened, and he was soon fast asleep.

She watched him for a while. They'd only been together for a short time, but she'd already lost track of how many nights she'd gotten him to fall asleep this way.

Nightmares.

She closed her eyes as she tried to drive the memory of his screams out of her mind. She could only guess at the things he'd seen in the war. She had seen the scars on his chest, but she knew his deepest scars couldn't be seen.

In some ways, she hated night. It was when Jack went somewhere she couldn't follow. While he dreamed, all she could do was whisper how much she loved him. And pray.

Jack groaned.

She made a fist and bowed her head.

41

THANKS FOR BEING ONE

Replacement pulled the blanket up to cover Jack's exposed shoulder, and the corner of his mouth ticked up.

Movement on her phone's screen caught her attention. Pierce was waking up. He stretched out and then froze. His head turned, and he stared at the camera. He gave a tired wave, rubbed his face, and got out of bed.

Replacement gave him a second. Then she put the phone on the nightstand and slipped out of bed. She pulled her shoes on and looked back at Jack. He hadn't moved. She quietly snuck out the door and started down the hallway.

The house was quiet. The sun was just starting to come up.

"Alice?"

She jumped but managed not to scream. Roger hurried out of the study but stayed at a distance. He must have fallen asleep in that chair.

"I'm sorry," he said. "I just wanted to say I was drunk. I know that. Please don't say anything."

Replacement tried to calm her pounding heart. "Have you been here all night?" she asked.

Roger's head seemed to nod in all directions. "I was wrong. So wrong." He rubbed his bloodshot eyes. "I need this job. If you tell Pierce how I acted… friend or not, I'm gone. I can tell he really, really likes you. I've just… I'm not justifying my actions." He waved his hands. "Okay, I sort of am, but I've been doing nothing but blowing up my life. I've decided to go get help. But if I lose my job…"

Replacement stared at him. He looked pitiful. "I won't say anything. Just go."

Roger nodded and scurried back down the hallway. "Thank you. Really. Thank you."

Replacement watched him hurry away.

The door to Pierce's bedroom opened behind her, and Pierce peered out.

Replacement spun around. "Morning."

"Was that Roger?"

Replacement nodded.

Pierce stepped to the side and kept the door open. Replacement walked in, and Pierce closed it behind her.

"What was that about?" he asked.

She crossed her arms and clicked her tongue. "He, umm… last night he saw me come out of your room."

Pierce's mouth opened and then snapped shut. "Sorry. If anyone would get the wrong impression, it would be Roger. Is that why he was apologizing?"

Her foot started to tap nervously. "I told him I wouldn't say anything."

"I want to know."

"He was drunk."

Pierce folded his hands in front of himself and waited for her to continue.

"He thought we were fooling around. He got this idea I was coming on to you." Replacement blew away a strand of her hair that had floated in front of her face.

"We both know that's not true." The corners of Pierce's mouth curled down. "And... why is that?"

Replacement blinked rapidly. "What?"

Pierce leaned against the bureau. "Remember when I asked you to be brutally honest?"

She nodded.

"It's my turn." He took a deep breath. His eyes danced around the room. When they finally locked on to Replacement's, she swallowed. "I'm sorry," he said. He crossed his arms. "Being around you has made me realize that I'm missing something. When you're around... I just feel we connect. Do you know what I mean? Do you feel that?"

"Yes, but..." Her voice was soft. "But the truth is I don't have many friends. *Any* friends," she added quickly. "I'm a girl computer geek. That'd be weird by itself; but me being me?" She smiled awkwardly. "When we talk, it's awesome. I love it. I laugh, and you make me feel good—as a friend."

Pierce's jaw muscles flexed. "I know. But I just..."

"Pierce, you're a great guy. You could have a hundred girls who'd throw themselves at your feet."

"Do you have any idea the kind of girl who throws herself at my feet?" He held his hands out to the room. "They're desperately in love with my money."

"Then find a nice girl. You want someone..." Replacement closed her eyes tightly and took a deep breath. "You want someone who says, 'All this doesn't matter. I don't care about the house or the cars or the money. I just care about you.'"

"That's what I've been waiting to hear. And then what happens? Do we run into the sunset and live happily ever after?"

Replacement nodded. "Something like that."

They stared at each other for a moment. The butterflies in Replacement's stomach stopped fluttering, and she smiled.

Pierce pushed away from the bureau. "Now what? Should we go talk to Jack?"

"Not yet. We should wait—he's only just now getting a little sleep. He was up almost the whole night."

"Okay. I'll get dressed, then meet you in the kitchen?"

"Sounds good." Replacement walked over to the door.

Pierce cleared his throat.

She stopped.

"You said you didn't have many friends?" he asked.

She didn't turn around, but she nodded.

"Neither do I. Thanks for being one."

Replacement smiled and walked out.

42

COLD

Jack heard voices coming from the TV. He rolled over and sat up, but the TV wasn't on. Then he looked at the nightstand. Replacement's phone was there. The voices were coming from the camera feed in Pierce's bedroom.

Jack picked up the phone and watched Replacement talking to Pierce. He turned up the volume.

Replacement lifted up her head and looked at Pierce. "All this doesn't matter. I don't care about the house or the cars or the money. I just care about you."

"That's what I've been waiting to hear," Pierce said. "And then what happens? Do we run into the sunset and live happily ever after?"

Replacement nodded. "Something like that."

They stared at each other for a moment. Pierce pushed away from the bureau. "Now what? Should we go talk to Jack?"

"Not yet." She shook her head. "We should wait—"

Jack clicked off the phone.

His throat tightened. Tossing the covers off, he got out of bed and walked over to the window. He put his hand against the cold glass and looked down at the lake below. The sunlight had just started to dance across the water.

He tried to drive what he'd heard from his mind, but he couldn't. His hand tightened into a fist. But the rage he'd expected wasn't there. Nothing was. He felt dead. Cold.

He looked at his reflection in the glass, and it stared coldly back at him. He inhaled and looked down at the phone.

The door to the room opened behind him.

"You're awake." Replacement sounded startled.

Jack slipped the phone in his pocket and stretched. "I just got up." He forced a smile onto his face. "Pierce awake?"

Replacement nodded. "He is. I'm going to take a shower and then go meet him for coffee. You should go back to bed."

"I just want to look something up first."

Replacement headed for the bathroom. Jack watched her go. She looked back and gave a little wave before closing the door.

And just like that, she was gone.

43

NOT YET

Jack sat in front of the laptop and stared out at the lake. Replacement turned off the shower, but he didn't move. He didn't want to. He looked at the monitor. He'd found what he'd been looking for last night. He knew who was behind the corporate spying. And now it would be easy to get the proof he needed.

It was also the last thing he wanted to do.

Should we tell Jack? Not yet.

The words echoed in his head. Why "not yet"? Was she waiting until the case was over?

If that was what Replacement was waiting for, he never wanted to solve this case.

He opened the browser window he'd been looking at last night. The website for the Northbank Players opened back up.

Someone knocked on the door.

As Jack walked across the floor, Replacement opened the bathroom door. "Who is it?" she asked.

He didn't know, but he could guess.

Jack turned the handle and let the door swing open.

Pierce's smile fell from his face, and he took a step back when he looked at Jack. "Jack… good morning."

"I found something." Jack turned and headed back to the laptop.

"What?" Replacement called out from behind the bathroom door. She opened it a crack. "Wait for me."

Jack sat down in front of the laptop.

"You look really tired," Pierce said.

"I am."

Replacement hurried out of the bathroom. She looked like she had pulled on her clothes without drying off first. "What did you get?"

Jack clicked the button for "past productions." A big red curtain pulled back and a poster for *Rent* appeared. He clicked on the "CAST" link and a page of portraits came up.

Replacement pointed. "That's Sophia."

Jack clicked on her picture, and her biography was displayed.

"Sophia went to New York University and received a bachelor's degree?" Replacement's voice went up. She nodded toward the keyboard. "Can I drive?"

Jack stood up, and Replacement slipped into the chair. She logged in to the Weston Industries database and pulled up her info. "That's not on the résumé she provided to Weston Industries."

Pierce rubbed his chin. "During a background check, we do search a résumé for inflated information—but I don't suppose we thought to look for omitted colleges."

"How did you know?" Replacement asked Jack.

"The way she talked," Jack said. "It didn't fit someone whose career was in domestic service. When I spoke to her, it felt like she was always playing a character."

Pierce nodded, impressed.

"Standard police work." Jack shrugged. "Canvassing a neighborhood. Knock on doors, talk to people, and hope for a lead. She told me she had danced and acted in that play, so I did some fishing." Jack reached for the mouse and opened another window. Now Nancy Bell's résumé appeared. "They both went to New York University. Same time. Same sorority."

"Wow," Replacement said. "But maybe Nancy hired her friend as a favor, but didn't want anyone to know?"

"There'd be no reason to hide it," Pierce said. "In fact, we have a bonus program for referrals."

"We should pull the records for her company phone," Jack said.

Replacement made a face. "A maid has a company phone?"

"Sophia was provided one so they can contact her. You won't need a court order for her records. How fast can we get them?" Jack asked.

"I can have security do that," Pierce said.

"Hold off on involving security," Jack said.

"But we know it's Nancy and Sophia. Security should be involved now." Pierce stood as though he was back in a board room.

"Look, I still don't think what happened to Gerald was an accident," Jack said.

Pierce shook his head. "Fine. Say I agree with you now and we say it wasn't an accident. It doesn't change who did it. Nancy's new. She was privy to the leaked information. Considering the fact that she hid her relationship with Sophia... that's enough for me."

"We still need to approach this slowly. Can you hold off on telling security until Alice can get the phone records?"

Replacement gazed at Pierce hopefully.

Jack looked away.

"Can you just wait until after your meeting?" Replacement asked Pierce.

"I'll just cancel the meeting," Pierce grumbled. "There's no longer any need for it."

"Don't cancel it," Jack said. "That'll look suspicious. Plus, the meeting will buy Alice time to get the records. Tell them whatever you want, but have the meeting."

Pierce nodded, but as he walked out the door, he was shaking his head.

Replacement grabbed Jack's hand. "Are you okay?"

"Yeah."

"Look at me."

Jack forced himself to. He stared into her green eyes, and she scanned his face.

"What's wrong?" Her voice was strained.

"Nothing." He pulled his head to the side. "I'm just tired." He marched to the door.

"You can go back to bed. I can tell—"

"No." He grabbed the door handle. The part of him that would have wanted to rip the door off its hinges was gone. His hand squeezed the metal, but the only thing he felt was the cold brass. "Call me if you hear something."

44

THE KICK IS UP

While Pierce held his meeting, Replacement worked in the server room, and Jack went back to helping Bruce and Phillip. Jack was relieved that the last of the APs were in place, and now they were on cleanup. They spent most of the day testing the connections and finishing up.

It was almost five o'clock when Jack went outside with Bruce and Phillip to load some of their gear into Replacement's Bug.

Bruce elbowed Jack. "Something's going on."

Leon and Manuel were just pulling up in a gray sedan. Behind them was a police cruiser. Jack recognized Mark Jenkins and Ray Miller.

Damn it. So much for Pierce waiting.

Jack dialed Pierce as he walked toward the side entrance.

"Where are you going?" Bruce asked.

Jack kept moving. When Pierce answered, Jack growled, "Did you tell him not to do this?"

Pierce raised his voice. "Leon confiscated Sophia's phone. She took photos of a confidential letter and sent it to Nancy. That's enough for an arrest warrant."

"I don't care if one of them *confessed*. I made it clear not to do this."

"That wasn't your call—it was mine. The time for waiting was over."

Click.

"Moron." Jack fumed. He dialed Replacement.

"The police are here," she said as soon as she answered. Her voice was labored. He could tell she was walking too.

"Did you talk to Pierce?" Jack asked.

"He just called."

"Where are they?"

"Living room on the second floor. I'm heading there now."

"Me too."

Jack and Replacement reached the upstairs living room at almost the same time and slipped inside. Roger, Lydia, Nancy, and Pierce were seated at the far end of the room and paid them no mind.

"Pierce shouldn't have moved yet," Jack whispered, still fuming.

"Why?" Replacement asked. "Pierce said Leon found evidence in Sophia's phone records."

"Something still doesn't add up."

They waited quietly at the side of the room for what they knew was coming. And sure enough, it wasn't long before the police came in—with Sophia in handcuffs. The maid's head hung low, and her shoulders rose and fell rapidly.

Nancy looked over and froze. Then she looked ready to bolt.

"Nancy Bell." Officer Jenkins walked over to her while he took out his cuffs. "I have a warrant for your arrest for the theft of company records."

"What?" Nancy turned to Pierce.

Pierce's whole stance changed. He looked at her with pity.

Sophia glared at Nancy. "I haven't done anything."

"Just be quiet," Nancy said.

"Ah, no. Look, I had nothing to do with this." Sophia's eyes darted around the room, as if searching for anyone who'd listen.

Nancy stood there for a moment, just staring at Pierce. Her lip curled up, and she shook her head. "No. I didn't… I didn't steal anything." She glared at Sophia.

"Don't look at *me*!" Sophia stepped forward, but Officer Jenkins held on to her arm. "I didn't even know what the hell she wanted me to do! I was ready to quit. This whole thing was ill-conceived. And I didn't *do* anything. She told me to keep my eyes and ears open. For what? This place is as boring as the town."

"Shut up!" Nancy yelled back. "Stop talking."

Officer Miller cuffed Nancy. When he read her rights, she broke down and started crying.

"Where's your phone?" Miller asked Nancy.

"My purse. You can't open that without a warrant."

"I'm sorry, but we can, ma'am." Miller opened the purse and took out her phone. "Is this your company phone?"

Nancy nodded and hung her head.

Miller handed the phone to Pierce.

Then Leon handed another phone to Pierce. "This phone belongs to Sophia. IT has already copied the files from it."

Nancy's head snapped up. She glared at Sophia in disgust. "You texted me that file from your company phone?"

"You told me to."

"Not on the company phone."

Sophia shrugged. "How else would I get it to you? Carrier pigeon? I'm broke. I don't have a phone."

"Is that why you did it?" Pierce frowned. "Money?"

Sophia scoffed. "Uh, yeah. Try not having any."

Replacement looked at Jack and made a face. "They're not the criminal masterminds I thought they'd be," she whispered rather loudly.

As the police started to take them out of the room, Nancy planted her feet. "Wait. Rutland Systems paid me. I'll make a deal with you."

Pierce stepped forward, but Leon cut him off. "You can talk after you're charged and processed," Leon said.

Nancy shook her head. "I won't."

"I'm sure you will," Leon said.

As the police led the two women out of the room, Sophia yelled out, "Wait! I'll deal too. Nancy told me everything. She's still working for Rutland. She gets two paychecks and they're giving her a ton of money. She's only given me a grand. That's it. I just needed a job. I didn't—"

"Shut up, Sophia!" Nancy screamed.

"*You* shut up. It was her idea. Please…"

Sophia kept yelling all the way out of the mansion.

Leon marched over to Jack. "Nice job, Stratton. I'd still like to have that talk."

"You moved too early," Jack whispered. "There's more to this than those two. Gerald getting hurt was no accident."

"Pierce conveyed your theory. You think there might be a connection. I think you're wrong, but don't worry, we'll look it over later. Right now, we have enough evidence anyway."

"You're making a mistake, sir."

"Like I said, we'll look it all over. My offer to you still stands. You have my card." Leon turned to Pierce. "Manuel and I will follow the officers downtown. They may need some additional signatures, and I want to know who these two will call. Gibson is on duty if you need anything."

Pierce nodded. "Thank you, Leon."

"Wow." Roger headed over to the bar. "I didn't see that one coming."

"It really is a shame," Lydia said.

Bruce and Phillip appeared in the doorway. Replacement waved them over to her and Jack.

"The cops just took Nancy and Sophia away in cuffs," Bruce said.

"What was that all about?" Phillip asked.

"And they arrested Sophia too." Bruce frowned. "She's a really nice lady. She gave me extra sandwiches."

"What did they do?" Phillip asked.

"Corporate spying," Replacement whispered.

"No way." Bruce's eyes grew huge. "Both of them?"

Pierce stood by the window and looked out at the lake, his hands thrust in his pockets. Jack walked over to him.

"Looks like everything's almost wrapped up," Pierce said. He extended his hand. "Thank you."

Jack kept his hands at his side. "They're not the ones who tried to steal the case."

Pierce rubbed his face. "You figured it out, Jack. Nancy and Sophia were behind everything. Now you sound like some conspiracy theorist." His raised voice caused everyone to turn around.

Replacement walked over. "Is everything all right?"

"*I* think we should be celebrating, but Jack…" Pierce rolled his eyes.

Jack felt his neck stiffen. His mouth pressed into a hard line.

"I've got it!" Pierce's hands shot out in front of him. "Lydia, can I borrow your laptop?"

"Of course." Lydia walked over to her bag.

Pierce marched over to the bar. Lydia handed him her laptop, and he turned it on. Roger moved over to make room. Jack walked over with Replacement.

"I'm connecting it wirelessly." Pierce took two phones out of his pocket. "Here are Nancy's and Sophia's phones." He set them down on the bar.

Phillip and Bruce joined the others, and now everyone was huddled around Pierce.

Pierce took the e-cigarette case out of his pocket, grinning like a science teacher about to perform his favorite experiment before the class.

"Now." Pierce turned back around. "The case is programmed to contact a phone when it's plugged in, right?" He looked at Jack.

Jack nodded.

Pierce plugged the case into the laptop. "As they say in football, the kick is up!" Pierce held out his hands to the phones on the bar.

Everyone watched.

After a few moments, Bruce cleared his throat. He leaned toward Jack, but Jack held up his hand.

"What's supposed to happen?" Roger whispered.

Lydia shushed him.

Roger sat down on a bar stool.

A phone played a cheery tune, but it wasn't one of the ones on the bar.

Pierce looked confused.

The phone rang again.

Replacement turned to Phillip. "Can I see your phone, Phillip?"

Phillip reached into his pocket and took out his phone. Jack quickly moved between him and Replacement, holding out his hand.

Phillip's eyes narrowed—

Then he threw the phone at Jack's face and ran toward his bag. His eyes went wide as his hand fumbled inside the bag.

Jack smirked. "If you're looking for the huge knife that was in your bag, it's not there anymore. I thought it was best if I took it out."

Philip reached behind his back. A utility knife flashed in his hand.

"I guess I missed that one," Jack muttered.

Phillip stepped toward the door, but Jack moved between him and the door, cutting him off.

"Back away." Phillip swung the knife in front of him.

"That's not happening," Jack said. He slid one foot back and bent both knees, getting on guard.

"I said *move*," Phillip growled.

Replacement grabbed a bottle from the bar and threw it at Phillip's head.

Phillip ducked, but the distraction was all Jack needed. He lunged. With one hand grabbing Phillip's wrist and the other on Phillip's shoulder, Jack spun him around and slammed him to the floor.

Pierce charged in and grabbed Phillip's other arm. When Phillip struggled, Pierce punched him in the face. Jack wrenched Phillip's wrist, forcing him to drop the knife.

Jack held both of Phillip's arms behind his back. "Do you have any zip ties?" he asked Bruce.

Bruce looked in the bag. "No. But I have some cord."

"That'll do."

As Jack tied Phillip's hands behind his back, Phillip continued to struggle. "Stop fighting me or I'll let Alice have a turn on you." Jack yanked Phillip to his feet and shoved him onto the couch. "Start talking."

"I want to talk to a lawyer."

"I'm not arresting you."

"You can't. You're not a real cop." Phillip sneered.

Jack's back tightened.

Replacement darted by Jack and grabbed Phillip's shirt. She spoke so softly that no one except Phillip could hear her. But whatever she said, it made all the color drain from Phillip's face. His cocky grin vanished. He swallowed and looked up nervously at Jack.

Replacement let go of Phillip's shirt and moved back to stand next to Jack.

Pierce moved to Jack's other side. "You took his knife," he said to Jack. "You suspected him?"

Jack nodded. "One of his tools had a European plug, but he said he'd never been out of the States."

Phillip cursed under his breath. "My Dremel." His voice was noticeably deeper and rougher now. "I had a feeling when you saw it."

"That and the code," Jack said.

"The date!" Replacement practically shouted. "In the code. The date's European."

Phillip sat forward on the couch and shook his head.

"Was he working with Nancy and Sophia?" Pierce asked.

"No. He wasn't," Jack said.

"But we caught Nancy and Sophia red-handed. The evidence is overwhelming. They were spying." Pierce stared at Jack.

"I didn't say they weren't guilty of corporate espionage. They are. Definitely. I'm saying they didn't make that e-cigarette case, and they didn't hurt Gerald."

Pierce stuck his finger in Phillip's face. "You're strong enough to pull that rack over."

"Should I contact the police?" Lydia asked.

"Tell them to send out a car." Jack glared down at Phillip. "Who else are you working with?"

Phillip closed his mouth and stared straight ahead.

Jack grabbed Phillip's shirt. He twisted the fabric tight and yanked him forward. "Someone broke into my apartment. They hurt my dog."

Phillip shook his head. "It wasn't me."

"I know. You were with us at the time. Who was it?"

Phillip pressed his lips tightly together.

"I'm so lost." Roger poured a drink.

"Shut up, Roger," Pierce snapped.

"The police don't have enough to hold me," Phillip muttered.

"You came at me with a knife in front of a roomful of witnesses. That gives them enough," Jack said.

Phillip glared at the floor.

"This is crazy," Bruce said. "Do you need me to do anything?"

"Just stick around," Jack said. "We need you all to give statements to the police." Bruce nodded.

Roger walked over to the door and looked out toward the front of the house.

"Now what do we do?" Replacement asked.

"Wait for the police." Jack nodded toward Phillip. "I can't wait to see what comes back when they run his fingerprints."

Phillip's shoulders slumped.

Two faint pops outside caused Jack's adrenaline to shift straight to overdrive. In the doorway, the drink fell from Roger's hand and shattered on the floor.

Jack ran up beside him. From here, a large window at the front of the house provided visibility straight down the driveway. Two sedans were driving toward the house, but that's not what caught Jack's eye.

A security guard's body lay on the ground outside the guardhouse. A growing stain spread on the tar underneath it.

"They shot him," Roger said. He looked as if he was about to throw up. "They *killed* him!" he shrieked.

"Alice, call nine-one-one now."

Jack yanked Phillip to his feet. But after one look at Phillip's pale face, Jack's chest tightened. Jack knew Phillip had guts—after all, he had almost killed Gerald and still remained undercover right among them. Yet that courage was now replaced with fear.

"They're here. The case called them, too." Phillip groaned.

"Who's here?" Jack shouted.

Phillip trembled. "We're all dead."

45

A CLUB TO A GUNFIGHT

"How many are coming?" Jack slammed Phillip against the doorframe. "I don't know. A crew. Five or six. They're going to kill us all. Me too." Replacement spoke into her phone. "I need to report a home invasion at the Bellmore estate. Six armed men. They shot a security guard."

"Who are they?" Jack asked Phillip.

"Ex-soldiers. They're crazy."

Jack looked down the hall and mentally analyzed the house. "Everyone head to Pierce's bedroom," he said. "Barricade the door. There's a staircase in the back. If they come to the door, go down the stairs, then run for the woods and scatter."

"They have guns," Roger moaned.

Replacement grabbed the e-cigarette case. "I'm going with you," she said to Jack.

"No. Take care of the others. And stay on the line with the police. I'm going to distract them, nothing more. It's at least an eighteen-minute response time." Jack pushed Phillip into the hallway and grabbed Roger. "You hold him." He put Roger's hands on Phillip's shoulders.

Roger pushed Phillip down the hall.

"Oh, Mr. Weston." Lydia gulped in air.

Replacement took her by the hand, but spoke to Jack. "I'm getting them to the bedroom, but then I'm coming back for you." She led Lydia down the hallway.

Jack grabbed Pierce's arm. "Pierce. Make sure Alice is safe. And don't let her come after me."

Pierce nodded.

Jack sprinted down the stairs while the others rushed to Pierce's bedroom. His feet clicked on the wooden floor. At the front entrance, he peered out. The driveway was empty.

Five or six guys. Three to a floor. They'll sweep left to right. Half in the front hall, half in the back.

Jack reached into the umbrella stand and grabbed a thick walking stick. Gripping it like a sword, he swung hard once, testing it. The old wood was solid. Jack ran toward the side entrance, which was just past the downstairs kitchen.

I'm bringing a club to a gunfight. Idiot.

Just before he reached the kitchen, he ducked into a room—some kind of library—and pressed himself against the wall. When the side door opened, he peered around the corner and counted five men. All carried pistols.

Three headed up the stairs at this end of the house. One of the others pointed down the hall in Jack's direction. "Tolyan, take right."

Jack ducked back into the library, once again pressing his back against the wall beside the door, which he left open. Sweat poured down his back. He gripped the walking stick tighter. Approaching footsteps echoed down the hall and rippled through Jack's chest.

Jack had faced death a hundred times, and each time he had wanted to run. The panic rising in him now made his hands shake. He fought against his survival instinct and the fear that clawed at him, but the dam of adrenaline broke. He felt it course through him. He felt the warmth spread in his chest, and his lips curled into a snarl.

Everyone deals with fear in their own way. Some pray. Some fall apart. Most battle back until they reach some strange standoff with their fear.

Not Jack.

Jack hated fear—and he used that hate. He fed off it and attacked the fear. He didn't just beat his fear; he destroyed it until only the hate remained.

Then he set the beast free.

The man's shadow appeared on the floor. His gun was slightly down and pointed along the hallway. Jack knew he'd look into the room, but just before he entered, he'd look the other way.

And the man did. As soon as his head started to turn, Jack sprang. He swung the walking stick down hard on the man's outstretched forearms. Something broke—and it wasn't the wood.

The man screamed.

Jack swung the stick down on the man's head.

The stick snapped. The man's scream cut off mid-screech, and he tumbled backward to the floor. The gun dropped from his hand and bounced in the hallway.

Jack lunged after the gun.

A gunshot echoed down the corridor, and the window in front of Jack shattered. Jack saw the second man standing at the far end of the hall. He fired at Jack again.

Jack grabbed for the gun as a bullet whizzed over his head. His fingers closed around the gun's handle.

The floor next to Jack splintered as a bullet shattered against the wood.

Jack aimed.

Another shot flew high over Jack's head.

Jack fired.

The shot slammed into the man's chest.

Jack fired again.

The second hit close to the first.

As the man started to crumple to the floor, Jack was already running. His head was on a swivel, and he tried to pick up any sound over the ringing in his ears. He reached the body and crouched low. He kept his gun trained on the staircase where the three men had gone.

He gulped in air and let out a low growl.

Calm down.

He fought to steady his breathing as he waited.

Listen.

The only sounds were his breathing and the ringing in his ears.

Jack took the clip out of the pistol and grabbed a fresh one off the man at his feet. He couldn't help but notice the bandage on the man's forearm.

Jack stood up and slapped the clip in place.

Two on this floor. Three up top.

He sprinted toward the staircase, hoping to come at the three from the back.

46

YOU DON'T KNOW JACK

Replacement ran down the hallway to Pierce's bedroom with the others. Lydia looked ready to hyperventilate, and Bruce was even worse. Replacement thought the possibility of him having a heart attack right then was high.

Pierce stopped at the door. "Go in. Go in," Pierce yelled, waving everyone inside.

Replacement helped Lydia and Bruce inside, but Roger struggled to force Phillip through the door.

"We need to run!" Phillip said. "We can escape into the woods."

"No. We stick to Jack's plan," Replacement said. "They could've sent someone around to watch that side. They'll shoot us before we reach the—"

Before she could finish, Phillip ripped one hand out of his bonds and punched Roger in the face. Roger stumbled back, and Phillip turned and bolted down the hall.

"Let him go," Replacement said to Pierce, who looked ready to take off after him. "We need to protect ourselves."

Nodding, Pierce came into the room and locked the door behind him.

"Can you guys help me move this bed in front of the door?" Replacement was pushing against the giant bed, but it didn't budge.

"Come on, Roger." Pierce grabbed the bed frame and heaved. It still barely moved. Even when Roger joined in, the bed slid very, very slowly.

"Phillip was right. We should run," Roger said, still pushing.

"They'll gun us down," Pierce said.

"The police will be here in ten minutes," Replacement snarled.

"We are so dead," Roger muttered.

Bruce let out a loud growl and slammed his body against the bed. Like a linebacker plowing through the offense, he kept his feet moving.

At last, the bed slid in front of the door.

"This belly's good for something." Bruce panted as he leaned against the wall.

"What about Jack?" Lydia asked.

"He'll come up by the back entrance," Replacement said. She opened the side door and peered down. The tiny staircase was narrow and dark. It ran straight to the outside wall of the house and then took a sharp corner.

"If we need to escape that way," Pierce said, "the stairs will put us right next to a rear exit from the house."

"How far to the woods?" Replacement asked.

"At least fifty yards. All open grass."

Replacement glanced at Bruce and Lydia and shook her head. "We'd never make it."

"We could try!" Roger said. "We're dead if we stay here. There're five guys out there." His hands went to the sides of his head. "What's your boyfriend going to do against *that*?"

Replacement grinned. "You don't know Jack."

She held her phone to her ear. The 911 dispatcher was still on, calling out to her. "Miss? Are you still there? The police are on their way. Miss?"

"I'm here. We've barricaded ourselves in a bedroom on the second floor. It's at the far right if you're facing the house."

"How many of you are in the room?"

"Five."

"Are you all currently okay?"

"Yes, but my boyfriend went to—"

"Tell him to stay in the room."

"He's already out there—" Replacement's voice cracked. She felt her eyes start to burn.

"You need to get him back. Stay where you are until the police—"

The bedroom doorknob turned, and the door rattled. Lydia gasped and stepped backward.

Something heavy slammed into the door. The wood creaked, but the door held.

There was a pause. Metal scraped against metal.

Then a distinct chopping sound echoed throughout the room.

"The police are on their way!" Replacement bellowed at the door. "They'll be here any minute!"

The tip of an axe sliced through the door. A chunk of wood flew across the room.

"We have to run!" Roger shrieked.

"What do we do, Alice?" Bruce looked at her.

Replacement rushed to the side door and ripped it open. "Everyone out," she ordered. "Go!"

Bruce and Roger dashed through, but Lydia stood frozen in place.

Pierce grabbed her shoulders. "Lydia, you have to move. Follow me."

The axe came through the door again. The hole was getting larger.

"Now!" Pierce grabbed Lydia by the hand and ran for the door.

Replacement dashed after them. As she grabbed the door to pull it closed, she looked back.

The barrel of a gun poked through the hole in the door.

Replacement pulled the door shut and darted down the stairs.

Gunshots filled the air behind her.

47

ACHILLES

Jack found Phillip's body in the upstairs hallway, lying in a pool of blood. Jack didn't bother to check his pulse; the man was clearly dead.

He stepped over the body and began sprinting.

When Jack rounded the corner toward Pierce's bedroom, he saw three men shoving open Pierce's broken bedroom door. Two men ran into the bedroom but the third turned to confront Jack. He was a huge man and held an enormous double-headed axe in his hands.

"Freeze!" Jack stopped and aimed.

The huge man dropped the axe and reached for his gun.

Jack fired.

The first round slammed into the man's chest. Jack expected the round to stop him, but instead the man groaned and took a step back.

Damn. He's wearing a vest.

Jack aimed for the man's head and pulled the trigger.

The shot went wide.

He pulled the trigger again.

Nothing happened.

Jack could see the slide on the gun wasn't fully back. It had double fed on his last shot. He knew there was no way to clear the jam on his gun in time. He sprinted toward the closest door to duck out of danger. The door was a good ten feet away, ahead on his left.

The man pointed his gun at Jack.

Jack let out a battle cry as he charged, praying that somehow the man would miss.

The man pulled the trigger.

Click.

The man tossed the gun aside. He hefted the battle axe with both hands.

Jack was trained to fight people using many weapons, and he had. He had faced people with guns, knives, and pipes. But a medieval axe... that was new.

The man swung. He aimed to cut Jack in half at the waist. His arms were long and the axe was longer. The heavy blade swung in a huge arc.

Jack's muscles burned as he stopped his forward momentum. The blade passed just in front of his stomach.

The head of the axe drove into the wall and stuck fast.

Jack lunged.

The man might be a giant, but all men have an Achilles' heel.

Jack punched him in the throat.

The man let go of the axe handle and staggered back.

Jack's foot drove into the side of the man's knee.

Cartilage snapped. The man turned sideways as he dropped to his knees. But he wasn't defeated. He pulled an enormous knife from his boot.

Howling in rage, Jack grabbed the giant Russian's head and slammed his face into the wall.

The man's body slumped to the floor.

Jack roared. The windows shook. One thought cut through the rage that swirled inside him.

Alice.

The giant's discarded gun lay next to a broken piece of the bedroom door. Jack picked it up. He ripped a fresh clip from the man's belt, slapped it into place, pushed his way through what was left of Pierce's bedroom door, and charged down the stairs.

48

RUN

Replacement wanted to move faster down the staircase but had to slow down because of Lydia. The older woman was bawling and stumbling. Pierce wrapped his arm around her and kept her moving forward.

At the bottom of the stairs was a door that led to the main front hallway. Another door stood on the right. Roger opened it, and Replacement saw the yard and woods beyond.

"Should we go?" Bruce panted.

"I'm running for it." Roger broke into a loping sprint for the tree line.

"Go!" Replacement pushed the staircase door shut, but not before she heard someone ripping the door upstairs open. "RUN!" she screamed.

Her throat tightened, and she gulped in air. The others ran across the yard. Lydia tripped and fell. Bruce turned back to help Pierce lift her up.

Replacement didn't follow. She knew they'd never reach the tree line before the men saw them.

Not unless she did something to slow the men down.

Or led them in another direction.

She shut the outside door, then sprinted down the hallway. She could hear footsteps pounding down the stairs. She stopped when she reached a corner, took the case out of her pocket, and watched over her shoulder.

Nicholai and Luka burst through the staircase door. Replacement paused only long enough to be sure they'd seen her.

Then she bolted.

And just in time. A bullet hit the wall just behind her.

But now she was sprinting down the long straightaway. Her legs were a blur. She kept her eyes focused ahead. She reached the carpeted area and the patter of her footsteps vanished. Her breathing sped up, and she pushed harder.

She dashed past the front door and chanced a look behind.

A thin man had just come around the corner.

As Replacement continued toward the other end of the house, she gasped. Up ahead, two bodies lay on the floor.

The window next to her exploded. The huge sheet of glass fell and sprayed her with pieces as it shattered. The echo of the gunshot filled the hallway.

Replacement just kept running.

Her eyes scanned the corpses. She fought to straighten out her stride. Black hair. Jeans. She couldn't see their faces.

Another shot zipped by her head.

It's not Jack, she realized, and a surge of relief poured through her veins. She leapt past the bodies.

The kitchen was just ahead on her left. She'd have to barricade herself in the pantry—

Pain ripped through her as a bullet hit her.

Replacement screamed. It felt as if someone had struck her with a bat. She started to twist. Her right leg landed, but she couldn't bring her left around. Her legs tangled together. Her arms shot out in front of her, but she was spinning. Somehow she made it into the kitchen, stumbling to the opposite wall, before she crashed down onto the tile on her side.

Her head smacked the floor hard. The kitchen lights seemed to burst into one bright light.

49

LIGHT IS MIGHT

Jack took the steps three at a time and slammed into the door at the bottom of the stairs. The door opened only half an inch before it hit something. Peering through, Jack saw that a cabinet had been knocked over in front of the door, and was jammed between the door and the wall. He wouldn't be able to shove it aside.

He stepped back and kicked out the left top panel of the door. The right panel broke out with one kick too, but the middle brace was solid. Jack set his foot against the staircase and thrust hard.

The wood shattered.

Far away, toward the other side of the house, he heard gunshots. Jack dove through the hole and scrambled to his feet.

A door next to Jack, a door to the outside, flew open. Jack's gun snapped up.

Pierce froze.

Jack exhaled. His gun was aimed at Pierce's face. "Where's Alice?" Jack asked.

"She didn't come with us. I came back to find her."

Jack sprinted down the hallway, toward the sound of the gunshots. Pierce ran after him.

They raced down the length of the house. Past the main entrance. Past the two bodies on the floor.

In the kitchen, two men stood at the far wall. But Jack barely saw them. His gaze flew to the body at their feet.

Alice.

One of the men fired. The bullet whizzed by Jack's ear.

Jack pressed himself against the wall. At the same time, he reached back and slammed Pierce out of the way.

Two more shots rang out.

"Back," Jack ordered Pierce.

Jack aimed down the sight of the pistol and leaned out.

Now one of the men was holding Replacement in front of him. She was alive. Tears ran down her face. She grabbed at the huge man's arm as her feet dangled off the floor.

"Let her go." Jack's hand was rock steady as he aimed at the man's head. The shot would be extremely dangerous even if he were using his own gun; with a gun that he'd never fired before, he knew he could easily hit her.

The second man fired, and Jack was forced to duck back out of the way.

Bullets slammed into wood across the hall from the kitchen. Some pinged off metal in the kitchen, the echo of the shots ringing like little bells.

Then he heard a man shout, "Get the door, Luka."

Jack leaned back out.

The kitchen had its own side exit, and the second man, Luka, had opened the door. Replacement's captor was backing toward the door, carrying Replacement in front of himself as a shield.

Jack stepped forward. "Let her go or I swear I'll kill you both."

"Stand down!" the man ordered. "Stay back or you'll give me a reason to kill her."

"Nicholai! Let's go," Luka yelled. He stepped outside after Luka, and Luka slammed the door shut behind them.

Jack growled at Pierce. "The garage." He ripped out his phone as they both turned and sprinted back the way they came.

Jack called the direct line for police dispatch.

"Darrington Pol—"

"Beverly, it's Jack Stratton. There's been a kidnapping at the Bellmore estate."

"We have every car already en route."

"They're driving now. Two armed men have a female hostage. Stop all traffic on Reservoir and Pine Ridge. North and south."

"Got it. Contacting Fairfield PD too."

They raced into the garage and Pierce grabbed the keys to the Porsche from the key box.

"I'll drive," Jack said. "Take my gun."

Pierce shook his head. "I'll drive. I don't know how to shoot."

"What?"

Pierce jumped into the driver's seat, and Jack swore as he jumped into the passenger side. Pierce pinned it. Tires squealed, and the Porsche flew out of the garage and down the driveway, past the guardhouse.

Jack looked both ways on the long, empty road. There was no sign of a car. "Head north." He pointed.

Pierce cut the wheel, snapped on the headlights, and punched it.

"You lose her, and I'll shoot you," Jack snarled.

"That's helpful," Pierce muttered.

The Porsche surged down the road. The trees whipped by. Jack craned his neck to try to see anything on the winding road ahead.

They approached a fork in the road. "Which way?" Pierce asked.

Jack pointed left. "Pine Ridge. It runs above Reservoir Road. We can see both roads from there."

"But Reservoir is faster."

"It's not faster than the Porsche. Punch it," Jack said.

Pierce turned left. The engine hummed as he flew around the corners and navigated the turns.

"We have to stop them before they pass the lake," Jack said. "After that, it's a maze of roads. And once they don't have a need for her…"

Pierce nodded. He slammed the gas pedal down.

Trees became a blur. Speed whipped the air between the guardrail and the car into an eerie cry that filled the car.

"I see the car!" Jack pointed to the road below them. "And there's a connector road ahead."

Pierce pushed the car, and its performance engine hummed. The dials flew up.

"The connector's coming up," Jack warned. "Slow down."

The road dipped at the turn. The tires screeched as Pierce hit the brakes. The screeching stopped only because the Porsche had left the tar.

The car landed hard and slid down onto Reservoir Road.

Pierce jammed down the gas and cut the wheel. The guardrail kept the car from hitting the rocks, but the whole car rocked as it slammed against it. Pieces of metal and plastic flew into the air, along with a shower of sparks. Pierce fought to straighten out.

Sparks stopped flying behind the Porsche as the rear quarter panel finally ripped free. The kidnappers' sedan had disappeared around a turn up ahead.

Jack undid his seat belt and checked the pistol.

"You can't shoot," Pierce said. "You could hit Alice."

"I won't."

"You *could*. We should do that PIT maneuver."

"You don't know it."

"I do." Pierce flew into the turn. "I told you I raced stock cars. It's just like a bump and run."

"This car's too light."

"It makes up for weight in power. Bruce Lee: light is might."

Jack looked down at the pistol. "If it starts to go wrong, I'm shooting the tires."

Pierce nodded.

The other car came into view. Like a fighter jet, the Porsche glided into place behind it.

50

THE MOTHER BEAR

Replacement kept her eyes closed as she lay stretched out on the back seat. Her hip burned. She flexed her toes. Her hand rested on her thigh, and she felt her blood-soaked pants. The bullet had struck her in the fleshy part of her butt.

Replacement examined the rest of her body. Besides her head pounding, everything else felt fine. But when she tried to move her leg, pain racked her body and her teeth clacked together.

"Headlights behind us," Nicholai said.

"They're coming fast."

She heard Luka pull on the front seat and guessed that he was hovering right over her, peering out the back window.

"That's no police car," Luka said.

Replacement tensed. She tried not to cry out as pain ripped down her leg.

"It's a Porsche." Luka continued to peer over the seat.

"They're almost on us," Nicholai said.

The sound of metal on metal clicked from up front.

"There are two people in the car. It's the men from the kitchen." Luka sat back down.

Replacement bit her lip as the confirmation that Jack was coming for her washed over her.

"Shoot them," Nicholai ordered coldly.

Something in Replacement snapped. The thought of these two animals shooting at Jack flipped some switch. Like a mother bear, she felt a need to protect him. It overran all other thoughts.

She jumped up and grabbed Luka's hair with both hands.

He screamed with a mixture of shock and pain.

She howled in rage and smashed Luka's head into the passenger side window.

Nicholai swore and reached for her.

The car swerved.

Replacement didn't let go of Luka's hair. She pulled his head back and then smashed it into the passenger window again.

Luka's gun tumbled to the floor.

Nicholai swung at her.

Her shoulder took some of the impact, but his fist continued up and hit the side of her head. Her left hand pulled free of Luka's head, yanking out a huge clump of his hair.

Replacement's vision blurred. But she still held Luka's head with her other hand. And all she could think about was him shooting Jack.

The pain in her thigh completely forgotten, she planted her right leg against the back seat and thrust forward as hard as she could. Her body dove over the front seat, and she smashed Luka's face into the dashboard.

Luka went limp.

Nicholai's fist came down like a sledgehammer in the middle of Replacement's back.

She screamed. Her arms and legs went out, and she collapsed on top of Luka.

Nicholai raised his arm again.

Metal ground together. The car groaned.

Nicholai swore and grabbed the wheel with both hands.

Tires screeched.

Above it all, Replacement heard her name being screamed by the man she loved.

51

NOT ALONE

"ALICE!"

Pierce had pulled up to the left of the sedan, and now he slammed the Porsche into it. Jack was thrown into the passenger side door. The windshield shattered. The Porsche's front quarter panel buckled.

Pierce's forearms strained, and he jammed the gas to the floor.

The sedan broke free, then it swung back and smashed the Porsche. The impact pushed the Porsche to the left. Pieces of the Porsche's front bumper crashed against the windshield. The right front tire blew.

Nicholai pulled away, but he cut back too far right. The sedan swerved straight for the guardrail that separated the road from a steep drop-off toward the lake.

The heavy car plowed right through it.

It disappeared over the edge.

The Porsche spun one hundred and eighty degrees. Pierce jammed on the brakes. The Porsche slammed into the guardrail on the opposite side of the road and slid down it.

Before it even came to a stop, Jack was slamming himself against the door, trying to open it, but it was wedged closed. Jack grabbed the roof of the car and pulled himself out the window. He ran across the hood and jumped to the ground. He raced past twisted pieces of metal and shattered glass as he sprinted across the road to the spot where the sedan had disappeared.

And he saw it.

The car had landed upright, fifteen feet out in the lake. Steam roared from the engine. The car's front end had started to sink.

Jack took two long strides, planted his foot on the guardrail, and jumped feet first. The water wrapped around him and he was plunged into darkness. He stretched his legs out, feeling for the bottom, but he didn't hit ground.

His head broke the surface and he swam to the rear of the car. He pulled himself along the side of the car to the passenger door, and looked inside.

Nicholai was slumped, motionless, over the steering wheel. Replacement was lying on top of Luka. She was conscious, but struggling to move.

"ALICE!" Jack pulled on the car door. Metal groaned as he wrenched it open.

"JACK!" Replacement tried to lift herself up, screamed, and fell back down.

There was a loud splash from the rear of the car.

Jack grabbed Replacement, and she wrapped her arms around him. He pulled her forward, and she screamed again. "My leg! It's stuck."

A blast of steam poured out of the dash. Jack shielded her face.

Pierce swam up next to Jack. Water was now pouring into the car; it was sinking rapidly.

"Where's it stuck?" Jack yelled.

"Next to the seat." Replacement was now barely keeping her head above the water.

Pierce pulled open the back door and moved into the back seat while Jack reached down to feel Replacement's leg. It was wedged fast between the seat and the frame of the car.

Jack pulled up on her leg, and she screamed.

"Can you get it from there?" Jack shouted to Pierce.

"I'm trying!"

Pierce pulled.

Replacement cried out.

The car listed toward the driver side. Water lapped at Replacement's mouth.

"Take a deep breath!" Jack shouted.

Replacement inhaled.

Jack filled his lungs with air just as water washed over them.

Jack started to pray.

Green eyes searched Jack's through the murky water as the car sank beneath the surface. The dashboard lights flickered and died, and darkness swept over them.

Desperation poured through Jack. It was as if Alice were being devoured by some beast. She had disappeared into the void, but not before he saw the look of sheer terror in her eyes.

He knew he couldn't save her.

He knew she was going to die.

But he knew that if she did, it wouldn't be alone.

Jack pulled his legs up and pressed them against the seat. He jammed his back into the dash and heaved.

All the air was being forced from his lungs as he pushed. He didn't care. He kept going.

Even underwater, he heard the metal grind.

Suddenly, Replacement started to pull herself up—and he knew she was free.

Jack wrapped his arms around her waist and swam for the surface.

As he pulled away from the car, he felt a hand grab his ankle. *The oaf in the front seat. Luka.* Jack kicked and broke the man's hold.

He swam hard. His right arm pulled down, and his legs kicked furiously. When his head broke the surface of the water, with Replacement beside him, they both gasped for breath.

A second later, Pierce appeared.

"Take her," Jack yelled.

Replacement coughed and shook her head.

"The guy down there is alive," Jack said.

"I'll go," Pierce offered.

Jack shook his head.

Pierce wrapped his arm around Replacement.

"Keep her safe," Jack growled.

Replacement reached out for him, but Pierce had already started to swim for shore.

Jack took three deep breaths and dove. He swam hard as he tried to keep the picture of the car in his mind. Bubbles floated past him, but he couldn't see anything below.

His hand hit the roof. He could feel the open door. Reaching in, he felt the body in the passenger seat.

Jack grabbed an arm and pulled, but Luka was stuck. Jack felt himself starting to rise, so he pulled himself partway into the car.

Just then the sedan finally hit bottom, and the car started to roll. The door hit Jack's back, pinning him inside, as the car inverted. At last it came to rest on its roof.

Jack couldn't see. He knew his eyes were open, but everything around him was a black void.

This is what hell will be like.

Jack gripped Luka's wrist tightly and braced his feet on the side of the car.

He pulled Luka free.

Wrapping his arm around the man's chest, Jack pushed off. Pulling with one arm and kicking as hard as he could, he struggled with the limp body.

Once again he broke the surface.

Pierce was swimming toward him.

Jack pulled Luka toward shore. The man wasn't breathing. His face was blue.

Pierce grabbed Luka's shoulder while Jack held the other one. Together they carried the man to the bank, where Replacement waited, lying on her back on the pebbly sand.

Jack stumbled out of the water and toward Replacement. He sank to his knees. She grabbed him, and he cradled her face in his hands.

Her green eyes filled with tears.

He pressed his forehead against hers.

Jack looked back to the water. "The driver." He panted as he started to rise.

Replacement grabbed his shirt. "You can't save everyone."

"We haven't saved this one yet," Pierce called out. "I need a hand."

Jack staggered over and knelt down next to Luka's body. They both started CPR. As Jack did chest compressions, Pierce did mouth-to-mouth.

Then Pierce sat up and turned Luka's head to the side.

Luka threw up.

Jack staggered to his feet and looked out at the water.

Pierce grabbed his arm. "She's right."

Replacement cried out.

Jack ran over to her. He saw the blood on her jeans.

"I got shot." She grimaced.

Jack grabbed the waist of her jeans, and her hand clamped over his. She shook her head.

"I have to see how bad it is," he said. Jack looked at Pierce, and he turned around. Jack pulled down her jeans, trying not to notice the grimace of pain on Replacement's features as he did so, and then examined the wound. "It looks like a through-and-through."

"A what-and-what?" Replacement asked through gritted teeth.

"It went straight through your left butt cheek."

"Will it scar?"

"Who's going to see it?"

"You should put pressure on the wound," Pierce said.

"Turn around." Jack glared.

"Stop it, Jack," Replacement said. "I don't care who sees my butt as long as it stops hurting."

Jack pressed his hand against the wound.

For the entire time until the ambulance arrived, Replacement let fly a steady stream of swears and tears.

52

I NEED TO TELL YOU SOMETHING

The next day, Jack paced back and forth outside Replacement's hospital room. He had a bouquet of Christmas roses tightly clutched in his hand. He wanted to talk to her, but now wasn't the time. He had no idea what he was going to say to her anyway. His eyes were dark and bloodshot. He hadn't slept. Every time he'd tried to sleep, he'd just heard her talking to Pierce.

The door to her room opened, and a nurse walked out and held the door open. "She's all set."

"Thanks." Jack started to go through the door, but the nurse held up a hand.

"She's on a morphine drip. She's a little loopy."

Jack nodded as he entered.

Replacement was propped up in the bed and grinning from ear to ear. Her smile widened when she saw him. "Hey, baby." She saw the flowers in his hand, and her eyes filled with tears.

"I ran across the street to the florist."

"You haven't gone home?" Her lip trembled.

"I called Mrs. Stevens. She and Lady are fine."

Replacement shifted her position and winced. "But what about you? Are you getting any sleep? You look terrible."

Jack held out the flowers. "I'm good."

"No, you're not."

"They're Christmas roses."

"They're my favorite, but I'm worried about you."

Jack exhaled. "Don't be."

"I need to tell you something." Her lips mashed together.

He stood up straighter.

"It's about Pierce. I gave it a lot of thought, but I wanted to talk to you first."

"Alice… we don't have to do this now. Let's wait until you're home."

She shook her head. "No. I need to get this over with. Well… while we were working on the house, Pierce and I worked together a lot."

Jack's chest tightened.

"He kept asking me ideas and such and… he kinda… he asked me to go to California."

Jack swallowed. "What did you say?"

"I told him I wanted to talk it over with you. What do you think about it?"

Jack scowled. "What do I think about it?"

She made a face. "Yeah? Do you think it could work? I never thought I'd have a chance like this."

Jack didn't answer. He scowled.

"I didn't think you'd get mad."

"What did you think I'd get?"

"I thought you'd be happy for me."

"Happy for you?" Jack's hands shot up. "What the hell are you talking about? You're leaving me, and I should be happy?"

"What? I'd never leave you."

"You just said you're going to California."

"No, I said I had to talk to you about it. Pierce said you could come."

"Wait. Is this the drugs talking?"

Replacement shut one eye. "Huh?"

"Look, I'm doing everything to keep from going medieval here. I just want to throw Pierce out the window and take you home. I know you have feelings for Pierce. You wanted to wait to tell me until after we caught the bad guys. Well, just get it over with, and tell me."

Replacement bit her bottom lip. "I have no idea what you're talking about."

Jack crossed his arms. "You and Pierce."

"What about me and Pierce?"

Jack glared out the window. "I heard."

"Heard? What?"

"The morning you went in to talk to Pierce in his bedroom." Jack walked close to the bed and gazed down at her. "You left your phone next to the bed."

Her lip curled. "You're right. I'm on some serious drugs, so you have to spell it out for me. I'm lost."

"You said you had feelings for Pierce."

"I what?" She made a face as if someone had poked her in the eye. "I didn't. I don't. I'd never say that."

Jack shook his head. "I heard you. You said you 'wanted him.' That you didn't care about the house or cars or—"

"I wasn't talking about *me*!" Replacement's head wobbled from side to side. "Wait a minute. Are you saying while we had Pierce on surveillance you heard what I said?"

"I wasn't eavesdropping. I hung up."

"Probably too soon. And you never told me?"

"I'm telling you now."

"Why didn't you tell me then?"

"Five guys came to kill us. Remember that? I got a little busy. And now you're telling me you're running off with him."

"What?"

A knock on the door interrupted them. Pierce walked in with a vase of flowers in his hands and a smile on his face. But that smile vanished when he looked at Jack's and Replacement's faces.

"If this is a bad time..."

"No," Replacement said. "It's a perfect time."

"No, it's not. Just give us a minute," Jack said.

"No, come in. Ask him." Replacement's hands went out. "Just ask Pierce."

"We'll talk about it privately."

Replacement blew a raspberry. "Right now I'm on some stuff that makes me feel all whoo-hoo, so it's now or never." She looked at Jack and blinked rapidly.

Jack stood up to his full height and faced Pierce. "I overheard when you and Alice were talking in your bedroom."

Replacement smacked her forehead with her hand. "I didn't mean talk to him about *that*. We can talk about that privately."

Jack turned back to her. "What did you want me to talk to him about then?"

"The job."

"What job?" Jack rubbed his face.

"I told her to discuss it with you," Pierce said. "I offered her a job. You too, Jack. Security."

Jack rubbed his eyes with his thumb and index finger.

Pierce's eyes went wide. "Wait, you could see us over the tablet's camera?"

Jack nodded.

Pierce held up a hand. "Nothing happened. Could you hear too?"

Jack glared.

"Did I, in any way, give you the impression I had feelings for you?" Replacement asked.

"No." Pierce dragged the word out while he shook his head. "It was the opposite, actually. You just talked about Jack."

Replacement crossed her arms. "See." She nodded, and her eyes rolled around in her head. "Oh, boy… that made me dizzy. Do you believe me now?"

"Wait a second. You offered her a job?"

"It's a computer job," Pierce explained. "But it's out in California. I know Leon would love to have you on his team too, Jack."

"I can't believe you thought that." Replacement looked at Jack. "I mean… after all we've been through…" Her lip trembled.

Jack reached out and took her hand. "Alice. I'm sorry. I shouldn't have doubted you."

"No, you shouldn't have." She pouted. "And I got shot."

The doctor knocked on the door. "Good morning." She smiled as she walked in. "Speaking of you being shot, I need to give you a quick checkup."

Two nurses came in as well. They looked at Jack and Pierce. "She'll need some privacy," one said.

Pierce set down his vase of flowers. "Feel better."

"Can I get you anything?" Jack asked.

Replacement's shoulders crept up sheepishly. "A steak and cheese?"

53

THE BIGGEST REQUIREMENT

Two Days Later

Jack stood in Pierce's upstairs living room and looked out over the lake. The sky was bright blue, and the water flashed white and gold. He smiled. Life wasn't perfect, but it was good.

Pierce strode into the room and walked over to him. "I want to thank you, Jack." He held out a check.

Jack took it and put it in his pocket.

Pierce chuckled. "You're not even going to look at it?"

"Nope."

"Okay. One last magic trick. Why?"

"Because you're a good man." Jack offered his hand.

Pierce hesitated, then clasped Jack's hand. "There's more to that answer."

"You're a fair man. You could be overly generous, but you're smart and know if you offer too much I won't take it. So you wrote the check for what you think Alice and I would accept. I know the check's going to be way more than what I'd ask for, so I'm not going to look. That way I won't feel guilty telling Alice I kept it."

Pierce laughed. "Are you both sure you won't reconsider my job offers?"

Jack shook his head. "We're very grateful, but our minds are made up." Jack's smile vanished. "Actually, I came out here for another reason, too."

"What was that?"

"They didn't find the driver."

Pierce straightened up.

"Last night, a couple with a house near South Pond came home from vacation. Someone had broken into the house, and their car was gone. The guy changed clothes while he was there. They had me take a look at the ones he left behind. They were his."

Pierce looked out over the lake. "I'll inform Leon. What about you and Alice?"

"We'll be fine. The guy had a target. I figure he'll cut his losses and keep going."

"I'm sure Leon will double security." Pierce cleared his throat. "There's an additional matter that I need to mention. I hope you won't think I overstepped."

Jack raised an eyebrow. "That depends."

"I was speaking with Mayor Lewis about a donation for a civic project. I happened to mention I was going to apply for a license to carry, but my instructor had his taken away." Pierce eyed Jack. "I tend to think they'll be rectifying that oversight shortly."

"Thank you for overstepping."

"No problem."

"So, an instructor? Do you want to go to the range?"

"If I'm going to spend any more time in quiet, nothing-ever-happens Darrington, I think I should learn."

Jack smiled at Pierce. "You asked me once about skydiving."

Pierce nodded.

"I didn't answer you because I don't like to talk about my time in the service." Jack turned to the window. "I served with Alice's brother, Chandler. He was my best friend... He died. I still feel like it was my fault."

"I guess you and I are a lot alike."

"I don't have any easy answers, Pierce, but I realized something when we went after those guys."

Pierce looked at the floor.

"If you'd died, would you have blamed me?" Jack asked.

Pierce thought for a moment. "No. And if it was reversed, you wouldn't hold me accountable."

"No. I would." Jack smiled. "I'd be ticked."

Pierce laughed. "Thanks."

Jack laughed too.

"What was that?" Pierce rubbed his eyes. "For a minute there, I thought you were trying to make me feel better about Tyler."

Jack stopped laughing. "I'd be mad as hell at first, but... if I really think about it, I wouldn't blame you. I'm just saying, I know Chandler wouldn't ever hold it against me. I don't know Tyler, but I know he chose to push you out of the way. From what I've seen of you, you would've done the same for him."

Pierce's face turned stern. "I didn't."

"You were busy getting pushed. But it doesn't matter."

"It does matter." Pierce's voice rose. "I'm here. He's not."

"Yeah. You know what Chandler would tell me? I'm glad you made it. Keep going. Live. Do you ever talk to Tyler?"

Pierce's mouth opened and closed. Jack watched as myriad emotions crossed his face. "Yeah. I apologize almost every night."

"I did the same thing for years. Do yourself a favor tonight. Listen."

"What?"

"Stop doing all the talking and listen to him."

Pierce's hand turned into a fist.

Jack shook his head. "I hated myself so much that I didn't want to think about what Chandler would say to me. I just wanted to keep on hating me. Blaming me. Tyler didn't save you for that. If you let him talk... I think that's what he'll say."

Pierce nodded slowly. "Thanks for that."

"Sure." Jack looked back out the window at the lake. His throat tightened as he thought about Replacement in the car sinking beneath the water. "I also want to thank you for saving Alice."

"That was all you."

Jack exhaled.

"You're a very blessed man, Jack Stratton."

Jack saw the angst in his eyes. "I can't even think about how long I'd have to work to pay off your Porsche."

Pierce shrugged. "They're customizing another for me now."

"Hard life."

Pierce's eyes connected with Jack's. "I have it good." Pierce smiled, but Jack could tell he didn't mean it.

Jack walked over to the far wall and looked at the huge mural that hung there. "So," Jack said. "How much longer will you be here?"

Pierce shook his head. "With everything that happened, I got sucked right back into work. I haven't even had any vacation time. I'm tempted to take another two weeks."

"You like art, right?"

Pierce nodded. "It's another interest of mine."

"I know this quiet place. Real peaceful," Jack said.

"You've been there, and it's still quiet?"

Jack laughed. "It's called Hope Falls. I have a friend there who could show you around."

"What's there to do in Hope Falls?"

Jack looked back at the painting and his lips pressed into a faint smile. "There's something about the town."

"You've piqued my interest. Why did you ask if I like art?"

"That's the biggest requirement." Jack grinned.

54

IF ANYONE ASKS

TWO WEEKS LATER

Jack held the door open to the small diner he and Alice liked to frequent. Replacement awkwardly navigated her way in on her crutches.

"Hi, Jack. Alice." The waitress smiled, grabbed two menus, and led them to a corner table. "I'll bring you coffee."

"Thanks, Debbie."

Jack took Replacement's crutches and leaned them against the wall. "You good?"

Replacement grinned. "My butt feels better."

Jack smiled.

"Figures I get shot there." She rolled her eyes. "If anyone asks, say I got shot in the hip."

Jack shrugged. "Shot is shot."

"No." Replacement made a face. "Listen to the difference." She cleared her throat and then lowered her voice. "So, where'd you get shot?" She held up her hand. "I could say: I took one in the hip."

Jack nodded. "That sounds cool."

"Or, I could say: Gee," her voice went way up, "I got shot in the butt."

Jack laughed. "Okay. I'll say hip. Have you talked to Gerald?"

"He's doing great. He's home and has a ton of jobs lined up. He offered me some work too."

"We're fine with money. You should rest."

Debbie came over with their coffee. "Pancakes and sausage?" she asked Replacement.

"Blueberry." Replacement smiled.

"Steak, medium, and three scrambled?" Debbie asked Jack.

Jack winked.

Replacement quietly stirred her coffee. "I didn't tell you something."

Jack raised an eyebrow.

"Pierce offered us money for catching Nancy and Sophia."

"And?"

"He offered a reward for catching Phillip and the others, too."

Jack waited.

Replacement looked nervous. "I turned it down."

Jack shrugged.

"Seriously? I thought you'd be at least a little upset I turned it down."

"Well, I don't think you should've turned it down. Pierce is loaded."

"But we didn't do it for the money."

"Actually, we did. He hired us, remember?"

Replacement nodded. "So you think I should've taken it?"

"Yes."

She sighed. "I'd feel stupid asking for it now." She gave him a please-do-this-for-me-because-I-really-don't-want-to smile.

Jack pointed at himself. "Now you want *me* to do it?"

"It would be better."

"No."

"You won't?"

He wondered how long he should leave her dangling on the line. "Actually, Pierce already talked to me about it." He grinned roguishly.

Replacement flicked a sugar packet at him. "Jerk. You should've told me you turned him down, too."

"I didn't."

Her mouth fell open. "You took the money?"

"Of course I did. He hired us. A worker's worthy of his wages."

"Well." She kept her eyes downward. "How much?"

"He was very generous. Two hundred and fifty."

Replacement let out her breath. "Oh, that was nice of him. You need some new clothes, and your sneakers are about to fall apart."

Jack grinned. "I said he was generous. Two hundred and fifty *thousand*."

Replacement almost spit out her coffee. "Dollars?"

Jack nodded.

"That's way too much."

"We caught seven people."

"Jack." She set down the coffee cup. "Really? Two hundred and fifty thousand?"

He smiled.

So did she.

"Wow. That was beyond nice of him." Her smile faded.

"What's the matter?" Jack asked.

She pinched her lips together, and her shoulders popped up and down.

He put both elbows on the table and stared at her.

"Fine. It's Pierce. I just feel bad for him," she admitted.

"I'm sure he's not crying himself to sleep on a pile of money."

Replacement scowled. "He's all alone in that huge house. He needs somebody. I wish there was someone we could hook him up with."

Debbie brought over their breakfasts.

Replacement bowed her head. "Dear God—"

She stopped when Jack's hand closed over hers. "Dear God," Jack said. "Thank you for keeping Alice safe. In Jesus's name, we pray."

"Amen. You need to switch up your prayer." Replacement picked up the syrup.

"Huh?"

"You've been saying thank you for keeping me safe so much it sounds like that's the only thing you care about." She giggled and grabbed her fork.

"Well, I guess I really mean it. Why did you get blueberry pancakes this time?"

"I was thinking about Hope Falls. Do you remember the pancakes? So good."

"Funny you mentioned Hope Falls."

"Why?"

"I was thinking about it too. When I was talking to Pierce. With everything that happened, he still hasn't had that vacation. His house needs to get repaired, so I thought he might want to go to a really quiet town."

"Hope Falls? Seriously? That's awesome. Maybe your grandmother could show him around. Or maybe Kristine?" Replacement's eyes went wide, and her mouth fell open. Her lips slowly pressed together, and she gazed at Jack.

"Yeah, I thought Marisa might make a great tour guide."

Tears appeared in the corners of her eyes, and she grabbed her coffee with both hands. "You're a good man, Jack Stratton."

Jack gave a little shrug.

Replacement's cup clinked off the plate as she set it down. "Aunt Haddie looked good today. And hey!" Replacement leaned forward and her chin jutted out. Her next words came out in a fierce whisper. "Why didn't you tell me that Aunt Haddie talked to you about sleeping with me?"

Jack tilted his head. "I didn't want to put Aunt Haddie under the bus."

"Under the bus? I'm the one who went under the bus. That was the most embarrassed I've ever been."

Jack covered his chuckle with a cough.

"It's not funny. She had me talk to her friends at the home. I was like—Aunt Haddie, I'm twenty. Then she threatened to have your mom call me."

Jack laughed.

Replacement picked her fork back up and pointed it at him. "Not funny. You should've told me that she made you promise not to sleep with me. Now *I* had to promise that I wouldn't sleep with you too. At least with just you promising we could have."

"What? So you think it would've been okay for me to break my promise?"

"You never do what you're told. Aunt Haddie always says that." Replacement's giggle trailed off as the color rose in her cheeks. She stared down at her plate. "We need to work on the whole communication thing, okay?"

Jack shrugged. "Sure."

"I'm serious, Jack." She leveled the butter knife at him. He kiddingly raised his hands. She rolled her eyes and put the knife down. "It's like the whole misunderstanding with Pierce. I'd never hurt you."

"I know." Jack reached out and grabbed her hand. Swallowing down the burn in his chest, he thought for the hundredth time what would have happened if the shot had been higher. He couldn't imagine a world without Alice. "And I hope you know I'd rather cut my arm off than see you hurt. But I think Aunt Haddie's right. We should wait."

"Or," Replacement winked, "we *could* both break our promises…"

Jack's mind raced as Replacement continued to talk. Aunt Haddie's words filled his head. *Marriage.* As panic gripped him, a dozen reasons—reasons why not—flooded his mind.

I'm too young. I'm only twenty-six. That's young, isn't it? He stretched out his body and felt the aches and pains that made him feel like an old man.

"I love you and you love me..." Alice continued.

Money! I have no money to start a family and support them. He pulled out his wallet and saw the deposit slip and its six-digit balance.

I'll lose my space. My independence.

"We've done so well sharing an apartment..."

Time. I just need some more time to think about it because... because...

"You've stopped eating." Replacement put a bite of pancake on her fork. "How're your eggs?"

She raised the bite toward her mouth.

Jack took a deep breath.

"Alice." He leaned forward and put his hand right over hers. "Will you marry me?"

THE END

THE DETECTIVE JACK STRATTON MYSTERY-THRILLER SERIES

The Detective Jack Stratton Mystery-Thriller Series, authored by *Wall Street Journal* bestselling writer Christopher Greyson, has over 5,000 five-star reviews and over one million readers and counting. If you'd love to read another page-turning thriller with mystery, humor, and a dash of romance, pick up the next book in the highly acclaimed series today.

AND THEN SHE WAS GONE

A hometown hero with a heart of gold, Jack Stratton was raised in a whorehouse by his prostitute mother. Jack seemed destined to become another statistic, but now his life has taken a turn for the better. Determined to escape his past, he's headed for a career in law enforcement. When his foster mother asks him to look into a girl's disappearance, Jack quickly gets drawn into a baffling mystery. As Jack digs deeper, everyone becomes a suspect—including himself. Caught between the criminals and the cops, can Jack discover the truth in time to save the girl? Or will he become the next victim?

GIRL JACKED

Guilt has driven a wedge between Jack and the family he loves. When Jack, now a police officer, hears the news that his foster sister Michelle is missing, it cuts straight to his core. The police think she just took off, but Jack knows Michelle would never leave her loved ones behind—like he did. Forced to confront the demons from his past, Jack must take action, find Michelle, and bring her home... or die trying.

JACK KNIFED

Constant nightmares have forced Jack to seek answers about his rough childhood and the dark secrets hidden there. The mystery surrounding Jack's birth father leads Jack to investigate the twenty-seven-year-old murder case in Hope Falls.

JACKS ARE WILD

When Jack's sexy old flame disappears, no one thinks it's suspicious except Jack and one unbalanced witness. Jack feels in his gut that something is wrong. He knows that Marisa has a past, and if it ever caught up with her—it would be deadly. The trail leads him into all sorts of trouble—landing him smack in the middle of an all-out mob war between the Italian Mafia and the Japanese Yakuza.

JACK AND THE GIANT KILLER

Rogue hero Jack Stratton is back in another action-packed, thrilling adventure. While recovering from a gunshot wound, Jack gets a seemingly harmless private investigation job—locate the owner of a lost dog—Jack begrudgingly assists. Little does he know it will place him directly in the crosshairs of a merciless serial killer.

DATA JACK

In this digital age of hackers, spyware, and cyber terrorism—data is more valuable than gold. Thieves plan to steal the keys to the digital kingdom and with this much money at stake, they'll kill for it. Can Jack and Alice (aka Replacement) stop the pack of ruthless criminals before they can *Data Jack?*

JACK OF HEARTS

When his mother and the members of her neighborhood book club ask him to catch the "Orange Blossom Cove Bandit," a small-time thief who's stealing garden gnomes and peace of mind from their quiet retirement community, how can Jack refuse? The peculiar mystery proves to be more than it appears, and things take a deadly turn. Now, Jack finds it's up to him to stop a crazed killer, save his parents, and win the hand of the girl he loves—but if he survives, will it be Jack who ends up with a broken heart?

JACK FROST

Jack has a new assignment: to investigate the suspicious death of a soundman on the hit TV show *Planet Survival.* Jack goes undercover as a security agent where the show is filming on nearby Mount Minuit. Soon trapped on the treacherous peak by a blizzard, a mysterious killer continues to stalk the cast and crew of *Planet Survival.* What started out as a game is now a deadly competition for survival. As the temperature drops and the body count rises, what will get them first? The mountain or the killer?

Hear your favorite characters come to life
in audio versions of the
Detective Jack Stratton Mystery-Thriller Series!
Audio Books now available on Audible!

Novels featuring Jack Stratton in order:
AND THEN SHE WAS GONE
GIRL JACKED
JACK KNIFED
JACKS ARE WILD
JACK AND THE GIANT KILLER
DATA JACK
JACK OF HEARTS
JACK FROST

Psychological Thriller
THE GIRL WHO LIVED

Ten years ago, four people were brutally murdered. One girl lived. As the anniversary of the murders approaches, Faith Winters is released from the psychiatric hospital and yanked back to the last spot on earth she wants to be—her hometown where the slayings took place. Wracked by the lingering echoes of survivor's guilt, Faith spirals into a black hole of alcoholism and wanton self-destruction. Finding no solace at the bottom of a bottle, Faith decides to track down her sister's killer—and then discovers that she's the one being hunted.

Epic Fantasy
PURE OF HEART

Orphaned and alone, rogue-teen Dean Walker has learned how to take care of himself on the rough city streets. Unjustly wanted by the police, he takes refuge within the shadows of the city. When Dean stumbles upon an old man being mugged, he tries to help—only to discover that the victim is anything but helpless and far more than he appears. Together with three friends, he sets out on an epic quest where only the pure of heart will prevail.

ACKNOWLEDGMENTS

Thank you! Thank you for taking the time to read this book. I hope you loved reading it as much as I did writing it. If you did, please leave a review and let your friends know about Jack and Replacement.

Word of mouth is crucial for any author to succeed. If you enjoyed "Data Jack," please consider leaving a review at Amazon, even if it is only a line or two; it would make all the difference and I would appreciate it very much.

I would also like to thank my wife. She's the best wife, mother, and partner in crime any man could have. She is an invaluable content editor and I could not do this without her! My thanks also go out to my family, my fantastic editors—David Gatewood of Lone Trout Editing, Faith Williams of The Atwater Group, and Karen Lawson and Janet Hitchcock of The Proof is in the Reading. My fabulous proofreader—Charlie Wilson of Landmark Editorial. My thanks also go out to my fabulous consultant—Dianne Jones, the unbelievably helpful Beta readers, including Megan Mason, Monica Hale, Francesca Bouvet and Michael Muir, and the two best kids in the world—thanks for all the help Laura and all the jokes Chris!

ABOUT THE AUTHOR

My name is Christopher Greyson, and I am a storyteller.

Since I was a little boy, I have dreamt of what mystery was around the next corner, or what quest lay over the hill. If I couldn't find an adventure, one usually found me, and now I weave those tales into my stories. I am blessed to have written the bestselling Detective Jack Stratton Mystery-Thriller Series. The collection includes *And Then She Was GONE, Girl Jacked, Jack Knifed, Jacks Are Wild, Jack and the Giant Killer, Data Jack, Jack of Hearts, Jack Frost,* with *Jack of Diamonds* due later this year. I have also penned the bestselling psychological thriller, *The Girl Who Lived* and a special collection of mysteries, *The Adventures of Finn and Annie.*

My background is an eclectic mix of degrees in theatre, communications, and computer science. Currently I reside in Massachusetts with my lovely wife and two fantastic children. My wife, Katherine Greyson, who is my chief content editor, is an author of her own romance series, *Everyone Keeps Secrets.*

My love for tales of mystery and adventure began with my grandfather, a decorated World War I hero. I will never forget being introduced to his friend, a WWI pilot who flew across the skies at the same time as the feared, legendary Red Baron. My love of reading and storytelling eventually led me to write *Pure of Heart*, a young adult fantasy that I released in 2014.

I love to hear from my readers. Please visit ChristopherGreyson.com, where you can become a preferred reader and enjoy additional FREE *Adventures of Finn and Annie*, advanced notifications of book releases and more! Thank you for reading my novels. I hope my stories have brightened your day.

Sincerely,